GUNS OF SEVASTOPOL

Empire and Honor 2

HAROLD R. THOMPSON

ZUMAYA YESTERDAYS   AUSTIN TX

2011

This book is a work of fiction. Names, characters, places and incidents are products of the author's imagination or are used fictitiously. Any resemblance to actual persons or events is purely coincidental.

GUNS OF SEVASTOPOL
© 2012 by Harold R. Thompson
ISBN 9781936144303
Cover art © Shaun Lindow
Cover Design © Tamian Wood

"Zumaya Yesterdays" and the phoenix colophon are trademarks of Zumaya Publications LLC, Austin TX. Look for us online at http://www..zumayapublications.com

Library of Congress Cataloging-in-Publication Data

Thompson, Harold (Harold R.)
 Guns of Sevastopol / Harold R. Thompson.
    p. cm. -- (Empire and honor ; bk. 2)
 Sequel to: Dudley's fusiliers.
  ISBN 978-1-936144-30-3 (trade pbk. : alk. paper) -- ISBN 978-1-936144-31-0 (electronic/multiple format) -- ISBN 978-1-61271-044-0 (electronic/epub)
1. Sevastopol, (Ukraine)--History--Siege, 1854-1855--Fiction. 2. Crimean War, 1853-1856--Fiction. 3. Great Britain--History, Military--19th century--Fiction. I. Title.
 PR9199.3.T4668G86 2011
 813'.54--dc22
                                2011030399

Dedication

This edition is for Ben and Maddy

CHAPTER 1

Ensign William Dudley stepped through a side door of the colossal Barracks Hospital. The March sun bathed him in its rich light, and he drew in a deep breath. Winter was over, and the air smelled of spring, a season that came early to the Turkish empire. It was now almost as warm as a summer day in Hampshire, his native county in England.

He clapped a wide-brimmed straw hat onto his blond and curly hair. As he adjusted the hat, he studied a batch of feathery clouds hanging low in the north. Somewhere beneath those clouds, a war was raging. The British army would be preparing a new offensive, and Dudley would join it just in time. In four days, he would return to the front, to the ongoing siege of Sevastopol, a siege that was five months old now.

Four days. Four days before he returned to the blood and carnage, the mud and the sleepless nights, and the endless crashing of the guns.

The prospect should have disturbed him, but it did not. He wanted to rejoin his men, and it would be a relief to leave

1

Scutari, to be free of the Barracks Hospital. So grand from a distance, the cavernous building had meant certain death for many a wounded man. For Dudley, it had meant sickness and misery. He would not miss it. There was only one thing about Scutari he would be sad to leave.

Movement caught his eye, and he turned to see a young woman approaching from his left. Quickly snatching off his straw hat, he said, "Good morning, Miss Montague."

The nurse who had saved him returned his greeting with a suppressed smile.

"Good morning, Ensign Dudley," she said. She did not pause to chat but continued on her way, following the perimeter of the huge building.

Dudley watched her, fingering his hat.

A hired caique took Dudley across the smooth surface of the Bosporus Strait. Other caiques plied the water, their slender hulls gliding between the pleasure yachts, fishing boats, and larger European vessels.

A trio of British men-of-war were on his left, solid and dominating where they lay at anchor. White birds swooped into the tangle of masts and spars, soaring and diving but never coming to rest. The French called the birds corps damné, for the Turks believed them to be the souls of unfaithful wives, condemned to perpetual motion for their sins. Angry husbands often bound such women into sacks and cast them into the strait to drown. To the Turks, it was reasonable to assume that the unworthy souls of those women would remain here in some form.

This was one of the strange customs that made Dudley uneasy about his hosts. He considered many of their practices barbaric. He knew the pain of a woman's betrayal, but he would never have considered murder. Yet in this country, such murders were legal.

2

Turkey was a paradox, a land of both great beauty and great ugliness. Sometimes it was difficult to say which was which. Constantinople was a fine example of such ambiguity. From the Bosporus, the tin plating covering the roofs in Stamboul, the Muslim part of the city, shone in the sun like silver. Distance made Constantinople a place of glistening magic. But upon closer inspection, one found houses that had not seen repairs in centuries, their walls chipped and crumbling. The streets were narrow and filthy, the broken pavement covered in rubbish and excrement. Through this streamed a constant and choking traffic—masses of pedestrians, donkeys with filled panniers, porters shouldering enormous burdens, and the occasional horse and carriage. Everywhere conversation, arguments, and music weighted the air.

The Turkish capital had not impressed Dudley on his first visit, but since then he had grown accustomed to its shabbiness and stink. Now it fascinated him. Constantinople was different from home. At once it was a sort of novelty but also a place of many fascinating layers. The city's three main districts—the Muslim, Jewish, and Christian—each contained a distinct collection of colourful citizens. There was always something to draw one's attention.

It was to the inner city he went once ashore. His aim was to browse one of the many markets to find gifts to send to his family. He wanted something for his aunt, his cousin Jane, and even for his uncle. He had searched for such gifts before but had never been able to make up his mind. Now that this was his last chance, he would seek out some of his earlier choices and at last commit to a few purchases.

The bazaar was crowded and noisy, and Dudley kept a firm grip on his purse as he pushed through the throng. He passed stalls selling fanciful glazed pottery, dishes in hammered brass or tin, Persian rugs, Kashmiri and Turkish shawls. Many stalls displayed weapons—muskets, swords, pistols and daggers, some inlaid with gold, silver or ivory, or studded with precious stones. Dudley wished he could buy a sword, but he saw nothing at a price that he could afford.

He came upon a vendor offering ladies' slippers at reasonable prices, the cloth embroidered in gold or silver thread. After much consideration, he chose a red pair for Jane and a dark-green pair for his aunt. The slippers would not be very practical in the old Georgian parsonage in Hampshire, but he knew Jane, in particular, would appreciate their delicate beauty.

For his uncle, Dudley searched the collections of pipes, which ranged from common clay to gold- or silver-mounted Turkish hookah. Tobacco was one of his uncle's few vices, and he chose a pipe with a bowl carved in the likeness of an aged monarch, his crown inlaid with mother-of-pearl. Perhaps his uncle would think it too fine, but there was no sense in sending him something plain. A gift from a foreign land had to bear some signature of that land.

With his packages under his arm, Dudley glanced at the sun and estimated the time as close to eleven o'clock. There was no sense in returning to Scutari at such an early hour. He *decided* instead to make his way to one of the city's most visited attractions, the famed Great Mosque of St. Sophia.

The nephew of an Anglican clergyman, he knew little of the Muslim faith. His one observation was that it seemed a religion that knew the power of a grand setting. He had always felt closer to God while fishing in a stream or wandering an open field than in church; church was a place for lessons and sermons. Yet the great mosque did inspire an otherworldly awe with its huge central dome and four corner minarets. Dudley found it more impressive than the cathedrals at Winchester and Salisbury. He did not mind one final visit, if for no other reason than to remind himself he was somewhere famous and exotic. The Turks encouraged visitors, even the heathen British.

An attendant greeted him at the door and reminded him to remove his shoes. When Dudley did so, the attendant offered a pair of slippers. Dudley glanced at the slippers and tried to keep his nose from wrinkling. He doubted they had ever been washed, despite the untold number of feet they had undoubtedly known.

"No, thank you," he said, smiling. "I'll go in my stockings."

"I may hold your shoes for you, sir, if you like," the attendant suggested.

Dudley had polished his boots so they shone like dark mirrors, and he did not feel comfortable leaving them with the attendants.

"Thank you, but I will carry them. It's no trouble at all."

The attendant bowed, and Dudley stepped through into the huge domed cavern, his boots in one hand and his straw hat in the other, his packages wedged under one arm.

As always, the sight of so much gold in one place took his breath away. The dome seemed to glow with its own radiance. Its rounded walls rose in three levels, two with columned galleries, the third with arched windows that let in the unlight. Below, on the floor to one side, an enormous book, perhaps the Koran, sat on a carved wooden rest. There were no seats or pews, for the faithful knelt on little carpets they brought with them. Over time, their weight had pressed the bare earthen floor as hard and flat as paving stone.

Dudley grinned at the sight of the worshipers, for between the carpets and their occupants strolled visiting British officers, all in stockings. Some of the officers wore scarlet uniforms and others blue. Each carried his forage cap in one hand and his polished boots in the other.

As he studied this curious scene, he caught the eye of a pair of officers in blue hussar uniforms, their jackets looped with gold. As they approached, one of them ran his eyes over Dudley's own threadbare uniform. Frowning, the officer glanced at his companion. Once they had passed, Dudley heard the fellow declare, "It's as I said—the army is going downhill with all this talk of reform. They'll let any ragamuffin in now that it's wartime."

Dudley felt his ears begin to burn, quick anger rising. The man had meant for him to hear the comment. He turned to look as the two fancy hussars moved farther away.

Like most of the officers in the mosque, the hussars appeared to be recent arrivals in Constantinople, part of a contingent of reinforcements. They had seen no fighting yet. Dudley resisted an urge to race after them and demand, "Where have you been in the last five months while better men have been dying in the mud?"

But he knew there was no sense in that. He did not want to cause a fuss in here, and he would only make enemies if he started a quarrel. Perhaps he would ruin his reputation as an officer before he even got started.

He glanced at his sleeve, at the gleaming brass buttons on his cuff. Those buttons should have been gold. He had done his best to keep himself looking smart, brushing his coat and Oxford mixture trousers until they were spotless. There was only so much he could do. The fact remained that his uniform was incorrect for a man of his rank. So many things about him, as an ensign, were incorrect.

He was not a *proper* officer, after all.

From boyhood, William Dudley had wanted to be a soldier. Perhaps all boys wish that at some point, but Dudley was more passionate than most. That passion had begun, as far as he could remember, when he was six years old and his father had brought him a gift from London. The gift had been a box of tin soldiers, and it had been magic, an antidote for his childhood loneliness. His mother had died when he was four, and after that his father had spent much of his time in the local tavern. Dudley had retreated into his imagination, a place where his best friends were tin soldiers, childish twins to his heroes from the long wars with Napoleon.

The greatest of those heroes was the Duke of Wellington, and little Dudley had named one of the tin soldiers "Wellington" in his honor. That soldier still survived. Attached to a slim length of chain around Dudley's neck, it hung inside his uniform coat as a charm of good luck.

When Dudley was seven years old, his father had toppled from a bridge in a drunken stupor and drowned. Little Master William had gone to live in the house of his uncle and aunt, the Reverend Robert and Mrs. Bronwyn Mason. There, he had enjoyed the company of his five cousins—four boys and one girl.

Uncle Robert was, to use his own word, an "educator." He wrote books and pamphlets on many subjects and managed a country boarding school attached to his church. Dudley had attended that school before completing his education at home under the private tutorship of both uncle and aunt. He had a sharp mind, and there had been talk of his attending university, something only one of his cousins had done.

Uncle Robert was a fair yet dominating man, sometimes severe in his opinions and notions of what was good for others. He had begun to believe it would be William Dudley's destiny to go away to Cambridge, as he had done himself.

Dudley had been in no position to refuse, although he had been unable to rejoice. His real interests lay far away from the little town of Cambridge. He wanted to follow in the footsteps of soldiers like Clive and Wellington, men who strove to uphold British justice in faraway lands like Spain and India. But he could never have explained that to his uncle. *Foolish dreams*, his uncle would have said. *Boyhood nonsense.*

The sensible part of Dudley's character had agreed, but his soul had rebelled.

Uncle Robert had done his best to help Dudley towards a sensible career. He had used his connections to find him a post as a tutor then had secured for him a place at St. John's College in Cambridge. All had been going as planned.

But the Reverend Mason had not counted on the presence of Martha Wilkes, the elder sister of Dudley's one pupil. Dudley had found something special in Martha, and she had returned his affections. They had even begun to discuss marriage. Then had come that terrible and momentous day, perhaps the defining day in his life. He had come upon Martha in the garden...in the arms of another man.

Dudley had thrown all caution and sense to the winds. Without Martha, his uncle's plans for him had seemed stale and hopeless. There had been nothing left but to follow his dream to become a soldier. And since he could not afford a commission—and his uncle would never have agreed to buy one for him—he had enlisted in the ranks.

It had been a rash move, and a betrayal of his family's wishes. It had wounded them all, but it had wounded his uncle the most. Dudley's aunt and cousin Jane still sent him letters, but for almost two years, Uncle Robert had refused to acknowledge that he had a nephew. In recent months, he had begun to refer to Dudley at last, but only as "that boy." That was a start on the healing road, but Dudley still considered himself an outcast. His new family was his regiment, the Royal Hampshire Fusiliers.

As it turned out, he had discovered he had a knack for military life. He had set about doing his best to master his drill and all aspects of the army's rather erratic protocol. In this he had discovered the advantage of his decent education, which led both to the label of "gentleman ranker" and an early promotion to corporal.

Then the war with Russia had come. Russia, the most powerful nation in Europe since Napoleon's defeat, had invaded the

Turkish empire. Britain and France, unexpected allies, had responded with outrage. Britain feared the Russian threat to both the Mediterranean and their passage to India, while France feared Russian expansion. The two nations had decided the Bear must be stopped.

Maintaining the pretense of helping "poor little Turkey," the allied armies of Britain and France had invaded the Crimean peninsula. Their objective was to destroy the important Black Sea naval base of Sevastopol.

For Dudley, the war began as a glorious adventure. Everything had changed in the terrible battle at the Alma River. He had received a field promotion to sergeant but had lost one of his closest comrades in murderous fire that left the dead strewn about the heights above the river. He had begun to worry that all of his romantic notions of soldiering were false. He had seen men blown to pieces before his eyes.

After that, he became obsessed with regaining his notions of glorious conquest, of triumph over an immoral enemy. In the muck of the growing siege trenches before Sevastopol, he began to convince himself that nothing had changed. The sight of the dead ceased to bother him as much as it had. When the Russians made a major push to destroy the British Army, Dudley had distinguished himself by leading his company against a field battery. That battle was now called Inkerman, and in its wake, Her Majesty Queen Victoria had issued a Royal Warrant authorizing the promotion of one sergeant from every regiment involved. Dudley had been the sergeant chosen from the Royal Hampshire Fusiliers.

He still wore his sergeant's double-breasted coatee, although he had made some modifications. He had removed the white lace chevrons and attached a worn and used pair of bullion epaulettes to his shoulder straps. Around his waist, he wore his sergeant's sash, and he had no sword. The army would give him an allowance of 150 pounds to purchase proper uniforms, but he did not think there was any sense in having them made here in Turkey. He loved fine uniforms, but once he returned to the Crimea, the harsh environment of war would not be kind to new clothing. It was better that he keep his makeshift rig for now.

But that makeshift rig had drawn the disapproval of the two hussars. Maybe they knew of the Royal Warrant and suspected that Dudley was one of its beneficiaries. Their attitude reminded him of the struggle for acceptance he was about to face.

The army believed that an officer should come from that class of men who owned property in Britain. Dudley's family had no land and no titles, and his uncle was nothing but a perpetual curate. Dudley was respectable and educated, but simple respectability did not matter a fig to most army officers. For them, blood and heritage were everything.

Most officers purchased their commissions. Under this practice, fools and incompetents with large pocketbooks could rise to the rank of general if they so wished. The danger was well-known, but men of great influence had and still defended the purchase system. The most famous defender was Dudley's hero, the late Duke of Wellington.

Wellington had believed that British army officers were the best in the world for one reason—they were gentlemen, born to owning land and thus born to lead. Keeping the price of a commission high was the only means by which men of inferior class could be kept out. If one had to contend with a few fools, so be it. As for the few promoted from the ranks, they were unfortunates. They had just joined a class in which they could never live up to expectations or the style of living.

All of this added to Dudley's predicament. Not only was he not a proper gentleman, and thus an inferior, but he had no money. An officer in the infantry required sixty to a hundred pounds a year of independent income. Dudley's new rate of pay was a minute four shillings and sixpence a day. That was about three times what he had made as a sergeant but was still not much, considering everything an officer needed to pay for. In the Crimea, an officer needed a horse, a saddle, a pack-saddle, horse accouterments, and a groom or servant. He would also have to pay a mess subscription when the war ended, as well as band subscriptions, subscriptions for theatricals and other social events. That was the stuff of an officer's life.

Dudley still had most of the salary he had earned as a tutor, which amounted to almost forty pounds. It would keep him going for now, but it would not last forever. In order to become a successful officer, he would have to find some source of income.

The extravagance of the Great Mosque suddenly seemed to emphasize his poverty. He looked again at the great dome, but the charm of this final visit was gone. With a sigh, he turned and began to wander back toward the door.

He tried to recall the names of the officers surviving in his regiment. He had never had much to do with any save his old company commander, a fellow who had lost a leg at Inkerman and was no longer serving. Dudley would have to get to know the others and adopt their habits to win their acceptance. Maybe his merit as a soldier would also help. He had risen in the ranks as a result of that merit. There was no sense in changing his philosophy now.

But he feared he would first have to endure many more insults like the one he had received today, here in this golden mosque.

Another day passed, bringing Dudley's return to the war that much nearer. He spent an afternoon sitting under the awning of a bell tent composing a letter to his cousin Jane. The tent was one of many on the hospital grounds, shelter for patients who no longer required beds. He had the tent to himself, which made it the most spacious lodgings he had occupied since joining the army.

A wooden crate served as his desk, a creaking camp stool his chair. At his feet lay a pile of old newspapers, their contents serving to jog his memory of the past months.

"The wound in my leg that I took at Inkerman," he wrote, "is almost completely healed, as is the subsequent ailment that seized my stomach and intestines. It is good to feel myself again, and as I sift through the reports from the front, I feel I am fortunate for having spent the winter here."

> Doubtless you have read William Russell's pieces in the *Times*, describing what our troops in the field have been suffering. Most Army officials dislike Mister Russell, while our Commander-in-Chief, Lord Raglan, thinks it a disgrace that the Army's doings should be reported in the papers. I for one am thankful for the reports, and trust their accuracy. They match the many tales told to me by the sick and wounded who have arrived here over the course of the winter.
>
> Taken together, Russell's reports are so bleak that my own experience seems trifling. The Barracks Hospital is far from a paradise, my dear Jane, but it is better than what my comrades have endured before Sevastopol. It is even possible that my second illness ultimately saved me, for it kept me here in Turkey for an extra month.
>
> However, I don't want to burden you with tales of starving men, dressed in rags, standing up to their knees in snow. You must

think that I take a perverse delight in re-
counting things evil, I do it so often. Perhaps there is some truth in that. I have felt
great rage in the face of the mistakes and
neglect, but I have come to accept the horrors of battle and war in general. Or I think
I have come to accept them, and learned to
see the good that may come of them.

A bad circumstance, my dear Jane, is
sometimes the best in which to foster gallantry and heroism. These are not mere
words. I believe in them now more than I
ever have.

For balance, and for your peace of mind,
you must remember that our foes seem to
have suffered as badly as our lads. An unde-
clared truce held throughout the winter,
perhaps because of the lack of ammunition
supplies. Now that spring is near, the trench
skirmishing has begun again. Fresh wounded
come to the hospital every few days, though
our fellows have fought no new battles yet.
Perhaps one last push will make the enemy
give in.

"Yes, one last push will do it," he said to himself.

This was a reasonable prediction, for the Russians now
faced a far superior force. According to the most recent issue
of the *Times*, the French army in the Crimea had received
reinforcements. They now stood at almost thrice the British
strength and occupied both the extreme left and extreme right
of the siege lines. The British remained in the center. Pied-
mont was also getting into the fray, having declared war on
Russia on January 26. They would soon be sending troops.

"I have heard the news of Lord Aberdeen's resignation," Dudley wrote.

> This gives me a certain amount of satisfaction. After all, it was Russell's reports of the bad conditions that forced the fall of the government. How does Uncle feel about Lord Palmerston becoming the new prime minister? The man seems eager to reform the army administration, which is a good sign. Another good sign is his strong talk of the successful prosecution of the war.
>
> We all thought something might happen when Czar Nicholas died a few weeks ago. They say that the new Czar, Alexander II, is a moderate. There was some fear that peace would come early, before we had finished our task in the Crimea. I dearly wish for peace, Jane, for this has dragged on too long, but I must be back with my regiment before that happens, and we must have something to show for it. Peace now, before we obtain our objective, would make a mockery of all we have suffered."

"Peace," he repeated aloud.

For a moment, he imagined the green meadows near his home in England, and the beautiful open downs he had so loved as a child. He wondered when he would see them again.

"Peace yourself, sir," said a nearby voice.

Dudley glanced up from his letter to see a gray-haired private approaching. It was Daniel Oakes, a member of his company.

Oakes touched his battered forage cap with his right hand in salute. The hand shaded his one good eye. A patch of black cloth covered his empty left socket.

"Private Oakes!" Dudley exclaimed. He set down his pen and stood, returning the private's salute. He had learned much from this grizzled veteran.

Oakes was at least fifty years old, although no one knew his exact age. He had never pursued nor accepted promotion but had remained a stabilizing force within the company, sharing the simple wisdom of an experienced campaigner.

"What news?" Dudley asked with a broad grin.

Oakes hesitated. "Bad, sir."

Dudley's smile faded. His friend did not look his customary cheerful self. He still wore a tattered uniform, his red coatee patched in many places with pieces of gray wool blanket. This was also strange. Oakes had come to Scutari because of wounds taken at Inkerman, but he had left the hospital weeks ago. Since then, he had been living in the camp outside Constantinople with other recovering members of the Royal Hampshire Fusiliers. That camp was bursting with new supplies.

Dudley asked, "You have still not been issued with new kit?"

The old private's one eye blinked.

"Well, it's like this, Mister Dudley. I'm to be discharged, sir."

"It's as we feared, then."

This was, indeed, bad news, although no surprise. He and Oakes had both fretted over the possibility for weeks. Dudley had tried to reassure his friend that the army would find a place for him, for Oakes was a good, steady man. Yet he had not really believed his own reassurances. The simple fact was that enlisted men had to be sound in mind *and* body. An officer could continue to serve without an eye—or an arm, as in the case of Lord Raglan—but not a private soldier.

Oakes sat on another crate next to Dudley's makeshift desk.

"What am I to do now, sir?" he asked, voice hollow. The army was everything to him, and now he was about to lose it.

"Well, you will have your pension," Dudley began, but he knew that was cold comfort. A soldier could never have lived even on his full regular pay if not for the food, clothing and shelter the army provided.

"Me pension," Oakes echoed. "Aye, there's that." He paused then added, "Perhaps it would 'ave been better that I'd died then, at the Barrier."

"Your wife doesn't think so," Dudley stated. Hester Oakes was the unofficial matron of Dudley's company.

"How shall I support her now?" Oakes asked.

Dudley could think of no other encouragement, so said nothing. In response to his silence, Oakes stood, face reddening.

"My apologies, sir. I never came to see you to bother ye with this. I just wanted to tell someone, that's all. Thought you should know, after all we'd talked about."

"It's all right, Oakes, I'm glad you told me. I wish there were something I could do."

He knew Oakes could still do his duty, one-eyed or not. He had been, and could still be, a good soldier. Now, without the army, he faced the possibility of life as a beggar.

"I'll try to think of something, Private," he at last promised. "Never you fear."

Oakes had regained his composure. His pride took over, and he declared, "That's all right, Mister Dudley. Hester and me'll be fine, you'll see. It's just a bit of a shock, that's all."

"Yes," Dudley agreed, "it is."

Private Oakes's situation remained foremost in Dudley's mind, but he tried to set it aside on his last day in Scutari. He did not want to spend his final hours here worrying about something he could not change. There was another matter more pressing.

Returning to his old ward, he moved along the aisle between the packed ranks of sick and wounded. The cots lay closer together than those in a barrack room, but every man had a shelf for his belongings. The ward smelled of soap and disinfectant, and the men, with their clean, fresh bandages, lacked for nothing. This efficiency was thanks to Miss Nightingale, the superintendent of female nurses, and her assistants. Assistants like Elizabeth Montague.

Elizabeth stood at the far end of the ward, bending over a wounded man who had just arrived. Dudley stopped and watched her for a moment.

He considered the horrible state of things before the arrival of the nurses. The patients themselves had never complained, but every able-bodied man had feared a wound more than death on the battlefield. The reputation of military hospitals had seen to that. Now, things were changing. There had never been a military hospital like this one.

The changes had begun with William Russell's articles in the *Times*. The Secretary-at-War in London, Sir Sidney Herbert, had read those articles and decided something must be done. He had then written to Florence Nightingale.

The men of the army worshiped Miss Nightingale, and knew her story well. She had been born to a well-placed Derbyshire family and had lived an active and frivolous social life. She could have continued in her place of privilege to the end of her days, but something in her heart had rebelled. While she had been living so well, the poor had suffered in the streets of the factory cities. To help correct the imbalance, she had decided to become a nurse.

17

The decision had horrified her family, but they could not dissuade her. She became devoted to her goal, her dream. Dudley could understand that.

Miss Nightingale had soon discovered there was no one to educate her in her chosen profession. Undaunted, she had studied on her own. She had consulted the great medical minds of Europe and had visited hospitals in Germany, Ireland, and France. By the time Sir Sidney decided to consult her, she had become a recognized expert on nursing and hospital management.

Upon her arrival in Scutari, she and her picked assistants had encountered the travesty known as the Barracks Hospital. There had been no furniture in the cavernous building, not even a single operating table. A sewer blockage had caused noxious gases to fill the wards. The various departments in charge had, in their squabbling, neglected everything, left everything undone, each pointing at the other. The blocked lavatories had leaked excrement into the halls. The muddy central courtyard had become a dumping ground for rubbish, animal corpses, and overflowing privies. The water supply, located in that same courtyard, was contaminated.

The Superintendent of Nurses had wanted to begin reforms at once, but prejudice had barred her way. Many of the army surgeons and physicians, although understaffed and overworked, had resented the presence of women. For most of her first month, Miss Nightingale found her services unwanted, and she could do nothing without official permission.

She could have given up, sat idle, but had instead persisted in an unofficial capacity. Her nurses had helped to feed and clean men who could not do so themselves, and had prepared bandages.

Then the wounded from Inkerman began to arrive, and everything had changed. The new wounded had crammed the wards to five times their capacity, men lying on the floors without clothing, shoes, or blankets. The few available surgeons had worked with their sleeves rolled up, covered in blood to their necks. Injured and sick men had called out for help that had not been available. The doctors had soon discovered the work was too much for them. At last they had called in Miss Nightingale's party.

At once she made an inventory of supplies. She found there were twenty chamber pots for every thousand patients. There were no drugs, no pillows, no washbasins or towels, and no combs or brushes. There had not even been a screen to hide the horror of surgery from those who waited to go under the knife.

With money from a fund created by the *Times*, Miss Nightingale had set about acquiring the necessary supplies. By December, she had cleaned and equipped ten experimental wards and had begun work on other sections of the hospital. That work continued still, but the bulk of the task was complete.

Before the arrival of the nurses, almost half those who entered the Barracks Hospital had died. The death rate had since dropped to a handful, and those were men with serious wounds who would not have survived under the best of conditions.

There remained a few who believed an army hospital was no place for women, but the majority had nothing but admiration for Miss Nightingale. She and her nurses often worked around the clock, and would never leave the side of a dying man until he had expired. They made attempts to appear drab and unattractive, but nothing could mask their beauty. The men called them "Angels of Mercy." Many a wounded soldier fell in love.

And then there was Elizabeth Montague.

Dudley wished he could have spent more time with her. Circumstances had not allowed for that, of course. It would have been scandalous for her to neglect her other patients for him.

As it was, he was uncertain about the nature of his attraction. It could not be love, for he did not really know her. It might have been simple gratitude, coupled with fascination. He had often wondered why this young woman would have left her comfortable home to come to this hell. She must be a cold machine, he had decided once, driven by duty more than true caring. He had noted her ability to control her emotions, to keep her face locked in an expressionless mask in the face of so much sickness and injury.

Yet in time, he had recognized a warm and cheerful disposition behind that mask, a caring soul. He supposed she must need to retain firm control over her behaviour in the company of so many men. Glimpses of her soul broke through now and then, in involuntary flashes she quickly hid. A tenderness toward a patient, or anguish when a man died. Best of all, Dudley had discovered he could make her smile and even laugh—sometimes, it seemed, against her better judgment.

He would miss her presence, her reassuring nearness that told him all was well. He would have to content himself with this last glimpse, although he hoped to see her again someday, when the war was over. Then, he would take the opportunity to learn whether his feelings could become deeper, and whether she truly had any feelings for him.

When she left her patient, he moved toward her and said, "Good morning, Miss Montague."

"Good morning, Ensign Dudley," she returned, stopping before him. "How may I be of service?"

"There is something I would like to ask you. I don't want to be in your way here, but I know that you're still very much overworked. I will be leaving tomorrow, and was wondering if perhaps there is any way I can be of help. To repay some of your kindness?"

She gave him a steady look, yet there was curiosity in her eyes. Her blue eyes.

He knew every aspect of her face. That face was perhaps too thin to be beautiful, although there were charming dimples at the corners of her mouth. The dimples were evidence that she smiled and laughed a great deal when she was not hiding behind firm efficiency. And her blond hair had a habit of coming undone, with small strands dangling over her smooth forehead.

"Help, Mr. Dudley?" she said. "Why, you're barely out of your sickbed yourself."

"But my strength is almost fully returned, thanks to your suggestion of taking walks every day."

She frowned, and he felt the beginning of disappointment. He did not want her to refuse him, and that was a possibility. Many recovered soldiers helped with the running of the hospital, but Elizabeth had a tendency to reject personal offers. Dudley had seen her reject help even when she could have used it.

Once, she had been struggling with a large load of blankets, yet she would allow no able-bodied man to intervene. It was a stubborn sense of honour Dudley admired, although he hoped she would make an exception in his case. Not because he was an officer, but because he was a friend.

His hopes were answered, for she at last said, "Your help would be appreciated, Ensign. Very much, to be truthful. I still have several serious cases to attend to, and there are bandages that need rolling. I was uncertain when I would find the time."

Dudley bowed. "Then I shall roll bandages for the rest of the day."

She showed him what to do, and he sat down to his task. He did not mind the tedium. When he had enlisted, an aged staff sergeant had told him to always help out when he could. If he did so, the old sergeant had insisted, he would go far in his chosen profession. Dudley did his best to follow that advice.

He worked in silence, but as time passed, his satisfaction gradually gave way to frustration. He found his mind wandering back to the problem of Private Oakes. It seemed absurd that he could help his nurse but could do nothing for one of his closest comrades.

Later in the afternoon, Elizabeth returned to collect some of the bandages for use. Dudley was no longer as cheerful as before, although he brightened when Elizabeth saw all he had done and praised his efforts.

"The men are always eager to help," she said, "although when other officers wish to contribute to the administration of the hospital they send their servants."

Then she smiled at him, her lips forming their graceful curve. Dudley tried not to stare at that smile, but in its warmth he realized something he been a fool to not realize before.

A servant! An officer's servant could remain with the battalion, and it did not matter whether the fellow had two eyes or not.

"Why are you laughing, Ensign?" Elizabeth asked, still smiling, although looking a bit perplexed.

"Because, Miss Montague," he replied, "I have just found a way to save a friend."

CHAPTER 2

March 23, 1855

Dudley shared a longboat with a detachment of the 68th Regiment. He watched the shore as the boat slid between the high bluffs flanking the harbor. The mid-morning sun lit the bare rock and cliffs of the western bluff, while on the eastern side the broken towers of an ancient Genoese castle stood in stark silhouette.

The village of Balaclava lay at the far end of the inlet, invisible for the crush of anchored naval vessels and transports. As Dudley's boat drew closer in, that tangle of masts and spars parted like prickly curtains. The houses at last came into view, a collection of plastered cottages and warehouses with clay tile roofs. Beyond the village, the ground sloped upward to meet the wide plateau of the Chersonese Uplands.

The boat came to a halt against a low wooden wharf. As the only officer present, Dudley was the first to disembark. The men of the 68th followed, filing past to form in line with another detachment that had come ashore before them. Dudley stayed on the wharf and waited for Oakes and his wife, still on the water in a second boat.

From the north came a dull thumping of guns. He listened, and a shiver ran along his spine. He had forgotten the unsettling impact of that sound.

He tried to ignore the cannon fire and studied the crowded waterfront. Rows of prefabricated wooden storage huts lined the quay, and at their feet sat piles of crates, barrels, and canvas sacks. A single railroad track ran along the shore and turned north to follow the road out of the village. The locomotive was not present, but a steady traffic of wagons, oxcarts, mules, and horses moved in and out of the supply base. No evidence remained of the harsh winter he had read and heard about. In fact, things seemed in a much better state than they had been last autumn.

When Oakes and his wife finally landed, Dudley said to them, "Things have changed here."

The first thing Oakes noticed was the railway.

"That they have, sir."

"Do you think we could ride on the train?" Hester Oakes wondered.

They waited, but the train did not appear. They decided to walk, trailing the marching files of the 68th out of the village and towards the camps.

A mile from Balaclava, they came to the smaller village of Kadikoi. There they at last found a locomotive and two cars. Smoke drifted from the engine's funnel, but the train had halted for a small herd of cattle blocking the tracks. The train drivers, an incongruous group of sailors, tried to clear passage, pushing and prodding the lumbering animals.

The two railcars were filled with shot and shell. Dudley wondered if the railway extended all the way to the batteries, but when he and his companions reached the far side of the village, they came upon an ammunition depot. Great piles of round shot and cylindrical shells lay beside the road. The railway ended at that spot. Stacks of wooden ties and steel rails suggested the tracks were still under construction.

Here, the supply road turned left, north toward the British camps. Dudley's camp was another four miles away. As part of Sir George Brown's Light Division, the Royal Hampshire Fusiliers held a position near the far right of the British lines. It was a fair walk, and Dudley convinced the driver of an ox-drawn wagon to allow Hester Oakes to ride on top of his load of biscuit barrels. There she sat with her carpet bag in her lap as the cart bumped along the rutted supply road. Dudley and her husband continued on foot. To them this was a familiar route, for they had travelled it many times last year when bringing up supplies.

Dudley welcomed the walk as a chance to keep warm, for the air held a damp chill. He shivered under his new wool greatcoat, and his toes ached within his knee-high winter boots. After Scutari, this came as a shock to his body; winter was not finished with the Crimea.

The French soldiers he saw stood huddled in their wool overcoats, kepis pulled down low over their foreheads. Many of the civilians wore furs, while the breath of men and animals alike came in puffs of steam.

Dudley thrust his hands deep into his pockets and gazed around at the barren plateau. Everywhere lay scattered rock and dull brown grass, gullies and deep ravines running at right angles to the coastline. A few trees had grown here, stands of slender cypress and scrub oaks, but they were now gone to feed the campfires.

Unlike Balaclava, with its abundant supplies, the signs of recent hardship were numerous in this region. The bones of animals, including a few complete skeletons, littered the bare ground. Here and there lay discarded bits of uniforms and equipment, broken wagons, crates, barrels, and ration tins. Much of the rubbish was half-buried in dry earth that had once been soupy mud.

"Looks like someone's been fighting a war," Oakes remarked.

When they reached the first of the British camps with its ordered tent streets, they encountered soldiers who were as shabby as the land. Save for their rifles and accoutrements, the men resembled bundled civilians. Most of them wore knee-high or thigh-length boots with mittens of colored yarn or sheepskin protecting their hands. Some had retained their standard gray greatcoats, but most seemed to prefer a fur-lined hooded cloak or a sheepskin coat. They wore the sheepskins with the wool on the inside, and many had painted strange fanciful devices, such as leaf and flower patterns, on the leather.

Save for their swords, revolvers, and dirty sashes, it was impossible to distinguish the officers from the men. For Dudley, this discovery came as a relief. He was one of thousands of dilapidated men, no matter what the two fancy hussars in Constantinople may have thought.

The last of the British camps was that of the Light Division, and there the journey ended. Oakes helped Hester down from the wagon while Dudley studied the perfect rows of conical tents. It was as if he had never left. Everything in this place was exactly as he remembered it, with the addition of a few prefabricated wooden huts.

But his sense of nostalgia was short-lived. As he and his companions strolled along the streets, he saw one unfamiliar face after another. Once he had known almost every man in the regiment, at least by sight, and many from his brigade. Many of those men were now gone.

"I suppose I shall have to report to Lieutenant-Colonel Freemantle," he said. He found the presence of so many strangers disorienting, and wondered if anyone was even aware he was coming back.

"As your servant, then, sir," Oakes said, "I shall go and see if I can't find out about our accommodation."

"Oh, yes," Dudley agreed. "I guess that would be the right thing to do."

Hester Oakes snorted.

"Fine army this is. No one here to greet us. Typical!"

"Ain't it, though?" her husband agreed.

They moved off together. Dudley stood in the street, trying to remember the location of his commanding officer's tent. It was then he finally spied a familiar figure coming towards him—Private Brian Barker.

Barker was a huge man with shaggy black hair and sunken, sinister eyes. When he saw Dudley, a wide grin split his bearded face.

"Welcome back, sir!" he cried, striding forward and giving Dudley a smart salute.

Dudley hesitated before returning the compliment. He had mixed feelings about this man, although he appreciated the friendly greeting.

"How are you, Private…" he began, and then his eyes widened in surprise. He had made a mistake. Barker wore a red sash around his waist, and there were three white lace chevrons on the upper right sleeve of his heavy coat. He was not *Private* Barker at all.

"Sergeant Barker?" Dudley said.

Barker shrugged.

"Amusing, ain't it?"

Dudley shook his head.

"Amusing if you have a black sense of humour."

Barker had been the most troublesome man in No. 3 Company. He might even have been the most troublesome man in the regiment. He had provoked the other men, been insubordinate to his NCOs, and had delighted in aggressive or cruel practical jokes. For all that, more than half the men of the company had followed him, either out of fear or respect. Barker knew how to rally others, and he knew how to intimidate.

He had been a problem for Dudley from their first meeting, but Dudley had refused to play his game or submit to his bullying. In slow increments, he had won Barker's respect and then his support. At Inkerman, Barker had been the first to follow Dudley when he took command of the company.

He had eventually discovered the reason for Barker's poor behavior. Barker had been a sergeant before, with dreams of reaching sergeant-major. His dreams had ended when a pair of lieutenants, men Barker had never named, ordered him to spy on another officer. The lieutenants had also expected the sergeant to plant incriminating evidence in the officer's quarters.

Barker had considered himself a man of honour, and had refused. Soon after that, he found himself on report time and again for the most trivial acts. At last, trumped-up charges of neglect of duty had led to his demotion to private, as well as the demotion of his closest friend, another sergeant. After that, Barker had lost his respect for the institution he had joined, the British Army.

Then came the war with Russia. Barker had found it difficult to maintain his bitter act when his comrades had need of his support. The bloody fighting and misery of the first months in the Crimea had pulled those men who survived closer together. Barker's conduct had improved.

Considering that improvement, Dudley thought, it was not so surprising Barker had managed to gain back his old rank.

"I suppose the company was in desperate need of NCOs?" Dudley suggested.

"That they were, sir," Barker replied. "In fact, after *you* were evacuated, there weren't any at all. A lieutenant was transferred from another company to make up our lack of officers, and they looked about to make a new sergeant. I had the experience. And since I'd taken part in your mad charge to take that battery, I got the promotion. So, I suppose I have you to thank."

Dudley smirked. "Forgive me if I doubt your sincerity, Sergeant."

He started to walk. He was still not ready to believe Barker wanted to be his friend.

"I'm hurt, sir, truly I am," Barker cried in mock indignation. He scurried to catch up as Dudley moved away.

"As long as you're following me, Sergeant," Dudley said, "maybe you can tell me what has happened in my absence. We seem to have received reinforcements."

"That we have, Mister Dudley, though a few of the old lads are still around. O'Ryan's back and promoted to colour-sergeant. We also got new rifles, an improvement on the Minié. The new Enfield, sir—five-seventy-seven calibre and a pound or two lighter. Very accurate, if I do say so myself. Oh, and all the boys threw away their shakos about a month or two back. Dumped them at the bottom of a mud-filled ravine. And good riddance."

"No doubt the quartermaster was happy with that," Dudley commented. "How was the winter? As bad as the reports?"

Barker uttered a sharp laugh.

"I'm sure it was worse, sir. The problem was that bloody supply road, which, as you know, sir, isn't a road at all. When the autumn rains came, it turned into stew, and the wagons couldn't move. Stores piled up on the docks in Balaclava, but there was no way to get 'em to the camps. We starved, sir. When the cold weather set in, the mud froze and the road was serviceable again, but by then things had slipped pretty far." Barker's jaunty tone changed, growing somber. "We had a poor bastard so frostbitten that, when we tried to take off his stockings, his toenails and half his toes came with 'em. There were plenty of cases like that. And horses standing around in the snow like bags of bones, eating each other's tails.

"Rain, sleet and snow every other day, the damned trenches knee-deep in water. Rats everywhere, somehow prospering. Men freezing to death on picket duty. There was so many men dying in January the sky was never wanting for vultures and ravens. Aye, it was bad."

Dudley sought to bring something positive out of this bleak description.

"Not a lot of fighting, though?"

"None to speak of. What was the point? The Russkies were as bad off as we were behind their walls. Not a soul about inside Sevastopol some days except the sentries when they were changed. We even got up a little trade—firewood for tobacco, that sort of thing. Officers trading letters. Some of the boys don't care much for our enemy and wouldn't go for that, but I told them they'd better if they wanted to survive till spring. And I'm still here, so I think I've proved the point."

Dudley could not help grinning.

"I'm sure you've proven a great many points in your lifetime, Sergeant."

"Thank you, Mister Dudley. The other boys knew that, too. I showed 'em how to make candles from rags dipped in pork fat, and how to make their coffee from those green beans the commissary kept giving us. Just find a piece of half-exploded shell, grind the beans with a nine-pound shot, and roast it in a frying pan over a fire of Russian firewood.

"It was also me that got them moving to bring up supplies when the wagons stopped coming. Paired the men off and had 'em carry a beaker of rum, pork or biscuits slung from a pole between them. Rough work and slow going, but better'n starving."

"You're a marvel, Sergeant. I trust things have improved with the weather?"

"That they have, now that it's no longer quite so cold as it was. We're getting our wood from the commissariat, as we ought to. And we have a divisional canteen where you can buy butter, cheese, bread, bottled ale for the men and wine for your lot."

Dudley gave Barker a sideways glance. "My lot?"

Barker shrugged. "Pardon me, sir, but...the officers."

Dudley halted where Lieutenant-Colonel Freemantle's tent had been; there was a wooden hut there now. He stared at the door and said to the sergeant, "So Number Three Company is under the charge of this transferred lieutenant?"

"Mister Arbuthnot? No, sir." Barker hesitated, and his eyes studied the ground for a second before rising again. "We have a new captain, came with the first parcel of reinforcements. Captain David Neville. Brought with him another sergeant, too. Chap named Hoskins." He scratched at his tangle of beard. "Unsavory chap, if you ask me."

"I'll pass judgement myself, Sergeant. So, we have a Captain Neville? I seem to remember there was a Captain Neville at Fairbridge when I was training. Though I don't recall dealing with him much. Just remember him standing there on the parade when on duty, and making his rounds. That's all."

"Yes," Barker said with a grimace. He cleared his throat. "*I* remember him well enough, though, sir. He was in the regiment before then got a staff appointment and left for awhile before returning to the depot."

"So, we have a Lieutenant Arbuthnot, Captain Neville, and then..." Dudley sighed. "...there's me."

Barker suddenly drew himself up, back straight as a ramrod.

"I'll deal with anyone who dares say you're not a real officer, sir. Beggin' your pardon, sir, no offence intended."

Dudley stared at the sergeant, his former adversary, and felt an unexpected wash of gratitude. With it came astonishment that he should be grateful to Barker for anything. Especially in the face of such presumption.

But grateful he was, and he found himself saying, "No offence taken. And I appreciate that, Sergeant. Thank you."

Lieutenant-Colonel Freemantle was in his hut when Dudley reported. The benign old man looked up from the papers on his campaign desk and said, "Welcome back, Ensign Dudley." His smile was genuine, for Dudley's promotion had been Freemantle's doing. "Have you met your new company commander, Major…er, that is, Captain Neville?"

"Not yet, sir," Dudley explained.

"Then you had best go and see him once he is off-duty. Out on picket now, I suspect, with your company. Or maybe they are helping dig. It's difficult to keep track, especially with all these reinforcements coming in day after day." He shuffled his papers for emphasis.

"I believe they may actually be off-duty, sir," Dudley said. "I just spoke to Sergeant Barker."

Freemantle's brows lifted in surprise.

"Oh, indeed. Well, as I said, it's difficult to keep track."

It was strange the colonel would make such a mistake, Dudley thought as he took his leave. He thought a commanding officer should know what was happening within his battalion at all times. But it was not for him to judge. He was nothing but a fresh subaltern.

He made his way to the regimental quartermaster's depot, and there, as he had suspected, he found Oakes. Oakes had come across some of his old comrades, and he and Hester were in the midst of a joyful reunion. Oakes was displaying his empty eye socket to a parcel of gaunt and bearded men. Dudley recognized them as veteran members of his company.

After exchanging joyful greetings, Dudley informed Oakes he was going to meet the company officers. He asked the men for the location of Captain David Neville's tent. They told him, and he excused himself to make his way there.

At the captain's tent, a servant let Dudley in before scurrying off to find his master. Dudley stood inside the flap and waited. He studied the tent's flawless order. Against one canvas wall stood a low cot, its blankets neatly folded. At the foot of the cot was a leather trunk, its brass furnishings gleaming. A camp desk sat at the opposite side of the room. On the desk was a bundle of paper, squared to the desk edge and weighted with an ink bottle.

Such exacting neatness seemed out of place in the Crimea. Whoever this Captain Neville was, Dudley thought, he was a fastidious fellow.

Fifteen minutes passed before the tent flap opened and Dudley finally met his new company commander.

"Ah, yes," the newcomer said, "Our queen's favoured promotion, former Sergeant Dudley."

"Ensign William Dudley, sir," Dudley replied, not caring for these opening remarks.

"Yes, of course," Neville said with a confident smile. He was a tall and well-built man, and it was easy to see he had not been in the Crimea long. His uniform was in as perfect order as his tent. The greatcoat he wore was new, while his high boots gleamed from toe to knee. His sword was just as well-polished. It looked as if he had just trimmed his reddish mustache, and he had oiled his hair and combed it back from his forehead.

Dudley recognized Neville as one of those aloof officers he had sometimes glimpsed during his training. Neville had often stood apart on the edge of the parade square, usually smoking a cigar. He had never looked as if he had anything to do with the procedures at hand. In that way, he was a typical officer.

"Ensign Dudley it is, then," Neville added. "I am Major David Neville, though I hold the position of captain in this regiment. Allow me to welcome you back." He extended his hand for Dudley to shake.

"Thank you, sir. It is indeed good to be back." Dudley attempted a bit of levity by adding, "I was afraid I might miss the end of the war, to be frank."

Neville gave him a polite grin, then narrowed his eyes.

"You don't sound like many ex-sergeants I've heard, Ensign. You strike me as an educated man."

"Yes, sir. I was to go to Cambridge but chose the army instead."

Neville chuckled in mild disbelief.

"In the ranks?"

Dudley swallowed. "Well, my decision was rather against the wishes of my family, sir. The ranks...were my only option."

"Ah, well, it has all worked out for you anyhow, what? I trust we shall get along quite well, Ensign."

Neville seemed on the verge of saying something more, but an artillery duel had broken out at the front. The tent walls rippled with each concussion, although the guns were several miles away.

"Does seem to be a constant thing," the captain muttered. Then he turned back to Dudley. "Have your servant take your baggage to Lieutenant Arbuthnot's tent. He's in there alone, so you may as well share. Er, you have a servant, don't you?"

"Yes, sir," Dudley replied. The only baggage he owned was his enlisted man's knapsack and its few contents, but he saw no need to mention this.

"Good, then."

That was the end of the interview. Dudley trudged off to find his new lodgings.

Sergeant Brian Barker wandered back from the Light Division canteen, a pound of cheese and some Turkish tobacco clutched in his left hand. He was worried, and aimed to have a sit-down and a smoke to sort things out. He always thought better when he had some activity to keep his body busy, even when that activity was just puffing away on a pipe. When the body was busy, the mind could not help but work along with it.

He thought of his chance meeting with Ensign Dudley. Dudley had been an upstart lance-corporal when Barker had first met him, young and inexperienced. He had possessed an infuriating educated bearing mixed with bewilderment and enthusiasm. Barker had not been sympathetic to anyone's situation but his own at the time, and had decided to make Dudley a target. He had tried to make Dudley's life as difficult as possible.

Dudley had been sincere in his passion for the army and all its notions of honour and glory, of duty to God, Queen, and Comrades. Barker had hoped to see him fall, to see his beliefs come crashing down. For that to happen, the army would have to fail, and Barker knew that it would, sooner or later.

This prediction came true with the onset of the war. The expeditionary force had waited for months in Varna, sitting idle and waiting for disaster. Then the cholera had struck. As Barker had hoped, Dudley had reacted with disillusioned outrage.

But instead of condemning the army, Dudley had looked for ways to improve things where he could. He insisted that if the army had made mistakes, it would not make them again.

At least, not if reasonable men were in charge, and the British were reasonable people.

This naive optimism—or perhaps it was not so naive after all—had been infectious. Bit by bit, Barker had come to like Dudley, to see in him the ideals and hopes he had once shared then lost.

Barker had thought he had lost those ideals forever, but in the mud and horror of last autumn's campaigning, he had found them again in the outstanding morale of his comrades. Their ability to prevail against overwhelming odds while fighting the enemy, their own administrators, and the earth itself had made him feel weak-willed and petulant. He was unworthy of their company, he had felt, and unworthy of the memory of his wife, who had been one of the many victims of the cholera epidemic.

Perhaps he would never trust or respect military authority as he once had. Respect would have to be earned from now on, and his standards were high. But he had regained his sense of duty to his comrades, and to the high dreams of his youth. He had also regained his rank of sergeant—and his determination to keep it.

That was why he was worried. Circumstances had changed, and now threatened that determination. Events had given his new-found confidence a bit of a check. He did not fear many things—not death, nor a stout flogging, nor the imposed will of another. But there was one thing he did fear, and that was losing his self-control again, and with it his self-respect.

He feared something would happen to cause him to slip back into the old frame of mind, the self-pitying frame of mind. He had lived with it for years, and its memory brought nothing but shame. He would not go back if he could help it.

He had once faced a charge of neglect of duty. His conviction had brought with it a demotion and a reputation for

bad character. The charge had not been true, but in his indignation, he had done nothing to clear his name. Instead, he
had become what he had denied being. At the time, he had
seen that reaction as a challenge to those who had destroyed
him. But in reality, it had been a form of self-pity, of self-
indulgence. Self-pity at the unfair treatment he had received
from two young officers.

One of those officers was dead now, killed at the Alma,
and damn his soul. The other was still alive. He was a gentleman, an officer whose word had meant much more than
that of a sergeant.

An officer named David Neville.

Lieutenant Arbuthnot's tent was on the same camp street as
Captain Neville's. Dudley ducked his head through the flap,
but the tent was unoccupied. Stepping inside, he surveyed the
scattered contents, the belongings of the man who would
become his closest companion.

A cot stood on the dirt floor, and beside it sat a small
iron-bound trunk and a pair of polished shoes. Other items
included a canvas camp stool, a small writing desk that could
rest in one's lap, and a campaign saddle and saddle bags.
From the central pole hung an oil lantern, and below it a
small looking-glass.

It was not the picture of tidiness Neville's quarters had
been, but Dudley was still reluctant to touch anything. He
chose a patch of floor near the flap to spread one of his two
wool blankets. This was all he had for bedding until he could
find something better.

He was still smoothing the blanket's corners when the
flap opened and in popped a man's head. When the newcomer spied Dudley on the floor, he exclaimed, "Oh!"

Dudley leapt up from his crouch and said, "Lieutenant Arbuthnot? I'm William Dudley, the new subaltern."

Arbuthnot blinked a few times, his mouth sagging in bewilderment. He had a round chubby face, a receding hairline, and a pair of oval spectacles on the end of his nose. After a moment, his cheeks rose in a broad grin, and he said, "Yes, of course! Ha-ha! Gave me a startle there for a minute, thought I was being burgled or something. William Dudley, eh? Well, I'm Harry Arbuthnot. Harry Arbuthnot, and pleased to make your acquaintance."

Arbuthnot stepped inside, and they shook hands. The lieutenant then glanced around and said, "I'd best move some of my things to one side, eh? I see you haven't brought much with you, though I'm sure you will be picking up some necessaries soon."

Dudley already owned what an enlisted man considered necessary, but he said, "I aim to send my servant down to Balaclava tomorrow to find me a pony and a packsaddle."

"You have a servant, do you? Well, that's jolly fine. We're all aware you're from the ranks, but I don't mind. After all, Sir Colin Campbell had a humble beginning, and there's no finer soldier in this army."

Dudley nodded, wondering if he should consider this remark an insult. He decided not to. This Arbuthnot seemed an agreeable character, and had spoken with obvious good will. Dudley's guard began to fall.

"So, you were in Scutari hospital," Arbuthnot went on excitedly. "Did you see Miss Nightingale there? We've all heard so much about her and her ladies. I say, that's an intriguing medallion."

Dudley's coat was undone, displaying his tin soldier where it hung from its chain. Arbuthnot stared at it in apparent fascination.

"Yes, that's Wellington," Dudley explained. "Last of a box of tin soldiers my father gave me when I was very young. I keep him for good luck."

"Well, he seems to work, don't he, given your career so far! I have a good luck charm, too, you know." Arbuthnot sprang to his trunk and threw back the lid. Reaching inside, he took out a small bundle. When he had brought the bundle into the light, Dudley saw that it was a braid of what looked like human hair. It was about a foot and a half long and tied on one end with a bit of green ribbon. Arbuthnot gazed on it with reverence.

"The hair of my dear Margaret," he said, voice hushed. "My fiancée, waiting for me in England." He lifted the braid to stroke one plump cheek with it. "She had to have it cut but gave it to me for good luck. As I said."

"That was a charming thing for her to do." Dudley felt his relief giving way to mild horror. Then again, he thought, some might have considered his tin soldier strange, while it was common for men to carry locks of hair—if not full braids—from their sweethearts.

"Yes." Arbuthnot caressed the length of brown hair for another moment then gently returned it to the trunk.

Dudley cleared his throat then asked, "So, how goes the conduct of the siege? Has the regiment been involved in any recent scraps?"

"The siege? Well, I suppose you arrived just too late for yesterday's sortie. And the French and their obsession with taking the Mamelon rifle pits."

"Mamelon?" Dudley did not remember a fort of that name.

Arbuthnot sat on the lid of his trunk.

"A detached earthwork the Russians have built several yards out from the Malakoff. It had been just a low hill the French were holding, but the enemy took it late last month, pushing back the French right-attack. Now the Russians have thrown up walls and dug a series of rifle pits in front. The French have been desperate to take those rifle pits." He shook his head. "The Russians have counterattacked several times, and last night made an attack all along the allied lines. We took about a hundred casualties, I am told, the French two hundred. But you should have seen the Russian dead. They left some eight hundred fellows lying in front of our trenches."

"So, really, the conduct of the war has not changed since last November," Dudley murmured, half to himself.

Arbuthnot removed his spectacles and began polishing the lenses with a handkerchief.

"No," he said, sounding disappointed. "I suppose not."

CHAPTER 3

April 4, 1855

The siege had not progressed, but as Dudley soon discovered, the daily routine in the camps had improved. Before the battle at Inkerman, he had been on duty round the clock, sometimes going days without sleep. Now his duties were light. He could not be sure if this was because he was an officer or because the regiment had been reinforced to near full capacity. Perhaps it was a bit of both. Whatever the reason, he could now go a day or two and have nothing to do.

During one of these idle evenings, he sat in his tent composing a new letter home. His uneasiness over what this officer's life might hold for him was giving way to excited anticipation he wished to share.

Arbuthnot had been kind enough to lend his lap desk, and Oakes had brought some writing paper from a general store in Kadikoi. Dudley bit the end of his pen and wondered where to begin. The small oil lantern burned on its pole, casting flickering illumination over the canvas walls and across the desk. Outside the tent, the raised voices of men sang an unfamiliar song:

> When I was young and in my prime
> I thought I'd go and join the line,
> And as a soldier cut a shine,
> In a lot called the hungry army.

> Sound the bugle, blow the horn,
> Fight for glory, night and morn,
> Hungry soldiers, ragged and torn,
> Just returned from the army.

The words seemed appropriate, Dudley thought. They expressed the bitterness of the winter of suffering yet hinted that something good could come of it. The song made him realize how much he had missed this life while in Scutari. That could have seemed perverse, for the horrors of this war had exceeded anything he could ever have imagined, but he had missed being here with his regiment, standing with them against the enemy in the field, despite the risk of death. His initial discomfort at the noise of the siege guns had passed. He was once again indifferent to their sound.

"I am glad to be back," he wrote near the top of his page. He wondered whether to address the letter to Jane or his aunt. That would depend on the contents. He wanted to describe his aims as an officer but he also wished to focus on some of the recent fighting. Arbuthnot had described the combat in some detail. His aunt found his depictions of battle unsettling, so he scrawled "My Dear Cousin Jane" above what he had just written. He would compose a second letter for his aunt.

His pen scratched across the page. First, he explained his relief at the promising reception he had received from the company officers. He also admitted his concern about having to buy a horse, for he had never been comfortable around the animals.

"On St. Patrick's Day last," he wrote, "which came and passed while I was on board ship, there were horse races here in the Crimea."

> I am told that it was a fine day and the ground dry, though the siege guns could be heard now and then in the background. After a while, however, you scarcely notice those guns, and horse racing seems to be a favourite pastime for most of the officers.
>
> I have vowed to embrace the officer's life as much as my pocket book allows, and will have to take part in one of these events. Though I must admit the thought fills me with dread. I was fine on the back of our old pony Daisy, but that was some time ago, and she was not capable of much more than an amble.

He paused, letting the pen rest in its ink bottle. Even writing a single line about home gave him a pang of regret and loneliness. He wondered if Jane ever showed his letters to his uncle. It would be strange if she did not at least try, knowing Jane. Dudley hoped that she did. If his uncle heard more of what he had endured and witnessed, perhaps some stirring of pride might emerge. That was a vain and desperate wish, he supposed, but not unrealistic.

He took the pen from its bottle. He suspected his uncle might even enjoy his accounts of battle if Jane could get him to read them.

"Let me tell you about what has happened here in the last week," he wrote.

The Russians have built a new fortification called the Mamelon, which is detached from their main line. In front of it are a number of rifle pits. Those pits are vacant by day, but every night Russian sharpshooters occupy them and keep up a galling fire on the exposed ends of the French right-attack trenches. The French were determined to seize these rifle pits, so assembled a force of their elite troops, the Zouaves, whom I have described to you before. You may recall that they were originally North African regiments, and though now most of their men are European, they still wear a North African uniform of fez caps and turbans, baggy pantaloons and such.

At any rate, the night of St. Patrick's Day, the French sent some six thousand of these fellows down to our positions. From there they moved into our advanced trenches at night. They sent their covering party forward to take possession of the rifle pits, thinking them still empty, but the Russian sharpshooters were already there! The fight lasted five hours. I was not there, of course, but some of the fellows explained to me how peculiar it was to hear all musketry with no accompanying artillery.

While this was going on, four of our divisions turned out in case the French needed assistance. Our lot waited as the fight continued, listening to the encouragement and cries of the Zouave officers between volleys, then the answering Russian volleys and Russian cheering. At length, the Russians gained the upper hand and forced the French to withdraw. They never called for British help, and our men all marched back to camp.

The next day, the French commander, General Canrobert (who had taken over from poor Arnaud), rode out with his staff to examine the rifle pits, the Malakov, and the Mamelon. At twilight, he sent out another strong force of Zouaves and a field battery. After a second hard fight, they managed to dislodge the Russians. They then reversed the sandbags and loopholes in the rifle pits and fired on the Mamelon.

But the struggle was not over, for on the night of the twenty-second, a day before I arrived, the Russians opened an artillery barrage on the rifle pits at 10 o'clock. There were only about five hundred Zouaves in the pits at the time, and the firing lasted about an hour. After that, the Russians attacked all along our lines, though their main aim was those troublesome rifle pits. The Zouaves were quite worn out by then. Their drummers sounded the 'pas de charge' to urge them on, but the superior Russian numbers drove them out of the prize they had just gained.

So the fight has gone, back and forth, though the French command had not made a coordinated attack. Lieutenant Arbuthnot, with whom I share a tent, tells me that one of our officers commented that

General Canrobert should have his name changed to 'Robert Can't.' Maybe there is something in that, because I have seen the Zouaves in action and they are excellent men. It seems a pity that their general is wasting them this way, in these piecemeal assaults, with no proper support.

Please don't think I am bloodthirsty, but I'm eager to get a crack at the Russians. A proper crack, that is, that will put an end to this siege once and for all. I have waited for so very long, that it would be nice to see some action, and to bring this all to a satisfactory conclusion.

As Dudley scrawled this last line, Lieutenant Arbuthnot ducked in under the tent flap and declared, "I have just had the most remarkable chat with some of our captured Russian officers."

Dudley looked up from his page.

"Oh? You had a chat?"

The lantern light played across the lieutenant's face, emphasizing its rounded contours.

"Yes. Some of them speak excellent French, much better than my own. They offered us cigars and did their best to be agreeable. I must say, they were rather complimentary to our fellows. One saw that I was an English officer, and said how brave he thought our men were. It surprised him how well we had all held up after such a winter, and here we were living in tents."

"I daresay the Russians had a better time of it in the Sevastopol barracks," Dudley commented, although he knew it could not have been much better.

"A bit maybe. But this fellow I was talking to also said that he wished the war over, he had seen quite enough. I then asked him if there were any ladies still in the town, and he said there were plenty. They had advised them to leave, but they were reluctant, this being their home. I said that I didn't like the thought of us shelling ladies."

"Of course not," Dudley remarked. He knew he need not say any more, that Arbuthnot would soon continue. The lieutenant loved to talk.

Arbuthnot sank onto his camp stool and removed his spectacles.

"The French officers were not very friendly. One fellow kept pointing to a large pile of Russian dead who had not yet been buried. I thought that quite rude."

"Perhaps they are dejected over their losses at the rifle pits," Dudley suggested.

This time Arbuthnot did not reply, for he had opened his trunk and reached inside. Bringing out the braid of hair, he said to it, "What do you think of our possibly shelling ladies, my dear?"

Dudley watched him with curiosity. The lieutenant was ignoring him now, stroking the braid with evident devotion. There was something ghoulish about the gesture.

He opened his mouth to ask if he had a picture of his lady then thought better of it. Arbuthnot appeared to be in a sort of trance.

He turned back to his letter.

The next day, the fifth of April, Dudley returned to the trenches. Lieutenant-Colonel Freemantle ordered all able-bodied officers to accompany the battalion, save those on special or detached duties. The companies assembled for parade in the morning and marched off to guard a section of the British right-attack.

The Royal Hampshire Fusiliers took a position in the most advanced British trench. The men of No. 3 Company arrayed themselves in a rough double line, half lounging in the bottom of the trench, the other half lying or crouching on the slope of the forward parapet. Over the course of the morning, the Russian guns kept up a sporadic firing. Several rounds of solid shot came bumping along the ground, and a few of the big mortar shells known as "Whistling Dicks" screamed overhead.

The incoming fire prompted the men on the parapet to jump or slither back into the trench and press against the walls. There, they waited for the shot or shells to land, praying that one would not make it into the trench.

Allied batteries then answered the Russian salvos. When all was quiet again, the men behaved as if the danger did not exist. They talked and joked, some playing dice or dominoes in the bottom of the trench. They had grown accustomed to this life.

The artillery duels continued off and on all day every day. Often, the exchange of fire continued far into the night, the orange flashes of the guns piercing the darkness. The men had learned to abide it without complaint.

Dudley had positioned himself on the forward parapet to watch for the enemy artillery and other signs of activity. The parapet was made of earth-filled baskets called *gabions* that creaked and prodded him when he shifted his weight. He shaded his eyes with one hand and studied the walls the Russian engineers had constructed to defend Sevastopol. Those walls loomed about a half mile away.

Sevastopol was a naval port that lay on the south side of a long harbor. Another inlet, jutting south from the harbour, split the city in two and served as a well-sheltered dockyard for the Russian Black Sea Fleet. Half of that fleet had been sunk in the harbour mouth while the other half was bottled up inside. The sunken vessels kept the navies of Britain and France out of the harbour, but the allies had still cut Sevastopol off from the sea.

This was step one in securing the port. Step two was still nowhere near to complete. The allies had yet to take the city, and yet to destroy the dockyard.

A half-circle of defensive earthworks, trenches and batteries protected Sevastopol on its landward side. The strongest of these earthworks were the Redan in the center and the Malakov on the allied right. The Redan was a huge salient angle projecting from the main defensive wall. It resembled a monstrous arrowhead pointed at the heart of the allied siege lines. In technical terms, this type of fortification was called a redan, but this one was so huge the British had dubbed it *the* Redan.

The Malakov, on the other hand, was a plain rectangular earthwork surrounding the remains of a white masonry tower. British artillery had knocked the tower to pieces months ago, but the earthworks, more formidable by far, remained.

Facing the Russian defenses were the allied siege lines, or *attacks*. Each attack comprised a complex system of trenches and artillery batteries. Holding the extreme left of the line was the French left-attack. East of that, in the center of the line, were the British left and right attacks, facing the Redan. On the extreme right, the French right-attack faced the Malakov.

The main feature of each attack was a series of parallel trenches, each closer to the Russian wall. Zigzagging approach trenches linked the parallels. In the rear lay the artillery batteries.

So far, the British had constructed three parallels, and work continued on further approaches. The third parallel was still not close enough to Sevastopol. It would be suicidal for the infantry to mount an assault across so much open ground in the face of Russian artillery.

When an assault did come, Dudley would join it as part of a company he only half knew. He would have to become better acquainted with his men before then, before he helped lead them against the enemy walls.

He turned to Sergeant Barker, who lay at his side.

"How have the new men been reacting?" he asked. "I remember that the old company was in remarkably good spirits before Inkerman."

"Those spirits suffered over the winter, sir," Barker said, "as was only natural. I'm amazed the lads were as cheerful as they were, which wasn't much. But, as you can see for yourself, things are picking up, thanks to the improving weather. These are good lads." He looked down into the trench then back at Dudley. "But they don't like these here rabbit holes. They want to get out and get at old Ivan."

Dudley nodded, for he felt the same way. It was a static war now, a war in which death could come from a random shell or a sniper's bullet. It was a war of waiting. The rumours did not agree upon the timing for the assault, and he could sense the general frustration in the battalion. He knew it was his duty to help the men through that frustration. He had to reassure them that no attack would come until all was ready.

"A few more weeks," he said. "It will only be a few more weeks."

Barker nodded. "Aye, I suppose so."

Dudley looked along the line of the trench, then lowered his voice to say, "I don't know many of these men, Sergeant. It is almost an entirely new company. I can use this time to familiarize myself with the new arrivals, and allow them time to know me."

"Plenty of time for that, sir. And they already know you by reputation. You're the fellow that took a battery at Inkerman."

"Well, I had some help." Dudley smiled.

Barker returned the grin. "Never mind that modesty, sir."

Dudley chuckled. He had every reason for confidence. As an officer, he had an obligation to offer his men something they could trust. He knew he could give them his ability to fight.

He had spent much of his convalescence in Scutari reflecting upon his performance in battle. His initial reaction in the face of enemy fire, he had concluded, was always fear, but somehow he managed to channel that fear into energy. It gave way to an overwhelming excitement, and a clarity of vision. Dudley was not the perfect soldier he wished to be, but he was more than capable on a battlefield. He had proven himself there, and he had proven he could lead men in combat.

"If you will excuse me, Sergeant," he said as he slithered down from the parapet, "I think I shall do the rounds."

"Enjoy yourself, sir," Barker remarked.

Dudley walked along the trench, greeting the men as he went. They returned his greetings, nodding and calling him "sir." They all looked neat and soldier-like, he thought, in their new greatcoats and round, visorless forage caps. Gone now were the furs and sheepskins. The weather was improving, and Colonel Freemantle had issued general orders banning all non-regulation clothing.

After passing several unknown faces, most of them bearded, Dudley came upon a red-haired Irishman named Aiden O'Ryan. O'Ryan was an experienced man who had taught Dudley much about soldiering, and was now colour-sergeant of No. 3 Company. He and Dudley had once been friends, although their reunion, now Dudley was an officer, had been strained. Dudley still sensed an awkwardness as he greeted O'Ryan.

"How are you, Colour-Sergeant?"

"Just fine, sir," O'Ryan replied, his expression a mask. He turned to the man next to him and added, "I don't believe ye've met Sergeant Hoskins, sir."

A man in an open greatcoat stepped forward and gave Dudley a crooked grin. So, this was Sergeant Hoskins. Dudley returned his salute, but found himself agreeing with Barker that Hoskins seemed an unsavory, brutish-looking fellow, with hollow pockmarked cheeks and shifty eyes.

"Were you at Fairbridge, Sergeant Hoskins?" Dudley asked.

"Yessir," Hoskins replied with a sharp nod. "I was an orderly for Cap'n Neville."

"Oh, I see. Well, it was good I finally met you."

He moved on, feeling dissatisfied and even a bit embarrassed. He hoped O'Ryan did not think him ridiculous, a sergeant playing at being an officer. In that respect, it was fortunate the company had so many new men. He would have a clean slate with them.

As for the rest, there were a few veterans Dudley knew he could trust. He noticed one of these fellows watching him as he moved along the trench and called out in greeting.

"Private Johnson, it's good to see you."

Johnson was a quiet man with narrow features that seemed locked in a sinister sneer. He had an almost fanatical enthusiasm for drill, his uniform, and his rifle. He was also one of the best marksmen in the battalion.

"How do you like the new Enfield, Johnson?" Dudley asked.

"Love it, sir!" Johnson said, shaking his rifle in a gesture of triumph. The Enfield was a slim weapon with a brass muzzle cap and three reinforcing bands holding the wooden stock to the barrel. Johnson's rifle brass and wood gleamed from polishing and oiling.

"It is, indeed, a fine rifle," another voice said. Dudley turned to see Captain Neville approaching with Arbuthnot close at his heels.

The captain stopped and frowned at the old Minié rifle slung from Dudley's shoulder. Neville wore both a sword and a holstered revolver, but Dudley's only weapon was the rifle he had carried before his promotion. Carrying a rifle also necessitated his wearing his old cartridge box, making him look more like a private than a junior officer.

Dudley was about to defend his need to go armed, but Neville did not pursue the subject. Instead, he jerked his thumb over his shoulder and said, "The blasted French next door have sent twice as many men to guard their trenches as we have." He chuckled. "They're afraid of another toweling like the one they got in front of the Mamelon."

Arbuthnot's eyes brightened.

"Do you know what I heard? A few weeks ago, an article in the *Times* mentioned that no general officer was present on duty in the trenches. Not long after that, Lord Raglan issued orders that a General Officer of the Week was to be given Superintendance of the Trenches." He laughed. "So now we know where Lord Raglan gets his orders. From the *Times!*"

Neville gave Arbuthnot a glare of evident distaste, and said, "I'd advise you not to pay attention to what the *Times* says, Lieutenant. And you, too, Mister Dudley. Neither will I care for it if I hear of anybody speaking to that man Russell. I agree with Lord Raglan that this reporting of the army's doings is a vulgar disgrace."

With that, Neville moved on down the trench. Deflated, Arbuthnot watched him go.

"I thought it was an amusing anecdote," he said to Dudley.

"Don't worry," Dudley said. "I thought so, too."

Arbuthnot was a peculiar fellow, but despite his quirks, Dudley was growing fond of him. He had a childlike innocence that made him an agreeable tent mate, if not terribly impressive as an officer. Dudley wondered how he would fare in action.

Neville had halted a few yards away to speak to Sergeant Hoskins. The sergeant grinned and nodded at something the captain said. Neville then returned to Dudley's side, and said to Arbuthnot, "Will you excuse us a moment?"

As he led Dudley away by the elbow, the captain remarked, "I see that you know Sergeant Barker."

"Yes, sir."

Neville halted.

"What is your opinion of his abilities?"

Dudley considered that question before replying. Doubtless Neville knew of Barker's reputation, and would not have had a chance to see for himself whether Barker had changed or not.

"The men will follow him, sir," Dudley said. "They trust him."

Neville's eyes narrowed. "Do you trust him?"

Dudley hesitated. He remembered Barker slouching on sentry, canteen filled with gin. He also remembered Barker rallying the men to move artillery and following him against the Russian battery at Inkerman. And Barker had saved Dudley's life during a skirmish in one of the old forward trenches.

"I trust him with my life, sir," Dudley declared.

Neville's eyebrows shot up.

"Really? Well, that's good to hear." He looked away for a moment then back at his subordinate. "We shall see how things turn out."

He turned and moved back toward Sergeant Hoskins. Dudley returned to the parapet to watch for the enemy.

CHAPTER 4

April 1855

The horse kicked a spray of mud as it charged across the Chersonese Uplands. The spring rains had begun, again transforming the barren plain into a sodden marsh. Dudley's legs were soaked, but he refused to check his pace. His backside kept slapping the saddle, and he had come close to falling off several times; but the best way to get over his fear was to keep riding. He would just have to push himself until the fear disappeared with familiarity.

Private Oakes had found the horse in Balaclava, a fine little brown gelding Dudley had named Bill. It had not taken long for him to form an attachment to the animal, which was affectionate and spirited. Bill's occasional wild behavior was the result of over-excitement rather than rebelliousness, he had already decided. The pony obeyed his commands without hesitation and hung his head when he knew he had done something to displease his new master.

Acquiring Bill had been a stroke of luck in more ways than one. Dudley had little use for a manservant and had searched in vain for things that Private Oakes could do for him. Mrs. Oakes had almost usurped her husband's place. She had mended Dudley's worn undress uniform and continued to do his laundry as well as that of any other man who could pay. Oakes had been left twiddling his thumbs and eyeing his rifle, doubtless thinking of sneaking off for trench duty.

Now that Dudley had a pony, Oakes would serve as his groom. The old fellow did not know much about horses, but he was already learning, asking the advice of other grooms and experienced riders. And he had made the acquaintance of a farrier with one of the cavalry regiments.

Dudley gave the reins a gentle and even pull, and Bill slowed to a halt. He leaned forward and stroked the pony's neck.

"What a good fellow you are, Bill."

Bill snorted and gave his head a vigorous shake. Dudley straightened and tried to catch his breath.

The music of a brass band came drifting over the plain, emanating from the little port of Kamiesch. Bill cropped new shoots of grass as Dudley gazed in the direction of the sound. Kamiesch lay partway between Balaclava and Sevastopol and served as the French supply base. A crowd of soldiers and civilians had gathered on the edge of the French supply road.

With a gentle squeeze of his knees and a click of his tongue, Dudley got Bill moving again toward the source of the music. From horseback, he could see over the heads of the spectators. Bill slowed to a halt, his ears twitching at the growing sound of the band, which had begun to play "Rule Britannia." The pony seemed as curious as its rider.

A moment later, the band came into view. The choice of songs must have been a compliment from one ally to another, for the musicians belonged to a Turkish column. The column was approaching from Kamiesch, the band in the vanguard.

The Turkish uniforms were simple and modern, consisting of blue frock coats, fezes and trousers. As the regiments passed, Dudley saw that some wore baggy pantaloons. At the head of each unit rode the colonel and his two majors, all mounted on small horses about the same size as Bill. The animals bobbed their heads with each step.

Behind the officers came their pipe bearers then the drums, fifes and trumpets and, finally, the men themselves. The soldiers carried old-fashioned flintlocks that gleamed in the April sunshine, and each unit carried a bright standard emblazoned with the crescent and star.

Dudley loved soldiers on parade, and was impressed with this spectacle. He doubted these fellows would be put to much use with their outdated weaponry, although he noted they had come prepared for a long campaign. A host of mules, tents piled on their backs, marched on the right of the column. The Turkish field artillery marched on the left, each bronze gun drawn by six horses.

The sight of so many Turks made Dudley think of Scutari. With that came thoughts of the Barracks Hospital, and of Elizabeth Montague. He had been trying not to think of her since his return to the Crimea but images and memories of her came unbidden.

He recalled a night at the height of his illness when he had been lying sick in the dark of his ward, unable to sleep. He had watched a tiny point of light draw near, moving from bed to bed. That had been Miss Nightingale, going from patient to patient with her little oil lamp. She always set the lamp down before attending to a man's complaint, where it burned as a beacon of hope for all those in need of care.

Elizabeth had accompanied Miss Nightingale that night. She must have recognized Dudley's suffering, for she had come directly to his side and placed her hand on his forehead. He had closed his eyes and felt a peaceful contentment spread through his body. Then her soft voice had whispered, "There, now, Mister Dudley, sleep and dream of home in Hampshire."

She knew he was from Hampshire, for he had told her one afternoon as she fed him with a tin spoon. He had been too weak to lift the spoon to his mouth but strong enough to speak between swallows. He had described his childhood, how he had enjoyed the wide, open countryside near his uncle's church and school. He had loved the brooks and the copses, and chasing butterflies, and going fishing. He had loved leading his little cousin Jane on long treks in search of whatever adventures they could stumble across.

Elizabeth had listened, smiling, and then he had learned she was from Hampshire as well. She had spent her childhood in a fine country house near Winchester.

When Dudley had grown stronger, Elizabeth had elaborated, describing her life in that house. She had begun with an account of her father's tenant farmers and how she had been ashamed of the disparity between master and servant. It was not her father's fault, she had insisted, but the structure of society. Papa, she said, was a Radical who believed in reform. He was kind to "his people." From him, Elizabeth had taken her inspiration and had decided to become a nurse, in part to right some of society's wrongs.

She had told this tale with a passion she usually kept in check. It had been Dudley's most telling glimpse of what lay behind her careful guard. He liked to think she had dropped that guard because he was not just another patient. As far as he knew, she had not told others the same things she had told him.

He sighed at these recollections. The last of the Turkish baggage animals had clomped past, bringing a touch of regret. His chances of seeing Elizabeth again were slim.

He turned Bill and moved at a canter towards the north and the Light Division camp. When the pony decided to gallop, Dudley let him and hung on for dear life.

On Easter Sunday, the Allied regiments paraded for divine service. Each regiment in the British Army formed three sides of a square to hear the words of the Protestant chaplains or Catholic priests. In the neighboring French camps, the regiments turned out for High Mass, attended with all the pomp and noise of their military bands.

At daybreak on Easter Monday, the whole line of allied artillery batteries opened fire on Sevastopol.

Before the bombardment commenced, Dudley rode out on Bill to watch. He made his way toward the Woronzov road, eager to witness this significant event. The Royal Hants had received no orders, but there was only one reason to bombard the enemy fortifications—the long-awaited assault was near, perhaps days away.

It would be a preliminary assault, Dudley reasoned, but still important. The British trenches were about three hundred yards from the face of the Redan, so that could not be the objective. The lesser Russian defences, such as the Mamelon, would have to fall first. The bombardment would pave the way for that attack.

Two main groups of British gun batteries lay parallel to the Russian works. The first was Chapman's Battery, in the rear of the left-attack trenches, and the second Gordon's Battery, in the rear of the right-attack trenches. Chapman's Battery actually contained six batteries, five of heavy guns and two of 13-inch mortars. Gordon's Battery contained six more batteries, four of heavy guns and two of mortars. An additional five-gun battery, manned by sailors, lay to the right rear of Gordon's Battery.

Dudley's company had helped build that emplacement months before.

A scattering of similar detached batteries lay here and there behind the trenches, bringing the total number of Royal Artillery and Royal Navy guns facing Sevastopol to one hundred and twenty-three. There was a like number of French guns.

Dudley guided Bill north along the Woronzov Road, the main route from the uplands into Sevastopol. The road followed the wide Woronzov ravine all the way to the Russian earthworks. The ravine ran at a right angle to the British gun emplacements and served as the natural divider between the left and right-attack. He knew he should not get too far forward, so turned his pony left off the road and up the ravine's western embankment.

The slope was a jumble of rocks, and Bill stumbled, almost pitching Dudley from the saddle. He gripped the pommel and managed to hang on as Bill scrambled up to the even ground just behind Chapman's Battery.

Moving to a safe distance, Dudley waited with a collection of other officers and enlisted men. He noticed that one officer had brought his wife, a slight woman with dark hair who held her husband's arm and huddled close to him. Lord Raglan and his divisional commanders were also nearby, positioned between two of the gun emplacements.

The air was cool, and Dudley glanced skyward. The sun was rising red in the east, but a gathering of deep-bellied and foreboding clouds hung overhead. The noise of the guns would reflect from those clouds. He wondered if it might rain.

A command rang out, and the first of the guns fired, lighting the early morning with a bright jet of flame. Dudley started, and Bill shied. The rest of the guns began to fire with a series of tremendous cracks, as if the earth itself were splitting. The spectators all flinched, and Bill tossed his head while

Dudley struggled to keep him calm. The officer's wife had clapped her hands over her ears.

By the time Bill had steadied, the noise of the guns had become a continuous rumble. A strange, cold ache grew within Dudley's inner ears. After a while, the guns no longer sounded so loud—they were too loud to hear. It was as if his ears refused to accept so much sound at once. The firing became muted, while the ground shook and the air quivered with each detonation.

Most of the Russian batteries returned fire, the most vigorous response coming from the so-called Flagstaff and Garden batteries across from the French left-attack. The Redan also gave a healthy response, but the Malakov and detached Mamelon remained silent. The bombardment might have taken their garrisons by surprise. Dudley could see where the allied shot struck home, casting great chunks of earth and debris into the air. The smoke balls of bursting shells dotted the sky above Sevastopol.

When the Russian gunners at last found the range to their targets, shells began to fall near and just in front of Chapman's Battery. The spectators retired farther to the rear, while some decided the danger was too great and went back to the camps. Dudley remained, fascinated by the conflagration.

A single heavy rain drop splashed across his nose. He absently wiped it away, but a moment later, another drop struck his forage cap. Others began pattering across Bill's neck and back. Dudley again glanced skyward.

The overhanging clouds burst, the rain coming down like a single sheet of water. A high wind rose, drawing the smoke away from the guns in long trails of dense vapor. Within seconds, the thick curtain of rain had obscured the sun and the flashing of the artillery. Dudley huddled in his greatcoat and decided he had seen enough.

"Come on, Bill," he shouted, turning the pony and nudging him forward. Bill gave a snort and complied.

When Dudley reached the camp, the streets were ankle-deep in mud. Clumps of rats, constant pests, sought the high ground of crates and parked wagons. The gale had blown down several tents, and men struggled with the flapping canvas, trying to undo the damage. He was relieved to find his own tent still stood but feared he would find the earthen floor in a sorry state.

Oakes scurried forward to grasp Bill's bridle, shouting, "Feels like hell broke loose, sir!"

Soaked and wretched, Dudley replied with a curt, "Take care of Bill, will you?"

He ducked into the tent to find Arbuthnot sitting in his camp chair, the braid of hair across his knees. The tent floor was well-drained, and the only water present had blown in through the flap.

Dudley had fashioned a makeshift table and chair from two empty crates. Without saying anything, he sat and began unbuttoning his greatcoat.

"Quite a storm," Arbuthnot cried over the noise of wind, rain, and guns.

"How long will it last, I wonder." At the sight of the dry floor, Dudley's irritation subsided. He would not have to sleep in mud.

"How long will what last?" Arbuthnot asked. "The rain, or the bombardment?"

Dudley shrugged. "Both. How long will either last?" He hoped the storm would end soon. More mud would hamper the attack. It would cost lives.

Arbuthnot returned his braid to its hiding place; then he and Dudley shared a cold supper. The rain drumming on the canvas overhead began to lessen. Before they had finished their rations, the rain had stopped.

The guns had continued throughout the storm, but they paused when darkness fell and Dudley took to his blankets. He had difficulty relaxing, his mind sifting through images of cannon fire and men storming across open ground, charging the enemy works. He hoped the wait would not be long.

Soon, he thought. The attack would come soon.

He drifted into asleep.

On April 12, the fourth day of the bombardment, orders came directing the Light Division to occupy the trenches. The Royal Hants paraded with its ragged and shot-torn Colours at sundown. The regiment, a little over five hundred effectives, formed in two ranks at open order to receive Brigadier Codrington's inspection. When the inspection was complete, the Colour party retired. Major Giles Willis, Lieutenant-Colonel Freemantle's second-in-command, then led the battalion down to its assigned section of trench.

The allied batteries had ceased firing to allow the guns to cool. The Royal Hants marched under this silence, following the 7th Royal Fusiliers. The men moved in two slender files in order to fit into the cramped space of the zigzagging approaches. So many soldiers jammed the trench that the traffic moved at a slow walk in either direction. Dudley disliked the confinement, and his inability to see what was happening outside the trench. It was no wonder the men preferred the thought of open battle to this.

As the battalion neared the third parallel, he heard the first Russian guns open fire. Moments later came the high whistling of a mortar shell. The men crouched as they continued to move forward, boots sucking in mud that had not dried since the storm. The first shell fell somewhere in the rear. Dudley heard the distinctive sound of bits of earth splattering against the trench wall and across men's backs.

The allied artillery again opened fire, this time to cover the advance. The regiment reached its position and halted. No one under the rank of captain knew what was going to happen, although they could guess. They had paraded in light marching order, without knapsacks. They would storm the enemy works tonight or in the early morning.

Dudley sweated under his greatcoat. He kept his hands in his pockets so no one could see them shake. He studied the men of his company, fellows he knew like Privates Geary and Johnson and those he had just begun to know like Forbes, Mitchell, Robertson, and Corporal Graves. They had looked decent enough at inspection, their greatcoats brushed and cross-belts cleaned as well as conditions allowed. Now, great spots of gray-and-brown mud covered their uniforms from their trek through the trench. One fellow had tiny blood spots on his face. An enemy shell must have found a human target, Dudley thought, spraying the poor victim's gore over his neighbors.

He felt a sudden and inappropriate urge to laugh at that thought, and took several deep breaths to steady himself. This was the closest he had been to combat since Inkerman. Despite what he had said in his letter to Jane, he had forgotten the precise feeling, the tightness in his chest that demanded release. He had to remind himself again that he was good at fighting, that he could keep a cool head under fire. He had to set an example for the other men.

He waded through the trench, seeking out Sergeant Barker. When he had located him he said, with affected confidence, "Do you think we shall go, Sergeant?"

Barker considered that.

"I can see us making a go at the Quarries, sir."

The Quarries were a group of large pits in front of the Redan. Russian infantry had occupied them in order to harass the British sappers as they dug their trenches ever closer.

Dudley agreed the pits were important, and said, "We can certainly make it there from this position. Though there are also a few other rifle pits we would have to take first."

Barker started to make a further comment, but something slammed into the forward parapet. Without thinking, Dudley closed his eyes and dropped. There was an ear-splitting explosion and a shower of dirt. A second later, a man began to scream.

He opened his eyes. A private lay against the back of the trench, face awash in blood. A shell fragment had cut out his eye, and the eyeball hung down his cheek by the little bit of remaining muscle.

Another soldier dropped his rifle against the trench wall and leapt to his comrade's aid. The moment he did, a voice cried, "You pick that bloody rifle up, Private Forbes!"

Sergeant Hoskins muscled his way forward. The man who had dropped his rifle hesitated in confusion. Hoskins grabbed him by the collar and hauled him away from the wounded man.

"Bloody hell, Hoskins!" Barker shouted, leaping to the wounded man's side. He tried to console the injured private, saying, "It's only an eye, lad. Quit yer bawlin' and get to the rear. There you go. Help this man get to the rear!"

As the wounded man hobbled off, Barker glared at the other sergeant.

"You're a surly bugger, ain't you."

Hoskins sneered, but Dudley stepped in.

"That's enough of that. Both of you desist, d'you hear?"

Barker drew himself up.

"My apologies, sir."

Hoskins released his grip on Private Forbes's coat, but not before hissing, "You keep a grip on that damn rifle."

"Sergeant Hoskins," Dudley said, "a word with you."

Hoskins blinked then approached. Keeping his voice low, Dudley said, "We are not in a garrison. I realize you have not been here long, but certain considerations must be given to conditions. It has been my observation that men commonly lay their weapons down in order to perform some other task. It is permitted as long as they treat their rifle with respect. Your principle is sound, I suppose, but I saw no negligence here."

Hoskins said, "Yessir, I understand." He paused then added, "May I carry on?"

Dudley nodded. Hoskins saluted and stepped back. He gave Barker a murderous glare before moving away.

Barker watched him disappear down the trench and growled, "That was bloody ridiculous. I don't care for that bastard."

"I admit that was a little peculiar," Dudley agreed, "as if he were looking for some reason to issue a reprimand. Any reason at all. But by the same token, I know you don't like him, and I don't want you feuding with him. Especially in front of the lads. Do you hear me, Sergeant?"

Barker sighed. "I won't, Mister Dudley. My feuding days are over, believe me. But I don't like to see the men treated like that, spit on when they've done nothing wrong. If they step out of line, they have only themselves to blame when they're dealt a firm hand. But if they don't know what's in line and what's out, if they're always looking over their shoulders and wondering, then they lose their efficiency, and they ain't happy."

"I agree, Barker. But just mind what I said."

"Yes, you bloody well mind what he said!" another voice interjected. A figure emerged from the growing darkness and jumped down into the trench. When the newcomer laughed, Dudley realized it was Oakes.

Barker was glad to see him, for they had both served in the army a long time together. Oakes had been one of the few men who could make Barker listen to reason during his bad spell. They chuckled and clapped each other on the back as the artillery duel continued.

Oakes wore his cartridge pouch and bayonet and had brought his Minié rifle.

"What are you doing here, Private Oakes?" Dudley asked, although he suspected he knew the answer.

"Well, sir, with your permission, if there's going to be a fight, I'd rather not miss it."

Dudley hesitated. This man was not meant to be in combat, but he still felt that Oakes was a good, steady soldier. He could see no reason for not letting him serve here, one eye or not. In fact, his presence was an unexpected comfort to offset his own fear and the incident with Sergeant Hoskins.

"All right, Oakes," he said. "Just don't let Mrs. Oakes know that I approve."

"Oh, she approves herself, sir. I wouldn't be here if she didn't." He looked aloft at the dark, overcast sky, the low ceiling lit by the flashing of artillery. "I don't mind spending another miserable night in the mud."

Dudley nodded. Oakes was right. They would be spending the night here. He settled against the parapet, trying to make himself comfortable.

At length, the guns fell silent. Hours passed, punctuated by murmured snatches of conversation. Dudley could not sleep; he was too anxious wondering what would happen. He could hear Russian voices shouting, and the sounds of men working in both the allied and enemy batteries. As usual, the Russians were repairing their works under the cover of darkness.

In the morning, the thundering exchange of fire resumed. The British infantry remained in the trenches, but no orders came to begin an assault. Instead, orderlies arrived to serve a breakfast of biscuits and salt pork. The men ate as Russian round shot slapped against the parapet, one after the other. The occasional shell exploded somewhere near or even inside the trench. The fire was heavier than that of the previous night.

"I'll have to go see to Bill," Oakes said when he had finished his rations. He began to climb out of the trench, but Barker grabbed him by the coat and hauled him back.

"You can't go across open ground under this fire!" Barker shouted.

"I'll be all right!" Oakes insisted, but as he spoke a round shot came over the lip of the trench. The heavy iron ball smacked into the rear wall where he had just been standing then bounced and struck Barker full on the side.

The blow knocked him flat into the muck at the bottom of the trench.

"Sergeant!" Dudley cried.

Barker was conscious and fumbling with his greatcoat buttons. When he had opened both his outer and inner coats and pulled up his shirt, he discovered that his wound was insignificant—nothing but a small scratch and a growing welt.

"The ball must have spent its force hitting the wall," he suggested.

Dudley and Oakes helped him to his feet, shaking their heads in amazement.

When Barker had caught his breath, he dug in the mud to retrieve the spent ball, saying, "I'll have to keep that as a souvenir."

"It's a bloody miracle," Oakes declared, sighing with relief. He turned to Dudley. "I would love to sit and marvel over this all morning, sir, but I should still see to the pony."

Dudley shook his head. "It's too risky, Private Oakes, even if you go back along the trenches. Mrs. Oakes can see to Bill. She knows what to do."

"I suppose she does, sir," Oakes agreed then chuckled. "I didn't want to miss the attack anyway, which will be more risky by far."

Dudley realized the truth of this as Barker hefted the ball that should have killed him.

CHAPTER 5

April 1855

On their second evening in the trenches, the Royal Hants received orders to return to camp. It was the beginning of a frustrating period. The artillery bombardment continued for six more days, and every evening, as the guns thundered, the Royal Hants were ordered back into the trenches. But on every one of those nights, after the guns fell silent, the Russians rebuilt their earthworks. The mornings revealed that nothing had changed.

By April 19, the allied command decided an assault was not yet feasible, and the bombardment ceased. That same day, work resumed on the British trenches. Sappers dug new approaches extending from the third parallel in front of Gordon's Battery. By dusk, the head of the new sap had come up against some forward Russian rifle pits. Those rifle pits would have to be taken.

A detachment of sixty men from the Light Division, mostly men of the 77th Regiment, volunteered for the task, eager to make up for the cancelled general assault. With fixed bayonets, they stormed the two nearest rifle pits, capturing both. The Russians counterattacked with field guns and managed to drive the British back part of the way. The British officer in command of the attack called for more volunteers, and in the morning, the Russians gave up and retreated to the Quarries. The British sappers then made the rifle pits part of their new parallel.

The skirmish was the talk of the Light Division the next morning. As Dudley and Arbuthnot shared a breakfast of biscuits softened with boiling water and soaked in molasses, the lieutenant rattled on, saying, "It's a shame that Colonel Egerton was killed in last night's raid. He was much beloved by his men."

"So I have heard," Dudley replied, only half-listening. The Royal Hants had not taken part in the raid, and he had never met Colonel Egerton. Death was so commonplace here that word of another faceless casualty could not distract him from the day's business, which might prove interesting.

The regiment was off trench and picket duty for the next eight hours, and Captain Neville had arranged for No. 3 Company to have its photograph taken. Neville had obtained the necessary permission from Lieutenant-Colonel Freemantle, and the company was to form ranks at ten o'clock.

"At least there is this talk of peace," Arbuthnot went on.

The camps were awash with reports that the new czar, Alexander III, had made peace overtures. The Austrians had agreed to mediate, and a peace conference had convened in Vienna. In the wake of the failed bombardment, this came as welcome news and a morale booster for the British Army.

Arbuthnot snapped open his watch.

"It's close to half-past nine. I suppose we'd best get ready."

Dudley nodded. "I'm looking forward to this. If there is peace soon, we will be able to look on this photograph as a memento of our time here."

He did not mention that he would prefer to have peace wait until after the fall or surrender of Sevastopol. In that case, the photograph would become a small monument to their triumph instead of just a souvenir. They had won victories in the field, of course, but their main objective remained unconquered.

The photographer was a man named Roger Fenton. Fenton had arrived in the Crimea in March, bringing a wagon that housed his portable photographic studio. He was not the first to photograph the war, for others had gone to record the Turkish struggles along the Danube, but he was the first to offer his services to the British. Officers had flocked to him to have their pictures taken in the field. Fenton offered prints of his work for five shillings each.

When ten o'clock arrived, Captain Neville formed his men in two ranks. The company was about fifty men strong, and in accordance with standard drill, the tallest stood on the flanks and the shortest in the center. For the first time in months they did not wear their greatcoats, and each man had done his best to make his red coatee and crossbelts look presentable. For some of the veterans of last year's campaigning that task had been difficult, their jackets having been patched and re-patched with bits of blankets and sacks. The regimental quartermaster had a small store of new uniforms, but he had not yet bothered to issue them.

Unlike Dudley and Arbuthnot, Captain Neville had come mounted. He sat his horse on the far right of the company and faced inwards. From this position he directed the officers and NCOs, telling them where to stand. The arrangement, he declared, had to be perfect. Colour-Sergeant O'Ryan was to position himself on the immediate right of the company. Dudley was then to stand on O'Ryan's right, and Lieutenant Arbuthnot next to him.

"Sergeant Hoskins will stand on the company's left," Neville said. "Sergeant Barker, you will take your place in the rear of the men."

Dudley watched as the two sergeants obeyed. Barker moved behind the ranks, where he would be invisible to the photographer.

He glanced at Arbuthnot. The lieutenant understood the unanswered question, but he just shrugged and continued to rub his spectacles with a white handkerchief. Perhaps Neville did not want Barker in the picture for some reason.

Barker did not seem to care. The men were standing easy, and Private Geary, one of the youngest in the company, turned to complain.

"All of us in the rear rank can't be seen, Sarge."

"No one'll be able to see your faces anyway, lad," Barker reassured him. "This is for the officers."

Roger Fenton assembled the large square box of his camera on its tripod in front of the company. He was a man of medium build with a neatly trimmed mustache and beard. A few paces away sat the mule-driven van that contained his darkroom equipment. Emblazoned on the side of the van was the photographer's name in elaborate lettering.

When all was ready, Fenton took off his hat and examined the sky.

"Captain Neville, I can begin whenever you are ready."

Neville nodded, then commanded, "Sergeant Barker, bring the men to attention."

Barker was fifth in command in the company hierarchy, and Neville's order should have gone to O'Ryan; but Barker was in a more convenient location. He filled his lungs and shouted, "Company, eyes...*front*! Attennn...*tion*!"

"We are ready now, Mister Fenton," Neville said.

Fenton brought a wet glass plate from the back of his van. He inserted the plate in the shaded back of the camera and took a few seconds to focus. When he was satisfied, he poked his head out from under the camera's hood.

"I will try a twenty-second exposure. It is imperative that everyone remains perfectly still. No one must move at all, not even a twitch."

Fenton removed the cap from the lens, and Dudley held his breath, waiting as the photographer studied his watch. When Fenton replaced the lens cap, he let out the breath. The photographer at once removed the exposed glass plate and took it with him as he clambered into his van, shutting the doors behind him.

"Sergeant Barker," said Neville, "stand the men at ease then stand them easy."

When the glass negative had finished developing, Fenton declared it a success, and the three officers crowded round to see. Dudley found the strange reversed image intriguing. In some sense, it seemed unnatural—the sky a dark gray, the men with dark faces and white coats. Yet this was no drawing or engraving, and he could imagine what the positive print would look like. Despite the odd colouring, these were men, looking as real as they did now, standing in their double line.

"There's me!" Arbuthnot cried, pointing. "It's really quite wonderful, isn't it! What would my Margaret think of that, I wonder?"

Neville gave him an irritated glance then turned to the photographer. He thanked him and arranged for the delivery of two prints. Dudley did not think it wise to spend five shillings on something so frivolous but placed an order anyway. He delighted in the image of himself as he really looked, standing with his men, his worn bullion epaulettes more than presentable from a distance.

With a sudden inspiration, he ordered a second print, asking Fenton if the photographer could send it to his uncle's address in Hampshire. His aunt and Jane would both love to see it, and it also might serve to soften his uncle's stance, perhaps more so than his letters. His uncle could see for himself how Dudley was serving Britain.

When the officers had finished arranging their orders, Colour-Sergeant O'Ryan approached Captain Neville.

"Shall I take the men back, sir?"

"No, Colour-Sergeant," Neville replied as he made his way back to where Hoskins held his horse, "let's have Sergeant Barker keep hold of the company. Sergeant Barker, carry on."

"Yes, sir!" Barker cried then added in a lower voice, "Looks like I'm the only trustworthy sergeant here, lads."

Though the comment was inappropriate, it was innocent enough, and the men chuckled. Dudley also could not suppress a smile, and was puzzled when he saw Hoskins glance at Neville, eyes wide. The captain's face clouded. Instead of mounting his horse, he strode towards Barker and halted before him.

"Sir?" Barker said, standing tall and steady in the face of Neville's obvious fury.

"You're lucky they raised you back to sergeant before I arrived, Barker," Neville said, voice loud enough for all to hear. "I know you better than they, don't I? We go back some, don't we? Well, you'd better not make any trouble. Remember, this is war, and in time of war there is no room for nonsense, is there? The army deals harshly with nonsense during wartime, Sergeant Barker."

"What sort of nonsense, sir?" Barker replied, his manner still serene and innocent.

"Damn your insolence, Sergeant!" Neville exploded. "I'm watching you, man! You had best remember that. Now, march the company back to camp and dismiss them."

Dudley stared at Neville in astonishment. O'Ryan and Arbuthnot seemed to share his surprise, their frowns revealing their discomfort with this public outburst. The men in the ranks looked around with nervous glances. The only man who did not appear uneasy was Sergeant Hoskins, whose face wore a satisfied grin.

Barker reacted with cool indifference. He snapped a salute, crying, "Yes, sir!" Then he turned on his heels and launched straight into his commands, bringing the men back to attention then giving them a right-face.

Captain Neville mounted his horse as if nothing out of the ordinary had happened. As Barker marched the company away towards the main camp, he stared down at Dudley, Arbuthnot and O'Ryan.

"Carry on," he said.

On their way back to the tent, Dudley remarked to Arbuthnot, "It seemed to me there was more to that than met the eye. Such a dressing down in front of the men seems highly improper."

The lieutenant agreed.

"I can't account for it. I am aware that Sergeant Barker has been a troublemaker in the past. We've all seen him flogged, haven't we? But he appears to have reformed, as far as I can tell. He was a valuable sergeant to me during the winter. I had never held the command of a company by myself before, and I admit that he helped take away some of the strain. Yes, he was very helpful, he and the colour-sergeant."

They had caught up to the rear of the company now and watched as Barker halted the files. Dudley turned to Arbuthnot.

"Please excuse me, sir. I would like to speak with him, if that's all right?"

Arbuthnot looked uncertain, but he removed his spectacles and said, "By all means. Of course. You've known him longer than I, after all."

Barker dismissed the men, breaking them off to go their separate ways. The sergeant then turned to face Dudley.

"What was that all about, Sergeant?" Dudley asked.

Barker hesitated. "I don't really like to say, sir."

Dudley sighed. That was not the answer he wanted. Neville had said he and Barker went back a long way. He wondered what that had meant.

At that moment, realization dawned.

"He's the one who had you before the court-martial. One of the fellows who wanted you to spy for him."

"Yes, sir," Barker admitted. "He was one of them. The other is dead, thankfully."

Dudley pushed back his cap, stabbing his fingers through his hair.

"This could be a serious business, Sergeant, if he still has it in for you. And it appears he does. You had better be on your best behaviour, and no more foolish comments." He bit his lip, knowing what a disaster this could be for the smooth operation of the company. An officer and a sergeant at continual odds would jeopardize morale, communications, and any number of other things.

Coupled with this understanding of the danger was sudden and profound disappointment. Neville was a gentleman who had accepted him, who did not judge him by his class. But here was evidence the captain was not above dishonesty and deceit, that he held a grudge and would not think twice about destroying another man's career for his own purposes.

"What should I think of him now?" Dudley murmured.

"He's just an aristocratic bastard, sir. I can take care of myself. I won't let him get me a second time."

He looked at Barker with a touch of sadness.

"If he wants to, you may not be able to stop him, Sergeant."

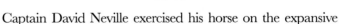

Captain David Neville exercised his horse on the expansive Chersonese Uplands, the plateau many in the army also called the "Balaclava Plain." He followed his preferred riding route and brooded upon what had just happened during the session with Fenton. He had not wanted Barker in the photograph. The man's presence would have ruined it.

He found himself boiling with fury whenever the sergeant was nearby. Boiling with fury, and prepared to push the man until he fell.

He brought his horse to a halt and absently stroked the animal's neck. He had to settle his nerves. There was no sense in letting his anger get the better of him. After all, Barker was nothing but a sergeant, while he was an officer and a gentleman.

Neville still held the rank of major in the army, and that was how he thought of himself. The position as captain was one of convenience, and temporary. With the conclusion of his recent staff appointment, he had found himself on half-pay and without an assignment. The best course of action, he had decided, was to return to his old regiment, the Royal Hampshire Fusiliers. As luck would have it, the Royal Hants had been in the process of expanding, anticipating further war in Europe. The regiment had a need for new officers. No openings for a major, but positions for company commanders.

Neville was still not satisfied with the appointment. Several years had elapsed since the last time anyone had addressed him as "captain," and it gave the impression his career was going backwards. Yet it would have been foolish to pass up an assignment with his old regiment, despite the initial sense of humiliation. This was a temporary posting, he told himself, something to tide him over while his family kept a watchful eye for other and better opportunities.

Meanwhile, he knew he should look for opportunities of another sort here in the Crimea. There was the possibility of his distinguishing himself in battle, of course, of furthering his reputation for soldiering. Perhaps he could even turn the presence of Sergeant Barker into an opportunity rather than letting it remain an affront. An opportunity for amusement, for diversion while he waited for combat.

He spurred his horse forward, standing in the stirrups as it leapt a slim gully. His blood began to surge with the excitement of the ride, his mood changing, lifting.

Life was little more than a chance for sport, he reminded himself. He was a country gentleman, born to privilege, and the world was his playground. That was simple reality. As landed gentry, his class had the greatest stake in the country and, thus, the greatest right to use the country as they would. And to use the country's inhabitants. No one could deny them that right, for the nation would collapse without the natural authority of his class.

Neville almost laughed aloud as the wind rushed in his ears. The people were his playthings. The servants on his family's estate in Kent, especially the female servants, were his responsibility and his pleasure. When they were no longer of any use, he got rid of them. That was as it should be, as nature dictated. As a child, his parents had made it clear to him that his nurse and his governess were his servants, and that he was in charge. If they did not like what he did, then Father would straighten them out. And Father did straighten them out. Little David had learned that if he did not like something, he could get rid of it. It was so easy! It hardly required any effort at all for someone of his station.

As an adult, he demanded the same. He could not bear to lose control of those within his sphere of influence. He had once beaten to death a hound that would not obey his commands. He had punished cheeky servants and could not abide a stubborn horse. Sometimes he felt flashes of guilt over this brutal behaviour, but it was necessary, and it was the way of nature. After all, it was his right to have his way. Perhaps that was unfortunate for some, but it was also unfortunate for the rabbit when it was taken by an eagle. The eagle could not be blamed.

Neville's lip curled as he remembered such a rabbit, a subaltern named George Peachy. Neville had met the man during his first posting with the Royal Hants. Peachy had been a thin and bookish fellow, always rattling off quotations from Shakespeare or Milton or some other rot. Poetry was fine, especially the old English masters, but not when some wretch was mutilating it while putting on such airs of learned superiority. Peachy had also cultivated an irritating jovial wit that had been a source of pride, and sickening to watch. The fact he had seen service in India and was popular with the men had made Neville hate him all the more.

Neville had not found it difficult to find another officer who shared his feelings. Together, they had decided to get Peachy tossed out of the regiment. They could do it via a campaign of vilification, or, they had decided, they could have a bit of fun with it, catch Peachy in an compromising position. To that end, they had called upon one of their sergeants, a big fellow named Brian Barker.

Corporals and sergeants were the officer's tools, men who had a duty to obey. Neville had instructed Barker to watch Peachy, report on him if he slipped up in any way. If he did not slip up, they had another option. Things could go missing from the mess and end up in Peachy's quarters. It was a marvelous plan!

But the plan had gone wrong from the start. With outrageous audacity, Barker had declined to play along, citing honour and duty to his fellow soldiers. Neville still felt his face reddening when he thought of it—a sergeant lecturing him about honour! Perhaps strict military law had given the sergeant the ability to refuse, but military law in the technical sense was not military law in the real sense. By refusing to help, Barker had destroyed his own career.

Neville's horse crested a small hillock. From here, he could see the little crossroads villa that housed Lord Raglan's headquarters, and the French headquarters just to the left. The villa also contained a post office, and he remembered he had several letters to send. Letters to his favorite ladies, describing his exciting adventures and how he was out here giving the Russians a good thrashing.

He should turn this situation into an opportunity, he thought again. Yes, it could be fun to break Barker a second time. Fun—and essential. Barker's presence was a further challenge to Neville's authority. The very fact Barker had regained his rank of sergeant said that Neville had failed, that he had not really destroyed the man after all. He could not tolerate that, the incompleteness of it all. It had always been that way with him. Once he started something, he had to see it through. He could not bear loose ends or frayed edges.

He felt a sudden craving for a cigar, but he could not turn back to camp yet. Just as he had to finish Barker, he had to finish his ride, take it all the way to the end of his course. He could not stand to leave a single gully or stream before his horse had leapt them all. If he did, the need would haunt him for the rest of the day. A man who did not finish what he started was not a man at all.

At least he had some idle time before his next bit of trench duty. He grimaced at the thought of that wretched task, standing up to the knees in mud. He detested being dirty. That was the worst thing about this war—it forced him to spend hours keeping his tent and his person clean.

He would complete this ride then have a cigar to help him consider his next move. Somehow, he hoped, this fellow Dudley could be of some use. In fact, Dudley was a prime candidate, a nobody promoted from the ranks for gallant behavior, without a friend save his old comrades, who were now beneath him. He was a learned man, and thus more respectable than most rankers who won commissions. But he was still alone and doubtless feeling inferior, as he should. Maybe,

Neville thought, Dudley might need a sympathetic ear, a sort of mentor.

He smiled. The tents of his regiment's encampment came into view, and he knew what he would do. He would become Ensign Dudley's mentor. He would show that young man he could fit in after all, if he only did what he was told. And he would do what he was told, or suffer for it. He would do whatever his captain wanted.

Neville chuckled, for he could see it all now. First, he would become Ensign William Dudley's friend; then he would buy his loyalty. Perhaps he could get him a sword, or some other physical symbol of acceptance. Maybe something like that would work, for these fellows were always hard-up for money. Quite often, it was their biggest worry. Neville would alleviate that worry, and Dudley would owe him his loyalty.

Then Neville would use him against Barker.

The second of May dawned fine and warm, and Dudley rode through camp intent on finding a horse race. His company had no need of him today. Half of the men were detached under an officer of the Royal Engineers to help dig a new sap, while Arbuthnot had the rest for supply detail to Balaclava.

He accompanied the supply party as far as the edge of camp, chatting to the lieutenant as they moved between the even rows of tents. Groups of idlers stood about, puffing on clay pipes and nodding as the small column passed. When the supply party emerged onto the plain, he halted to say his farewells.

"Good luck, sir," he said.

Arbuthnot shrugged. "Supply runs are not so odious now that we have partial transport."

That was true, for the railway now extended past Kadikoi. The train transported ammunition, men, prefab huts, and commissariat supplies up from the front then took fatigue parties and sick and wounded down in the other direction. This system was a far cry from the congested, mired supply route Dudley remembered from last autumn. Slowly, things were improving.

Now if only the conduct of the war could be a little more swift, he thought.

The days had dragged on since the failed bombardment, with no indication of when the next assault attempt would come. Dudley could sense the growing frustration within the company. None of his men would have dared complain to him, but he knew they were sick of the unending rotation of guarding trenches, bringing up supplies, providing outlying pickets, and digging new approaches. The only fighting they saw consisted of sniping with the Russians and watching for incoming artillery fire. Men died or were wounded one sudden casualty at a time, often struck from nowhere. Save for the few trench raids, the enemy remained aloof behind their walls. For the British infantry, this created an impression they could not fight back, that they were helpless against an invisible foe.

He shared and understood this sentiment. Except for a few prisoners, he had seen little of the Russians since his return to the Crimea. He had watched their guns spit fire, had listened to accounts of the struggles for the rifle pits, but he had not seen the face of the enemy. Even the few distant figures glimpsed running from place to place had been half-obscured by smoke.

Even so, he had to admit the officers did not have it as bad as the ordinary soldiers. Officers were, of course, as vulnerable to frustration and enemy fire as the rank-and-file, but they were under fire less often. Their ample free time allowed them to read the newspapers, to discuss and hope for the success of the Vienna peace talks, and to pursue simple entertainments and diversions. Dudley's favourite diversion—improving his riding skills by exercising Bill on the plain—was a common one. Riding was a fundamental pleasure for many officers. That was why they had arranged another steeplechase.

Dudley left Arbuthnot's supply party and bore away for the racecourse. The course was a flat run along an oval track of bare earth, the same that had hosted the event on St. Patrick's Day. A crowd had already gathered on the perimeter before he arrived. Within its ranks, he saw the uniforms of every allied army—British, French, and Turkish. Even a few Russian prisoners stood about, keeping up amicable chatter with their captors.

Most of the British officers present were from the cavalry. They had the most idle time of anyone, for the war had become a show for the infantry, artillery, and engineers. The horse soldiers had found themselves with little to do since the Battle of Balaclava, and their appearance reflected that fact. Most still looked fine enough for dress parade, the dragoons in their polished brass helmets and the hussars with their tight blue jackets and busbies.

Dudley felt an instant dislike for the hussar officers, recalling the insulting pair in St. Sophia's Mosque. He tried to suppress the feeling, for it was pure prejudice. This was a day for making friends, not enemies, and petty resentment had no place here. His growing interest in horses was one way to find some common ground with these fellows. Racing was an activity that could help him become a part of their society.

The races had yet to begin, and he rode along the line of noisy spectators. As he passed a large group of French infantrymen, he spied the familiar face of a sergeant of the 17th Lancers, a cousin to Sergeant Wellman of the Royal Hants. The cavalry sergeant was a survivor of the Light Brigade's mad charge at Balaclava. Dudley was pleased to see that the man had also made it through the winter, and called out a cheerful, "Well, how do you do?"

"Well, good day, Sergeant Dudley!" the lancer replied before noticing the ragged epaulettes on Dudley's jacket. When he did, his right hand jerked up in a startled salute. "Oh, I apologize, sir!"

Dudley gravely returned the salute.

"A natural mistake, Sergeant. Don't worry yourself with it. You couldn't have known of my good fortune." He maneuvered Bill to stand beside the other man's much taller mount and asked, "So, what is the nature of this race?"

The sergeant cleared his throat, but a moment later, his smile was back as he explained.

"It's a race of fine Arab horses only, with a purse of twenty pounds to the winner. All of the entries are French, and I suspect it's a bit of a good-will thing for them, sir."

Dudley nodded, noting the high number of French soldiers present. Near the head of the track stood a clump of *Chasseurs d'Afrique*, an elite French light cavalry regiment. He admired their powder-blue jackets and tall, striking red shakos. In general, he preferred the French uniform styles to those of his own army. Most of the French infantry wore smart peaked caps called kepis, and trim blue frock coats or jackets. Here and there stood a few Zouaves, the officers in kepis and the men in turbans.

The assemblage began to cheer as the five entries in the race, two chasseurs and three infantry officers, took their positions at the start of the course. Their horses stamped in impatience, and the onlookers shouted encouragement or derision in both French and English. A British dragoon officer, one of the organizers, raised his pistol towards the sky. The starting shot rang out, and the contestants bolted onto the track.

Dudley leaned forward in his saddle as the crowd cheered and the horses thundered toward the first turn. The turn was a sharp one. Too sharp, in fact, for two of the horsemen, who crashed to the ground in an explosion of dust, screaming horses, and exclamations from the spectators. A third rider also missed the turn and charged straight ahead, far off the course. As the dust began to clear, the two fallen men and their mounts scrambled to their feet, unhurt but shaking their heads in disgust.

Two riders remained in the race, a chasseur and an infantryman. They rounded the next bend, neck-and-neck, and charged for the finish line. Each flogged his mount, but at the last second the chasseur surged ahead to win.

The British officers exclaimed "*Bono Francais!*" as the chasseur wheeled about in victory. He galloped back and forth along the edge of the crowd, laughing and waved his right hand. Many of the other riders slapped him on the back and shoulders. When it came time for him to claim his prize, his eyes widened as the master of ceremonies placed a series of heavy English coins in his hand, one by one.

"Quite something, eh, sir?" the sergeant of the Lancers said to Dudley.

Dudley agreed. The spectacle and the prize had both been impressive. He realized that if he could race and win, he could gain a substantial supplement to his income.

There were no other races scheduled, and the crowd began to disperse. Dudley said goodbye to the sergeant, but as he moved off he saw Captain Neville riding toward him.

He tensed. Neville had given no reason for mistrust, but Dudley had been uncomfortable in his presence since Barker's revelation.

"Ah, Ensign Dudley," Neville began, "were you here for the race?" A broad grin lit his handsome face. "Quite the thing, wasn't it? We shall have to have more in the future, if we can."

"I would like to compete myself, actually, sir," Dudley ventured, doing his best to sound casual.

"Smashing, Ensign, smashing! But that is not what I have come to you to speak about. I have good news. Some of the boys have managed to get their hands on one of those pre-fabricated huts that have been piling up on the wharves in Balaclava. Quite a large one, in fact. It has already been assembled, and we thought we would use it as a sort of officer's meeting place. Not an ideal mess, of course, but the closest we can come under these conditions."

Dudley swallowed. "That's good to hear, sir."

"Yes, isn't it? You have not had a proper introduction to the life of an officer of the Royal Hampshire Fusiliers, Dudley. Unfortunately, at least half of the regiment will be on duty at any given time, so we will only ever be able to assemble half of our fellows together for supper and so on. I'm afraid the victuals will certainly not be up to snuff, either, but we do have a proper cook, if not a chef. So it will not be an ideal mess, you understand. Just a hut where we can go and be comfortable and have good company. But we shall treat it as a proper mess, with rules in effect."

"Yes, sir. I, uh…I am not very familiar with the rules, Captain."

Neville shook with warm laughter.

"Of course, not, Ensign. No one who first comes on board can be expected to know everything. But it's not to worry, for it is the custom of the officer's mess to assign every junior officer a ward who will show him the ropes. I think it only makes sense for Lieutenant Arbuthnot to be your ward, and he has already agreed. He will tell you all you need to know."

Dudley nodded. "Oh, very well, then. I shall look forward to it, sir."

"As well you should. Ah, look, there's my old chum Carthright from the Eleventh Hussars. We'll have to invite him to come to the hut some night. In fact, I think I shall do so now." He gave Dudley a parting nod. "Good morning, Ensign."

"Good morning, sir."

Dudley wandered back across the plain. Instead of delighted anticipation, Neville's news had brought only added anxiety. So far, he had encountered no resistance from his fellow company officers, but he had not had many dealings with others in the regiment. This mess hut would bring the true test of his acceptance. The officer's mess, proper or not, could be an intimidating place for those not used to its sort of society, with its tight rules and traditions and stiff penalties for breaking them. It could also be an expensive place.

Dudley cursed himself for his nervousness. He was an educated man, and his aunt had always insisted on good manners. He knew he did not stand out among the officers as he had stood out as a so-called "gentleman" among the sergeants. His continued fear had no basis, for none of his worries about his commission had come true. Arbuthnot could not have been a friendlier companion, and Captain Neville had done all he could to make him feel at home, despite what he had done to Barker in the past. With their support, Dudley had no reason to believe that any of the other officers would treat him differently.

The Royal Hants prided themselves on their fighting prowess, and in that he was lucky. His regiment held merit and personal valour in high regard.

Dudley nudged Bill into a canter then a gallop. He wanted the wind in his face, the good spring wind. There was still the war and the Russians to consider, but things were unfolding well for him. His luck was holding.

Dudley and Arbuthnot crouched under the light of their single lamp. Arbuthnot had agreed to explain the rules of the mess, and Dudley was thankful for the diversion. It had been a trying afternoon.

The company had been guarding a new trench in the fore of the right-attack, closer to the Redan than any other British earthwork. This had put them under heavier artillery fire than usual, and Dudley had seen seven men wounded by shells, splinters, or flying debris. One man had died after he had thrust his head over the parapet at the wrong time—a piece of grape shot had split his skull. Dudley wanted something else to think about.

He and Arbuthnot tried to enjoy a supper of normal rations while Oakes brewed them some coffee. Arbuthnot spoke on a variety of topics, working his way towards the mess rules. Between sips from his steaming earthen mug, the lieutenant expressed his concern over the health of Miss Florence Nightingale. She had come to Balaclava to set up a field hospital, thus alleviating the pressure on Scutari, but had become sick herself with a fever. This was now a popular concern for the entire army, and Arbuthnot spoke for them when he said, "I do hope she will be all right."

Dudley hoped so as well.

"She isn't the only one sick. It seems as the weather grows warmer, incidents of fever, even cholera are again increasing. I hope we aren't reduced to a skeleton army again, with everyone doing double duty with hardly a chance to sleep."

"Well, more reinforcements have arrived," Arbuthnot declared. "Did you hear? An entire army of Sardinians has joined us. They came in three steamers today, arriving all ready for the field, with transport horses, carts, mules and vehicles. They're going to reinforce the French on our right."

"A lot of good that will do us. The French already have more men in the field than we do."

They sat in silence for a moment, sipping their coffee. Then Dudley asked, "So, what about the rules of the mess?"

"Of course!" Arbuthnot exclaimed. "I'm a great fan of the mess. I think this hut is a wonderful idea and can't wait for them to have it ready." He paused, staring at the canvas wall of the tent. "Now, where should I begin? I've never been a ward before, though I had my own, of course. I shouldn't let that worry you, though. The old Royal Hampshire Fusiliers does not stand on as much ceremony as some regiments. As Major Willis would say…" He knit his brows and lowered his voice in imitation of the second-in-command. "…the Royal Hants is a fighting regiment!"

As Arbuthnot chuckled at his own performance, Dudley confessed, "I have never spoken to Major Willis. In fact, you and Captain Neville are the only officers I have had much contact with. The others I know by name alone."

"Well, that will certainly change soon. You will meet everyone in this mess hut. As they say, there you shall learn 'courage, honour, and truth.' Ha-ha! I think you may already have a smattering of that. That does not worry me. No, no. Though I do hope the price of the subscription will not be high. Normally, there is the considerable expense of maintaining the mess itself, providing newspapers and such, as well as replacing the inevitable broken glass and dishes. However, we have very few of those things here, so the subscription should not be a burden for you."

Arbuthnot began to polish his spectacles.

"Whoever is in charge of this will have to hire a butler and waiters and so on. Our own servants will have to do, I suppose, though no one has actually informed me of such a decision. I have to admit that I don't know who is arranging this whole thing. Usually, the management is by a committee—a major, a captain, and two subalterns, each responsible for a different department. We shall need something like that, but I have not heard who it shall be. It's a shame we couldn't turn everything over to a private caterer, but I doubt there are very many caterers to be had here. Ha-ha!"

Dudley chuckled politely.

"I'm sure Private Oakes will be willing to chip in some time."

"Yes, of course. Oakes is a fine fellow. Now, where was I? Ah, yes, mess rules. They are similar to what you must have had in your sergeant's mess. Certain conversational topics are forbidden. Those are women, religion or politics, to avoid unpleasant disputes. You must never quote Latin, for that will make it look as if you are trying to upstage the others. General discussions on philosophy and literature are permitted, though not when they have to do with any of the aforementioned topics. And of course, you mustn't discuss anything pertaining to your duties or the running of the regiment. The mess is a place where we should avoid such things, a sort of sanctuary.

"What else?" He replaced his spectacles and squinted at the air. "I know there are a very many things. No swearing, of course, and…ah, yes, very important! As a new subaltern, you must not speak at table unless you are spoken to. In fact, I would advise you not to express any sort of strong opinion on any topic whatsoever. If anyone asks, try to determine what that person asking wants to hear. That's your safest bet."

"Sounds like good advice," Dudley agreed.

Arbuthnot looked around as if the next important item lay somewhere in the tent.

"There are a number of other things. No smoking until after dinner, and during dinner the wine must always pass from right to left. If you break any of the rules, you will have to pay a fine. Though I don't know how much the fine will be here. It's often fun when someone breaks the rules, actually, for you get to say, 'Aha! Now you have to pay up!' Though many consider rule-breaking an insult, which, in truth, it is."

Dudley rubbed his neck. His head was aching. There was too much to remember.

"What about mess uniforms?"

"Oh, I shouldn't worry about that here. Hardly anyone has a proper uniform at all, from general to the lowliest private. But there is one thing. In the Royal Hants, we traditionally wear our swords in the mess, ever since our officers were attacked at dinner in India during the Maharatta Wars, at the end of the last century. They were all slaughtered except the surgeon, who hid under the table. So now we are always prepared. As I said, a fighting regiment." He ran a hand through his thinning air. "And along with that, it's been common in the past for our officers to challenge each other to duels in the mess itself."

Dudley chuckled. "I trust that won't happen here."

"No, I suppose not. That sort of thing is frowned upon these days, especially during war. Illegal, you know. But our dear old Colonel Freemantle might not mind, if he thinks the generals will turn a blind eye. He's fought several duels, all as the injured party. Made the challenges in the mess itself! Doubtless you'll hear the tale before long."

Dudley could not picture his lieutenant-colonel fighting a duel. He seemed too mild a man.

"I would like to hear the full story of the Maharatta massacre someday," he said. There was reason to look forward to the mess now, if it would allow him to hear more tales of his regiment's history. "Though I'm afraid I won't be able to honour the tradition it began. I don't have a sword." He glanced at Arbuthnot's sword where it lay across the lieutenant's trunk. It was an old-fashioned light cavalry sabre with a stirrup guard. "That's a fine looking specimen," he commented.

"Really?" Arbuthnot examined the weapon. "Oh, it's nothing special, just a standard issue sabre, seventeen-ninety-six pattern. My father carried it in the Peninsula, and now it's mine. Would you like to look at it?"

He said he did, so Arbuthnot drew the blade and lay it across Dudley's outstretched hands. The blue steel was well-oiled and sharpened, the curled guard polished. The metal was a bit worn in places, and the leather-and-wire grip looked like a recent replacement.

"Your family has a long history of service?" he asked.

"Yes, I suppose we do. At least two of us have served in this very regiment. My father was at Waterloo, you know, though he was knocked on the head early. A Froggie cavalryman split his hat in two, and he sat out the rest of the battle in the field hospital. He was all right, however, once he had regained his senses, though he carried a sizable scar for the rest of his life."

"He must have, if he was knocked on the head with something like this." Dudley hefted the sabre. "I suppose I shall have to enter the mess hut swordless."

"I shouldn't worry about that," the lieutenant reassured. "As I said, none of us has a proper kit. This war has forced us all to make do with what we have." He tapped his head. "I feel that I am forgetting something. Though I suppose it can't be anything too important if I am. I would say you've got everything you need to know. You won't make an ass of yourself."

"If I do," Dudley joked, "can I blame you?"

Arbuthnot laughed, rather too loud.

"Yes, but nobody else will!"

CHAPTER 6

May 1855

Despite his self-assurances, Dudley could not marshal much confidence before his first visit to the mess hut. He rehearsed Arbuthnot's instructions time and again, but still he worried he would make a mistake. Worse than that, he dreaded the possibility the others would ignore him, excluding him from the conversation altogether. There were more than thirty officers in the regiment, and if they wanted to, they could let him fade into the background. He could not speak unless spoken to.

When he entered the hut, a third of the officers were on duty. Aside from himself, only nine others were present, and two of those were the young ensigns—just boys—who carried the battalion's Colours on parade and in battle. Dudley took a deep breath to steady himself. He could not become buried in such company.

The mess hut smelled of new wood. Eight hanging lanterns provided light while an iron pot-bellied stove supplied heat. A long table with a collection of mismatched chairs dominated the room. The table was set with linen tablecloth, silver cutlery, and chi all items belonging to the regiment's travelling mess. The travelling mess had come to Turkey and the Crimea last year but had remained in storage. In the early months of the war, with so many officers sick and the others on duty round the clock, there had been no use for it.

The senior officer present was Major Giles Willis, a lanky man with bushy iron-gray side-whiskers. He took his place at the head of the table. Along the sides sat the three officers of No. 3 Company, two other captains, two lieutenants, and the other ensigns. Dinner came in the form of disguised army rations and locally obtained supplements, all prepared in an adjacent tent. The pork had been soaked to remove the salts then marinaded in something sweet; it was served with turnips, carrots, cabbage, and a mixed-meat pie. Following the main course came cheese and a suet pudding. Three corporals provided the service, bringing each dish in through the back door.

Dudley ate in silence, although by now he was past caring whether anyone spoke to him or not. This was the best meal he had eaten in almost two years. It brought home to him the disparity between the officers and the enlisted men. He had not tasted such fare since before joining the army, not even in barracks where supply problems did not exist.

After dinner, the servants brought in a bottle of fine port, a luxury now available at the commissariat. As the bottle passed round the table, Dudley refused, preferring to drink water. Water would cost him nothing, and he could still use it for the toasting.

The officers of the Royal Hampshire Fusiliers toasted the queen every night they sat down together. With everyone's glass filled, Major Willis, acting as mess president, said to Captain Neville, "Mr. Vice, the Queen." Dudley took hold of his water glass, stood with the others, and said with them, "The Queen, God bless her." Then he sipped.

It was a curious scene, he thought, these nine men in worn and ragged uniforms standing in a wooden hut, raising their glasses as guns boomed off and on in the distance. But raise their glasses they did, again and again, going from man to man. They toasted absent friends who were sitting in the trenches then the Church of England. Next, Arbuthnot raised his glass to "Our wives and sweethearts," while Neville replied with the old joke, "May they never meet," before drinking.

When it came to his turn, Dudley said the first thing that came to his mind: "Mister Vice, to our men of the Royal Hants." His voice was as strong as he could have wished, and he was pleased the ritual went as it should, the others echoing his words.

When the toasts had ended, the conversation resumed. One of the other captains, a smooth-faced fellow named Edward Rowntree, began with, "I say, David, I was thinking of that time in London when we made off with that baby carriage." He then addressed those assembled. "We left the hysterical mother behind, chasing us through Hyde Park and wailing for her child! Ha-ha!"

Dudley did not think this very funny, and when Major Willis asked Neville to explain, it got less funny still.

"You see, sir," Neville began, his face flushed and lit with good-humoured pride, "we were just out for a bit of fun—new lieutenants at the time, wandering the town. We'd been to a luncheon at Hammond's and were in high spirits when we came across this grand pram with a baby inside. The mother was sitting on a bench and was fast asleep. Fast asleep, mind you!"

Neville then went on to describe how they had removed the baby and hidden it in the hedge next to the path. Then they had made off with the carriage. The mother had awakened in time to see them go.

Thinking two army officers were kidnapping her child, she had chased them through the park shrieking at the top of her lungs and waving an umbrella. Neville and Rowntree had eventually let her catch them. When the two witty young men had pointed out the infant's true location some yards back, the mother had turned around and gone shrieking the other way.

More than half the assemblage received this incredible story with uproarious laughter. Dudley, not seeing the joke, did not join in. He noted two others, Major Willis and a fellow named Norcott, captain of the Grenadier company, also offered nothing more than polite smiles.

There followed other anecdotes about similar pranks. There was the time when Neville had shouted "Police!" in a crowded and illegal gambling institution, and another when he had loaded a gentleman friend's gun with blanks during a pheasant shoot.

When the laughter over this last tale had subsided, there was a brief silence. In the distance sounded the pounding of artillery.

"Oh!" said Arbuthnot. "There are the guns again."

"Well, they never stop, do they?" said Captain Rowntree.

"No, indeed," said Neville. "Let us hope we have peace soon, and we can all go home. This is a very fine little hut, but it ain't our familiar old rooms back in Hampshire. How I miss it."

There was agreement in this from all save Dudley. In the pause that followed, Major Willis said, "You're a native of Hampshire, are you not, Mister Dudley?"

Dudley was startled to hear his name but collected himself and replied, "Yes, sir. My uncle runs a public school there."

Major Willis looked satisfied.

"Ah, that's good. Whereas most of our enlisted men are from the county whose name our regiment bears, too many of our officers are not. And if I am not mistaken, Dudley is a noble old English name. Would I have heard of your uncle, by any chance?"

"I don't know, sir. He does write some on the subjects of religion and education, and has made a bit of a name for himself. But his name is not, in fact, Dudley. He is the Reverend Robert Mason, of Addington."

"Robert Mason," Willis repeated. "No, I'm afraid I don't know of him."

Not wanting the conversation to end there, Dudley added, "He was a classmate of Lord Palmerston's, at St. John's College, Cambridge."

As soon as he said these words, he wished to take them back. His uncle had worked as Palmerston's servant in order to help pay his tuition. The two men had been friends, but Dudley knew there was no excuse for his implied untruth. He had made it sound as if his family were on a social footing with the prime minister.

But the statement had its desired effect, and Willis said, "Oh, indeed? Well, that can't hurt these days, eh?"

There was a polite rumble of laughter, and Dudley tried to accept his mistake. Maybe there was nothing wrong with a bit of name-dropping now and then, he decided, if it helped him settle in. But he would have to be careful not to try passing himself off as something he was not.

"But on the subject of education," Willis said, "I am reminded of a man I met in Paris who had some very new and unusual ideas."

As the major's anecdote developed, Dudley relapsed into silence. No one addressed him again, save when Neville said at one point, "I say, Mister Dudley, can you pass the bottle round?"

Later, the gathering made an attempt at singing, and Dudley did his best to join in, with much laughter and encouragement from Arbuthnot. He managed to enjoy himself, although when the singing ended, so did his evening. The others rose from the table to smoke their cigars, and Dudley found he had no reason to linger. He did not smoke and had no desire to start. He could never have afforded cigars anyway.

He emerged from the mess hut feeling a mixture of satisfaction and uneasiness. The meal had been good, but his performance left him feeling dissatisfied. He had not broken any rules, but he had also not bothered to offer anything substantial to the conversation when the chance had presented itself. All he had managed was the foolish comment about Palmerston.

As for the storytelling, he had nothing to say to fellows who thought torturing civilians made good fun. He thought of himself as a humorous man by nature but did not consider such "pranks" harmless or amusing.

Then again, it had been Neville and Rowntree telling those stories. The others had spoken of more normal subjects, such as horses and fox-hunting, while Arbuthnot had talked about his boyhood wish to become a portrait artist. Dudley could have ventured a comment or two there. He would have to try harder next time. If he allowed himself to relax and did not expect too much, the mess hut could become a haven.

He moved into the camp street. It was a lovely evening, with a hint of sunset in the west and a few stars glittering through the ragged cloud. He had not heard the artillery for about half an hour. As he began making his way towards his tent, he noticed Colour-Sergeant O'Ryan approaching from the other direction. O'Ryan saw him and saluted.

"Good evening, sir."

For a second, Dudley wanted to say, "Don't call me sir." O'Ryan had once been a senior sergeant, one of his drill instructors and teachers. But that was all in the past. Dudley returned the salute and replied, "Good evening, Colour-Sergeant."

O'Ryan did not stop to chat. Dudley watched his receding form with regret.

He and O'Ryan had once been friends, but apparently the Irishman thought Dudley did not want his friendship anymore. Or perhaps it was the other way around. Either way, he knew O'Ryan was lost to him.

He looked back at the mess hut, where the lanterns burned inside. The others were still in there, puffing away and chattering in loud voices. The light in the door's tiny window made a pale-yellow glow.

Stomach full, Dudley slept well that night. He awoke to the bugle sounding reveille. As he dressed, an orderly corporal came to the tent to tell him the company had trench duty. Arbuthnot, groggy from the previous evening's indulgence, groaned. Dudley was thankful for his decision to drink water instead of wine.

Under a sky still filled with stars, he followed his men through the maze of trenches in the right-attack. Captain Neville was in the lead, trying to find a position identified as the "Number 2 Left Demi Parallel." Like Arbuthnot, Neville was bleary-eyed from too much drink, and he took the company down the wrong approach trench.

When he discovered his mistake, he let loose a string of angry curses. Doubling back in a counter-march would take precious time, and the company would soon lose the safe cover of darkness.

They moved along the old third parallel. Scarlet light outlined the horizon now, but the Russian guns stayed silent. The enemy artillery had not been active for the last few days, perhaps to conserve ammunition. No fire rained down as Neville took his men along the "Number 1 Left Demi Parallel." From that, he found an angled approach that led to the their assigned position.

The Number 2 Left Demi Parallel was a short trench fashioned from the captured Russian rifle pits. It was one of the closest positions to the Redan. The company that held it, waiting for the arrival of No. 3 Company, was from the 23rd Fusiliers. They were a band of muddy and haggard men, their captain wrapped in a non-regulation tweed overcoat. With them was a company of sappers and an officer of the Royal Engineers. The sappers looked clean and rested, and must have arrived moments before.

"You are relieved, sir," Neville said to the man in the tweed coat. His voice was cracked and hoarse. He did not look well, nor did Arbuthnot.

The sappers broke out their breakfast rations as the men of the 23rd filed away in the growing light. The Russians saw the movement, and several musket shots rang out. Dudley's company huddled under cover as the bullets struck the parapet. When all seemed quiet again, the sappers resumed their meal. The infantry settled in to do the same, the men taking off their knapsacks and pulling out their dried pork and biscuits.

The sky was gold-tinged azure when the sappers began their work, extending a new approach from the parallel. It was the infantry's job to protect them. Dudley's section of the company arrayed themselves along the parapet to watch for the enemy snipers or the jet of smoke from artillery fire.

It was shaping up to be a fine day, although the chill of night lingered. Dudley wished the company had not gone on duty without their greatcoats, and began to strut back and forth in the bottom of the trench to keep warm. He could feel the tin soldier around his neck under his coat. The metal was cold.

In the middle of the morning, Private Oakes arrived by way of the approach trench. He carried his rifle and cartridge box, and announced, "Bill's all fed and cozy, sir."

"You didn't have to come here to tell me that, Private," Dudley replied. "You simply can't stay away from the front lines."

"I'll leave if ye order me to, sir."

"Of course you will, Private Oakes." Dudley managed a smile. "But you know I won't do that."

As he spoke, two rifle shots sounded from the left of the company line. In their wake came a low rattle of laughter. With Oakes trailing behind him, Dudley moved to investigate.

The men who had fired were Private Johnson and another first-rate marksman named Mitchell. Both leaned over the parapet with their rear rifle sights adjusted for three hundred yards. Sergeant Barker stood with them. At Dudley's approach, he turned and said, "We can see one of the Quarries from here, Mister Dudley."

Dudley stepped onto the narrow earthen firing step that let him see over the parapet of gabions and muck. Ahead stretched a wide expanse of rising ground, ending at the dark wall of Sevastopol. An unmistakable feature of that wall was the Redan, and at its foot was a ditch and an abatis of sharpened stakes. In front of that abatis, between it and the British positions, was another stretch of obstacles.

During the winter, the Russians had begun digging a series of short trenches and rifle pits far out in front of their main fortifications. One trench was a long parallel almost two hundred yards from the Redan. Zigzag approaches extended from this to a group of depressions that offered cover for large bodies of men. These depressions were just large rifle pits, but the British had dubbed them the Quarries.

Dudley wished for a telescope to examine the depressions in more detail, for he would have to fight for them soon enough. The Quarries were to the British what the Mamelon was to the French. Before an assault could be made on the Redan, they would have to seize the Quarries. Then the Russian trenches could be incorporated into the British works.

"That Quarry straight ahead," Barker said, "can hold a strong party, maybe about fifty men. But they keep coming out, you see, sir, because they don't seem to have dug a proper latrine. They go about fifteen yards to the edge of the Woronzov ravine, and there they do their business. That is, if we let 'em."

Private Johnson chuckled and took a fresh paper cartridge from his ammunition pouch. He bit open the end, poured the powder into the muzzle then pushed the greased paper and bullet in after it. The conical bullet was of a slightly smaller diameter than the barrel, and it was no effort to thrust it home with the ramrod. When fired, the bullet would expand to grip the musket's rifling.

Mitchell, a gaunt young man with a straggle of beard, reloaded in turn. Oakes joined him at the parapet. Oakes had cast away his old Minié rifle in favour of a new Enfield. Dudley suspected the old veteran had taken the weapon from a corpse. He was eager to try it, and began loading.

Almost every man in the company now waited for a Russian to emerge from the Quarry. As Oakes fitted a copper percussion cap over the breach nipple of his rifle, there was an expectant silence.

The head of a Russian soldier appeared as if from the ground, then his shoulders and upper body. The fellow wore a floppy green forage cap with a red band, a long brown coat with a red collar, and dirty leather cross-belts. Slung over his shoulder was a big smoothbore musket. As he emerged from cover, he glanced around like a rabbit coming out of its hole. He did not see the silent British snipers waiting behind their parapet. He began moving off at a crouch.

The parapet erupted in rifle fire. Bullets struck the ground at the Russian's feet, throwing up little jets of earth. Grasping his cap, the man turned and dove back into the Quarry.

The British soldiers shouted and cheered him. Barker commented, "That was probably as good as a dose of opening medicine for him!"

The men in the trench hooted and slapped each other on the arms and back. No one had actually tried to shoot the Russian. There would be plenty of time for that later.

<hr />

Near the end of May, word came that the peace talks in Vienna had ended in failure. The war would go on. This news was too much for the French commander-in-chief, General Canrobert. He decided he had seen enough, that others could command better than he. He resigned, relinquishing command to General Pelissier.

In the British camps, Dudley continued to ease into the life of an officer. Activity along the front continued, although it did not intensify, and No. 3 Company continued to have two or three nights off at a time. The break allowed him to visit the mess hut on a regular basis. He met most of the other officers and was becoming more comfortable with the general atmosphere of the hut. He had also decided he liked Major Willis. The major seemed a fair and reasonable man, if perhaps a bit dull, and a welcome foil to Neville and Rowntree with their aggressive sense of humour.

As for Neville, Dudley had still not decided what to make of him. He seemed a contradiction. It was obvious he despised Barker, and his delight in stories of cruel practical jokes fit with what he had done to the sergeant when he was a lieutenant. Yet he had been fair and welcoming to his new subaltern, and Dudley had no cause to dislike him on a personal level. He also included Dudley in the dinner conversation every evening and encouraged him to take part in other social activities.

One of those activities was a test of marksmanship. As a sporting venture, Neville had set up a small pistol range on the edge of camp. There, the officers could wager on each other's skill with a revolver. Neville suggested Dudley test his ability to shoot.

Dudley had never fired a pistol before, but Arbuthnot offered to teach him. As his tent mate, the lieutenant had become Dudley's closest companion. They accompanied each other on rides across the uplands, sometimes engaging in short races. During these rides, Arbuthnot would speak at length about his betrothed at home, about how much he missed her. Dudley sometimes found this tiresome, but for the most part, Arbuthnot was an amiable companion and a competent teacher.

Arbuthnot carried a five-chambered Adams revolver when he and Dudley first visited the pistol range. Dudley thought the Adams an ugly weapon, but it was said to be reliable and accurate.

"Very handy in trench skirmishing, I imagine," he said as he hefted the two-pound revolver.

"Now, hold your arm at full extension," Arbuthnot instructed, "and don't close one eye to aim. Keep them both open and focus on your target. I find it much easier."

Dudley obeyed, stiffening his arm and applying gentle pressure to the trigger. He sighted on the first in a line of empty wine bottles twenty paces away. The pistol barked, leaping in his hand. He did not see where the bullet went, but it was nowhere near the target.

"Try again," Arbuthnot said, sounding a bit smug. Perhaps he was enjoying this bit of practical superiority, for Dudley had a reputation for excellent marksmanship with a rifle. "Watch where the shot strikes, to determine how the pistol shoots, high or low or to one side. Relax your arm."

The Adams was self-cocking, so there was no need to pull back the hammer. Dudley sighted again and fired. The bullet struck the dirt in front of the bottle. Encouraged, he fired a third time. Again he missed. A group of watching officers began to chuckle, and he sighed in frustration.

"Try tracking your target," Arbuthnot suggested. "Find the proper elevation then move the pistol from side to side, firing when it lines up with the bottle. It will eliminate quivering in your arm."

Dudley paused, waiting for his irritation to subside. There was no reason why he could not do this.

He raised the pistol, this time tracking across the row of bottles until he sighted his intended target. He squeezed the trigger and saw the bottle's spout leap from the neck.

"Aha!" he said in triumph. Encouraged, he aimed for his fifth and final shot. A cloud of powder smoke had formed around his head, but he disregarded its sulfurous stink and concentrated. Once again, he moved the revolver from right to left, firing when his target came in line. The bottle shattered into sparkling fragments.

"Bravo!" Arbuthnot exclaimed. "See, all it takes is a bit of relaxation. Practice like that, and soon it will become second nature."

"I rather enjoyed that," Dudley declared.

"Well done," Captain Neville said, striding up from the edge of the range. "Is this the first time you have fired a revolver, Ensign?"

"Yes, sir. I never had much occasion to before."

Neville unbuttoned his holster and drew his own pistol, an attractive brass-framed Colt Navy pattern revolver.

"Allow me to have a go."

The captain effected a ready stance, right toe pointing down-range, left foot to his left. The watching officers began to whisper among themselves.

Dudley studied Neville's actions, hoping to learn something. The captain pulled back the hammer of his pistol with his thumb then extended his right arm. He took great care in aiming. Dudley was able to count to ten before he fired.

The second bottle in line shattered. Neville pulled the hammer back again and shifted his arm to the right. Again he took great care, but when he fired the third bottle shattered. The watching officers applauded, and Neville bowed.

"Perhaps when you have practiced," he said to Dudley as he returned the pistol to its holster, "we can have a little contest."

"I think I could agree to that, sir."

Neville smiled and put an arm across Dudley's shoulder, drawing him away from Arbuthnot and saying, "Excuse us a moment, Lieutenant, will you? Now, Ensign Dudley, I'd like you to accompany me to my tent for a moment. I have something for you."

Dudley was intrigued but cautious at the same time.

"Something for me, Captain?"

"Yes, Ensign. If you will come with me." As they made their way back among the rows of tents, Neville continued, "Because of the circumstances surrounding your becoming an officer of the Royal Hampshire Fusiliers—this being wartime, that is, and everything being so unsettled—we in the mess feel that you have not had a proper introduction. That does not sit well with us. We are all gentlemen of action, you see, and we respect another man of action. We value a man who achieves something by gallant deeds, and it is common knowledge that your commission was granted as a result of your leading the very company I have the pleasure to command. Leading it and subsequently capturing an enemy battery."

"I am told my actions were a factor, sir, as well as the Royal Warrant."

"Yes, of course. Well, we thought that things have turned out rather shabbily. So, we would like you to know that if you need anything to help ease you in, you are not to hesitate to ask the other fellows. As a mark of my sincerity in this, I have, as I said, something for you."

They had come to Neville's tent, and the captain led him inside. There, he produced a rectangular wooden box more than half a foot long. He placed the box in Dudley's hands. Dudley opened it. Inside rested a brass-mounted telescope, collapsed for storage.

"It's not much, I'm afraid," Neville was saying, "and rather old. But it is given as a token of welcome, and I think you will find it useful."

Dudley shook his head and stared at the beautiful gift.

"I'm afraid I don't know what to say, sir."

"You don't have to say anything, lad. Just remember that all of the fellows in the mess are your comrades. You are uncomfortable for having been raised from the ranks, but there is nothing in that. You have a humble background, it is true, but a respectable one. I am aware that your uncle is a man of some means, and rather famous in certain circles. At any rate, we stick up for our own in the Royal Hants."

On this last comment, Dudley could not help thinking about how Neville had "stuck up" for Barker. He wanted to feel thankful for this gift, but his skepticism would not allow it. Neville was either a changed man…or a hypocrite.

Or perhaps he had misunderstood Neville's meaning. Barker was a sergeant. When Neville had trumped up the charges against him, the other officers had gone along with the game. They had all known Barker was a good man, but they had never listened to his side of the story, nor any testimony on his behalf. They had sided with Neville because he was an officer, and Barker was an enlisted man.

Officers stuck up for officers. The enlisted men were just the enlisted men. Dudley wondered if that meant his new messmates would support him, no matter what.

Then again, the root of Barker's troubles had been his refusal to help Neville destroy another subaltern.

Dudley despised this doubt, this suspicion. He wanted to believe Neville had changed, that this gift was sincere. He ran his fingers along the edge of the box. It was so foolish and unfair to condemn Neville without any evidence. Neville was his company commander, a man he had to follow.

He forced a smile and said, "I don't know how to thank you, sir. You've done a great deal to make me feel welcome."

Neville's eyes sparkled. "Not at all, Ensign," he said. "Not at all."

A Russian mortar shell resembling a black football rose against the bright blue of the sky. On its downward arc, the shell left a smoking comet's tail, shrieking as it plunged toward the forward British positions. From the lookout in front of the Light Division camp, Dudley saw the dirty burst when the shell struck short of its target. The distant bang of the explosion followed a few seconds later.

Two more shells came after the first, rising from beyond the Redan then falling toward the British trench. Dudley tried to fix them in his telescope to see what damage they would do, but they were moving too fast. By the time he had focused, the shells had burst and the smoke was clearing.

"Our old friend Whistling Dick," Sergeant Barker said at his side, "and his two abominable brothers."

Dudley lowered the telescope and shaded his eyes with one hand. It was a bright June afternoon, still and warm. He waited, but the Russians fired no further shells.

It had been like this for weeks now, the artillery exchanges becoming fewer and fewer. When there was firing, it came like this mortar attack, two or three rounds and then silence. A strange state of neglect had fallen over the war, each side waiting for the other to make a move.

Until today.

"They're saving their ammunition," Dudley said.

Barker bit into an apple, and the juice ran into his beard.

"Let's hope most of 'em have gone to sleep," he said after some noisy chewing.

Dudley raised his telescope again. He and Barker stood on a wide hill on the northern edge of the Light Division camp. The hill made a natural balcony with a good view of Sevastopol and had become the camp lookout.

At the moment, officers and men crowded the space, waiting for three o'clock to arrive. With Dudley and Barker stood Privates Mitchell, Forbes, Geary, Johnson and Oakes. The Allied artillery would bombard Sevastopol once again, and everyone wanted to watch. Three hundred British and French siege guns opening fire at once would make for quite a sight.

Dudley swept the telescope back and forth, pushing the eyepiece in and out to focus on various features of the land. The maze of the French right-attack spread out below the lookout. Beyond those trenches rose the low walls of the Mamelon redoubt, now notched with gun embrasures. Dudley swung the telescope to the left, and the angle of the Redan popped into view.

He studied the huge salient angle and its two sloping edges. For the first time, with the aid of the telescope, he could see the many gun emplacements. Some were like square notches in the parapet, others like windows or gunports cut into the side of the scarp. In some places, he noticed gunports below gun embrasures. The Russians had mounted some of their cannon on platforms above other guns, as in the broadside of a man-of-war.

The structure was a brilliant feat of military engineering. Curtains of thick rope known as mantlets screened the gun positions, protection that not even rifle bullets could penetrate. Flanking fire from the west curtain of the Malakov and from another structure known as the "little redan" covered the approaches. The allied artillery would have to destroy much of these defences for an infantry assault to succeed.

"We have our work cut out for us," Dudley commented.

"Where did you buy that spyglass, sir, if you don't mind my askin'?" Barker asked.

Dudley hesitated before replying, pretending to focus on something.

"It was a gift."

Before Barker could say anything else, the entire line of allied batteries blasted smoke toward Sevastopol. The spectators on the lookout jumped. The force of the combined detonation made Dudley feel as if someone had just boxed his ears.

"Three o'clock, sir," Barker shouted, grinning under his shaggy beard.

Dudley turned his telescope into the west to watch the activity in the batteries. He focused on a position in Gordon's Battery that held four 32-pounders on siege carriages. All four of the guns had fired at once for the opening salvo, and he watched their respective crews reload according to the ritual drill. One man sponged the barrel to extinguish any remaining embers while another man sealed the vent with a leather thumbstall. On the far side of each gun, three other men worked together to bring up ammunition. The man who had sponged then rammed powder cartridge, wad and projectile home in turn. With the gun thus loaded, its crew ran it up so its muzzle thrust through its embrasure. One man inserted a copper friction primer into the vent then attached a lanyard to the tube by means of a tiny hook. Meanwhile, the officers in charge watched for targets through telescopes or binoculars, occasionally giving instructions to their NCOs.

The guns now fired whenever they were ready, making a constant rolling thunder. A heavy cloud of pinkish-yellow powder smoke settled over the allied positions. Dudley shifted his telescope back to Sevastopol to watch for damage.

The five-gun naval battery on Victoria Ridge had targeted the Redan, and he could see the heavy shot striking home, spraying up gouts of earth. The guns of the Redan jetted smoke and flame in reply.

After about an hour, the smoke began to screen Sevastopol from view. No one moved from the lookout, and Dudley could hear cheering in the camp behind him. He turned to find out what this was about, and spied a group of riders moving among the tents. Some were French and others British. Dudley recognized Lord Raglan, the grandfatherly—and, some said, dotty—British Commander-in-Chief. The empty right sleeve of his dark-blue coat was pinned up, and he held his plumed cocked hat in his left hand. With him rode a French general officer who could only be General Pelissier, who had taken over from "Robert Can't." Behind the generals trailed a small host of aides.

The men on the lookout took up the cheer as the procession came closer. Private Johnson cried, "If the generals are on parade that means something's up for sure, and all this noise ain't for nothing!"

Dudley knew Johnson was right. The generals' tour could only be a morale boost prior to an attack.

When the riders had gone, the people on the lookout milled about, some staying to watch and others moving off. At one point, a black ball, clear against a backdrop of smoke and sky, hurtled toward the position. It thumped into the ground, spraying turf and bouncing three more times before coming to rest on the edge of the camp. This produced some nervous laughter, and a few more spectators left the lookout. Dudley and Barker remained, enjoying the novelty of the telescope.

Through the haze, Dudley could still see the hump of the Redan. When shells struck it, they blasted bits of wood, clods of earth, and parts of bodies into the air. He watched a round shot dismount a gun before his eyes, the bronze barrel sliding forward through its smashed embrasure and crashing into the ditch.

It was a satisfying sight. One less Russian gun would make the attack that much easier.

The artillery thundered and crashed until dusk, and in the morning No. 3 Company received orders to proceed to the trenches. In the last minutes of darkness, the men filed through the approaches to a position in the old third parallel. There, they waited. When the sun at last emerged in the east, the allied bombardment resumed.

The Russians had repaired some of their damage in the night, and they returned fire. One of their first shells scored a lucky hit and exploded an expense magazine in Chapman's Battery, eliciting an audible cheer from Sevastopol.

The men of No. 3 Company tried to relax within the shelter of their trench. All around them waited detached sections from other regiments. Everyone suspected there would be some kind of assault soon.

Hours passed, shot and shell screaming overhead. Early in the afternoon, Captain Neville called together Color-Sergeant O'Ryan, Dudley, and Lieutenant Arbuthnot. Neville's eyes glowed with excitement.

"We are to assault the Quarries later today," he shouted over the noise of the guns. "Most likely at five or six o'clock this evening. The French will storm the Mamelon. Our attack will be carried out by parts of all four divisions." He seemed pleased with himself. "The Light Division was not supposed to be involved, but a few companies of the Connaught Rangers and the Seventy-seventh have volunteered. I could not let them show us up, and volunteered Number-Three Company. We will be the only company from the regiment to take part."

He paused to let this sink in. Dudley nodded, trying not to acknowledge the stab of alarm that trilled through his stomach and intestines. Today he would go into battle.

"I expect every one of you to do his duty," Neville added, looking at each man in turn.

"Very good, sir," O'Ryan said with a blithe grin.

"My Margaret would not be proud of me," Arbuthnot declared, "if I did not do my duty."

Neville stared at his lieutenant with evident annoyance.

"Lieutenant Arbuthnot, this is not a time for your fantasies. Practically every one of our messmates knows that your Margaret is dead, and has been for these four years. You will end up in a lunatic asylum if you don't cease your nonsense. I am ultimately responsible for my men, and I will not have an officer of mine prattling on as if he were not right in the head. Is that understood, sir?"

Arbuthnot had gone very pale, but he nodded.

"Yes, Captain Neville."

"Good. Then we shall wait for the signal."

Neville glanced at Dudley once then moved away several paces. O'Ryan cleared his throat and scurried off to pass on the news of the assault to the other sergeants. Arbuthnot turned to Dudley, his lips quivering.

"I am not deluded," he said, voice almost inaudible under the guns. "I know she is gone, and am sorry I misled you.

But that does not mean she does not hear me when I speak to her."

Dudley had noticed Arbuthnot never wrote or received letters from his oft-mentioned fiancee. Now he understood why. For some reason, he felt no shock or disgust. He found he could forgive a man for talking to a spirit through a lock of hair. Perhaps that was even more reasonable than speaking to a live woman in the same way.

"It's all right, sir," he said. "Maybe she can hear you from heaven."

"Yes." Arbuthnot managed a nervous smile. "I do believe she can."

The company waited, the men not speaking. Idle talk was not worth the effort. As two o'clock neared, Private Oakes came along the trench, carrying his rifle. He saluted Dudley and said, "Permission to join the assault, sir?"

"Does Mrs. Oakes approve of what you are doing?"

Oakes's face hardened. "She knows she married a soldier, Mister Dudley."

Dudley had not minded Oakes's presence before, but for a moment he considered telling him to go back. He knew this could be a hard fight. If something happened to the old fellow, he would feel responsible, if only because he had the power to keep him from combat.

But Oakes was a soldier, and Dudley had made him his servant in order to let him be a soldier. There was no sense in pretending there had been any other reason save rescuing the man from a hopeless life in the gutters of London. That was something no one who had fought for Queen and Country should ever have to endure.

"Okay, Private Oakes," he said, "permission is granted. But stay close to Sergeant Barker."

Oakes grimaced. "He's the first person they'll shoot at, sir."

They continued to wait in the trench, waiting and waiting as shells detonated outside, unseen but felt as the ground trembled. The sound of the guns became a monotonous pounding. That and the arrival of Private Oakes heightened Dudley's impatience. Again and again he found himself reaching into his coat front to finger his tin soldier charm.

He understood the significance of this attack, and its difficulty. The struggle for the rifle pits in front of the Mamelon during which so many Zouaves had been killed was finally reaching its climax. The Russians had since formed those pits into parallels, and the French would have to cross five hundred yards of open ground to reach them. On the British side, the men would have to cross about two hundred yards to make it to the Quarries.

Captain Neville suddenly appeared and said, "We're going forward to the Number Two Left Demi Parallel. Right now, Ensign."

Dudley found Sergeant Barker and relayed the order, and a moment later, Barker had the men moving. They filed along an approach trench carrying their rifles at the trail. Neville led, and this time had no difficulty locating the position. It was the right-attack advance trench, the closest to the enemy. Other companies were already there. So were several senior officers.

As No. 3 Company filled their section of trench, Neville shouted, "Form a single rank. Right marker, position yourself here. Move!"

The men hurried to form a line along the bottom of the trench. The right marker—the tallest man in the company—took his place, and the rest formed to his left. When each man was ready, he stood at attention, rifle at the order. Dudley took up a position on the left with his section while

Arbuthnot took the right section. Neville squeezed in behind the center of the line.

"Company will fix bayonets," he shouted, "Fix!"

Every man in the rank grasped his rifle in his right hand and the socket of his bayonet in the other.

Then Neville cried, "Bayonets!"

The men dragged seventeen-inch bayonets from their scabbards with a single metallic swish. In a chorus of rattling, they fitted the bayonets over the muzzles of their muskets.

With bayonets fixed, Neville stood the company at ease then stood them easy. They held on to their rifles in silence. They waited some more. It was about half-past four in the afternoon. Captain Neville passed the time by trying to brush some fresh dirt stains from his uniform.

Dudley's mouth was dry, and he kept swallowing. This tension was different from what he had known before the Alma or Inkerman. He shifted from foot to foot and licked his lips. He realized he was afraid again, and this brought a flash of panic. He drew in several deep breaths, and the panic eased.

Before his other battles, he had needed to concentrate on his foot and arms drill. Drill was a familiar procedure. It took all one's concentration and diverted the mind from the possibility of being killed, or of seeing comrades killed. Here was none of that. The company was not to march into battle; it was to emerge from the ground to face the struggle all at once.

Dudley looked at the trench parapet inches above his head. In an hour or so, they would clamber up the ladders and storm the Quarries, if all went as planned. In the attack, they would be met with a storm themselves—a storm of bullets and grapeshot.

He had never had a chance to dwell on these things before, and that, he decided, was the key. He had nothing to stop his imagination from working, thus producing this unexpected fear. All of his loose bravado in his letters to Jane had

been genuine, but now he knew what he was about to face—
a nightmare come true. He knew the perils of combat too
well, for he had seen them and felt them.

Barker came up beside him and muttered something, but
he could not hear over the pounding of the guns and did not
reply. He knew he was pale and sweating. It was no comfort
to look down the line and see that many of the other men,
Arbuthnot included, were in the same plight.

He hoped that, once the fighting began, he would launch
into it and let it carry him away. There was no question of his
going forward, fear or no fear.

He tried to take himself back to the capture of the battery at Inkerman. The memory of that time and place was
hard to recall. It was a confused jumble. That action had oc-
curred in the thick of things, where action could have come
from anywhere at any time. He wondered if he had been
afraid. He supposed he had but had not noticed it. There had
been none of this *waiting*.

Neville had wandered off to the left where the senior
officers stood. When he came back, he said to Dudley, "The
assault will be later than expected. Let's have the men fall out
of line. They may have their supper as well."

Dudley sighed. There would be more waiting still.

CHAPTER 7

June 6, 1855

In the French right-attack, the Zouaves and Chasseurs of the Guard crowded together in their advanced trenches. At six o'clock in the evening, as the sun began its descent toward the horizon, the bombardment eased, the gaps of time between each shot lengthening. The French soldiers tensed and watched for the signal.

On the lookout in front of the Light Division camp, those not involved in the assault watched the low dark form of the Mamelon. The Russian guns there continued to flash and boom, and several balls sped toward the lookout. One took a man's head off, his body flopping down and blood pouring from his stump of neck. The other spectators fled, anticipating more incoming fire. When it did not appear, they returned to their choice seats.

As they watched, three rockets shot into the air, trailing long lines of smoke and glowing brightly. It was the signal for the attack. The French infantry scrambled over the parapet and rushed across the open ground in one great mass.

Russian gunners in the Mamelon saw the attack and shifted their aim. Their guns belched flame and grape, mowing great gaps in the French advance. But the guns could not stop the huge attacking wave. The Russian sharpshooters in the rifle pits emptied their muskets then fled from their positions. Few got very far before the attackers had engulfed them.

There was a brief play of bayonets; then the French swarmed up the side of the Mamelon in a tide of blue coats and red trousers. The Zouaves led the attack and revenged themselves on the redoubt that had dealt them so many cruel defeats. Within ten minutes, they had torn down the cross of St. Peter and hoisted the Tricolour on the parapet.

Some of the attackers continued to run over the fort, down the far wall, and across open ground toward the Malakov. They stopped at the edge of the abatis and ditch, and there they milled about, fodder for the guns. Blasts of grape and canister shot tore into them. A moment later, the French swarmed back the other way, shattered.

The Russians who had fled from the Mamelon saw their enemy retreat and gave a cheer. Inspired, they charged back toward the redoubt. The Mamelon was now on fire, black smoke pouring from its center. The Russian counterattack charged up the far wall and smashed into the French defenders inside, forcing them back, back, until they withdrew from the fort they had thought taken. The Russians snatched the Tricolour from the earthen wall, while the French ran all the way back to their original trench.

The guns on both sides ceased, and there was a profound and eerie silence. The ground outside the French trench was littered with torn bodies.

But the French reserves had been creeping up on the Mamelon from the shallow ravines on either side. In the silence, they burst from their cover and charged back up the wall. Again, Russians went down under French bayonets. Those Russians who survived the charge ran for their lives. The attackers raised the Tricolour once more.

Some of the French continued to the Malakov as they had before. When they retreated under the blasts of its guns, no Russian infantry followed. The Mamelon had fallen.

Three British mortar shells whined overhead. Dudley started when he saw them, thinking they were rockets. He cursed under his breath when he realized his error, but at that moment, a single rocket also shot into the air. It was the signal for the British to assault the Quarries.

The waiting was over.

Captain Neville drew his sword and leapt onto the trench parapet. With his sword outstretched, he cried, "Number Three Company of the Royal Hampshire Fusiliers—advance!"

"Here we go, sir," Dudley heard Private Oakes say.

All along the trench men began climbing the little ladders and pulling themselves over the parapet. Dudley scrambled up behind the left wing of the company. Sergeant Barker was right beside him, Oakes in the line in front.

As they rose out of the trench, a Shrapnel shell burst in the air nearby, its deadly rain striking down two men. They lay on the ground two yards beyond the parapet, while their comrades surged forward. Dudley hesitated a moment, frozen at the sight of the bodies, trying to determine who they were. Then he realized he was being left behind. He began to run, forcing all of his nervous energy into his legs. He felt exposed, vulnerable, but he refused to panic. He was still in control.

The red backs of the company grew nearer as he ran, faster and faster, rifle gripped hard. His forage cap blew off his head, and he heard the distinctive whine as a bullet passed his ear. Puffs of smoke appeared near the ground where the Russians hid. More men fell, but Dudley passed their stricken forms without a second look. Then, with a great cheer, the line ahead of him dropped out of sight.

Three paces later, he also came to the edge of the nearest Quarry. The men were locked in a hand-to-hand struggle within. With a scream, he jumped in after them, bayonet thrust out before him. Using the force of his falling weight, he drove the triangular blade deep into a Russian chest.

He wrenched the bayonet free and felt something smash into his left shoulder. It was the butt of a Russian musket, and its glancing blow knocked him on his back. His assailant stood over him. Dudley pulled back the hammer of his rifle, but there was no percussion cap in place, and he had no time to pull one from his pouch. The Russian stabbed with his bayonet, and Dudley rolled to one side. The bayonet crunched into the ground and stuck. Before he could rise, a British private stabbed the Russian in the side.

Dudley leapt to his feet, fumbling to fit a percussion cap in place. He chose a target at random and fired. His bullet entered a handsome blond man's eye and lifted off the top of his skull. He lowered his rifle and assumed a bayonet stance. He saw Captain Neville cleave the arm from a Russian officer who had leveled a huge dragoon pistol at him. The officer fell back in shock, blood spurting from the stump of his arm. Neville coolly stabbed him in the throat.

Brown-coated shapes were now fleeing from the pit, and Dudley was surrounded by red-coated British only. He saw Arbuthnot and Barker, Johnson, Mitchell and Forbes, all safe but looking confused in their moment of victory.

"Get these gabions onto the opposite side!" Neville shouted, pointing with his bloody blade at the Quarry's forward parapet, now behind them.

Dudley's took a second to note that his anxiety and fear were gone, but he had no time for relief. He joined the others in grabbing the heavy wicker baskets and taking them to the opposite side of the pit. They piled them anew, leaving gaps for loopholes.

They had re-positioned about half a dozen gabions when the Russians made their first counterattack.

"Stand to!" Colour-Sergeant O'Ryan shouted.

The troops grabbed their rifles and formed a rough line. The Quarry was shallow enough to fire over the edge. Without thinking, they began biting cartridges and loading their rifles. Dudley did the same.

"Fire on my command," Neville shouted.

A formed column of Russians marched toward the Quarry in normal quick-time. When the Russians were a scant twenty paces away, they gave a hoarse cheer and doubled forward.

"Present!" Neville shouted.

All save two of the defenders aimed. One who did not cursed his broken hammer spring, while the other had spilled the contents of his percussion cap pouch and was searching in the dirt.

"Fire!" Neville cried.

Dudley's rifle jarred his shoulder; then, without pausing he dropped the butt to the ground to reload. The close-range volley had cut down the entire front rank of the enemy column. Some members of the second rank stumbled over their fallen comrades to continue, but most had halted.

Neville and Arbuthnot drew their revolvers and began shooting into the decimated column. Rifles banged, and the smoke settled in a dense, foul cloud. More Russians fell, and the rest gave up and withdrew. In the dim twilight, Dudley did not see how far they went.

"They'll be back," he heard Barker say.

"That's enough of your comments, Sergeant Barker," Neville remarked. "Continue reinforcing the parapet."

"Yes, sir," Barker replied with unnatural enthusiasm.

The next Russian attack came in the darkness. The British volleys lit up the faces of both attackers and defenders. The Russians were more reckless this time and charged all the way up to the gabions. Some even made it into the Quarry before the attack was repelled.

The next attack was more daring still, coming from three directions at once. The defenders could only hear the enemy coming on, and muskets boomed and flashed in all directions.

Dudley began to feel ill from breathing the thick powder smoke. He fired without knowing whether he hit anything and lashed out with bayonet and stock when the Russians managed to get back into the pit. He did not see them retreat. Between one minute and the next, they simply disappeared.

It was to be a sleepless night. There were four more counterattacks, confused and unnerving. The Russians seemed to be everywhere, while their dead were thick along the edges of the Quarry. The British defenders were nearing exhaustion, mouths dry and shoulders bruised from firing. Their casualties lay bleeding and untended at the bottom of the pit. At one point, Dudley realized he had not seen Oakes for a long time, but in the darkness he had also not seen Barker or Johnson or Arbuthnot.

Early in the morning, the Russian infantry attacks ceased. The British began to wonder if they had succeeded, but minutes later the Russian artillery took its turn. The Quarries lay within close range of the batteries, the Redan in particular. A storm of shot and mortar shells began to fall, exploding all around, smashing into the gabions, tearing some men apart and spraying others with dirt and rocks and metal fragments.

The defenders hugged the forward wall. Some even burrowed little depressions where they could hide. Dudley thought this seemed like a good idea so began digging with his hands. He tore the flesh of his knuckles and broke his fingernails, but that was a small price to pay for safety.

Huddled in his small pit, he managed to get some sleep.

Dawn came like a gray mist, bringing a coating of sticky dew. Dudley awoke half-buried in mud and took a few minutes to remember where he was. He was amazed to discover how complete a burrow he had made for himself. From within, he could see the bottom of the Quarry, knee-deep in British dead and wounded. He guessed that about a third of the company had been struck down. The Russian artillery was still firing the occasional shell. The morning air smelled of sulphur and blood.

When it was light enough, the allied bombardment resumed. The Russian fire turned from the captured Quarries to target the allied batteries. Dudley fought his way out of his hiding place, brushing wet earth from his jacket and trousers. For a moment, he made a frantic search for his cap then remembered it had come off at the beginning of the attack. His rifle was gone as well, and as he looked for it, he saw that Captain Neville was the only other man on his feet. Neville was meticulously loading each chamber of his revolver.

"The men will eat what rations they have with them," he said. "An account of the dead can wait until things are a bit more quiet."

The survivors began to stir then settled down to what pork, beef and biscuits they had in their knapsacks. Many tried to make the groaning wounded comfortable, sharing water from their canteens. The artillery duel continued almost unnoticed over their heads. Few bothered to speak, conserving their energy. Amid the groans and cries for help, Dudley heard a few jokes and a few snatches of quiet laughter.

Sometime after noon, the artillery duel ceased. A last gun fired, and after a series of angry echoes, there was silence.

"Hey!" shouted Private Johnson as he leaned over the parapet. "The white flag's gone up!"

White flags of truce flew from three Russian batteries—the Flagstaff, the Malakov and the Redan. Soon, answering white flags fluttered over the British and French gun positions. There would be a parley.

A delegation of Russian officers met Lord Raglan and his staff near the center of the siege lines. The Russians requested an armistice to collect and bury their dead. Raglan's staff advised against the request. It was a ruse to halt the bombardment, they said, to give the enemy time to repair their defences in case of a further assault. Lord Raglan listened, but perhaps more persuasive than words was the sight of so many dead, a red-and-brown stain on the land. He agreed to a cessation of hostilities from one o'clock in the afternoon until six in the evening.

The men in the Quarries watched the parley from afar. When it became apparent there would, indeed, be a truce, they prepared to sort the wounded from the dead. It was a strange situation, for the British would have to carry out this grim task side-by-side with their enemy. Corpses in red coats lay intertwined with those in brown-and-gray.

The hidden gates in the walls opened, and the Russians made their deliberate way down from Sevastopol. Dudley watched them come. They moved in small groups, sluggish and uncertain. Many carried stretchers. Despite the warmth of the June day, they still wore their long overcoats, some with red facings, others with sky blue. They approached the British and moved among them, tending their fallen.

He eyed them with wonder. After the fury of the Quarries, this peaceful mingling did not seem real.

On the British side, horse-drawn ambulances and bandsmen with litters arrived. Others with spades began to dig a large pit to bury the enlisted dead. Dead officers were carried away to the rear. Each officer's body would be laid out in his camp and eventually placed in one of the many allied graveyards on the uplands.

Dudley supervised a group of men in sorting the dead from the wounded. Many of the dead had swollen faces, their features unrecognizable. They sprawled amidst the debris of broken muskets, bayonets, pouches, belts, fragments of clothing and broken gabions, a scene of utter destruction. Here and there, some of the living tried to lighten the mood by striking up conversations with the Russians, thus adding to the dream-like quality of the scene.

Dudley watched one such exchange, the Russians grinning and saying, "*Bono Inglais.*" This prompted the British to respond with, "*Rooso bono,*" at which the Russians then shook their heads and said, "*Français no bono.*"

Dudley saw a Russian officer approaching, an elegant man with a neat mustache and goatee, dressed in a smart green tunic. Though he had lost his headdress, Dudley snapped a salute. The Russian returned the gesture.

"Your men are very fierce," the Russian said in perfect English. "Our fellows call them 'red devils.'"

"Thank you, sir. Your men are putting up a stalwart defence."

The Russian lit a slim cigar and drew on it. He blew a jet of smoke and asked, "When do you think the war will end?"

Dudley almost replied, *When we have taken your city*, but such talk did not suit the strange politeness of the occasion. So, he said instead, "Soon, I hope. Everyone hopes it will be soon."

"Yes." The Russian smiled. "Yes, as do we."

There was an awkward silence. Dudley wished he had more to say but could think of nothing. At length, the Russian officer nodded, touched his hat and moved on. Dudley watched him go, finding it impossible to feel hatred. He had despised the enemy as barbarians last year when they bayoneted British wounded on the field. Now that he faced them as men, it was hard to reproduce that anger.

With this on his mind, he wandered back toward the Quarry. The mass grave was now a deep pit, and men were heaving bodies into it. The burial seemed a poor reward for those who had fought for the glory of their country.

"Hey," he heard a private down in the Quarry say, "here's old One-eye."

Dudley stopped, his blood turning to ice. He looked in the direction of the speaker, hoping he had not heard aright. "Old One-eye" could be only one man.

"Who said that?" he demanded, running towards the Quarry.

The men gathering bodies looked at him then snapped to attention in response to his obvious displeasure. Two had been in the process of lifting a stiff corpse, and they set it down.

Dudley stared down at the body then knelt to get a closer look. It was Oakes. A gaping hole in his chest was crusted with dried blood. No fresh blood flowed from the wound. He had been dead for some time, by the looks of him.

He slowly stood. His body felt hollow.

"Take him back to the rear. He'll be buried on the uplands."

"Sir?" one of the men, still at attention, questioned.

"You bloody heard him!" roared Sergeant Barker as he approached. "Take him back to the rear!"

"Yes, Sergeant," the men said in unison. One of them scurried off to find a litter.

When they carried Oakes away, Dudley watched and felt nothing. He had seen so many die.

"Damn," he heard Barker say. The sergeant sighed and stared at the littered field.

"We'll have a funeral for him," Dudley promised. It was the least the old veteran deserved.

There was no time to grieve, no time even to come to grips with the loss. The body collection continued. The wounded were carried off. In Sevastopol, Dudley could hear the noise of work parties, repairing what damage they could. Under the terms of the armistice, the Russians had agreed not to do this, but their workers were invisible.

The little exchanges between enemies here had been polite, but this was not a polite conflict. It was cruel and merciless. Dudley thought again of how the Russian troops had bayoneted helpless British wounded.

When six o'clock arrived and the white flags came down, the allied artillery opened fire. The five-gun naval battery was the first to speak.

That evening, the assault companies left the Quarries and fresh troops took their place. The next morning, the engineers and sappers began turning the new positions into new approaches.

The Russian trench beyond the Quarries became the starting point for a fifth British parallel. The French also began to extend their trenches beyond the Mamelon. General opinion held that the assault would continue in a few days, carried on the momentum of this preliminary victory. Sevastopol could fall soon.

In the afternoon, Hester Oakes chose a place on the edge of the Light Division graveyard for her husband's final resting place. Dudley arranged for the funeral to take place on June 11. Oakes had been well-known in the regiment, a veteran of more than twenty years service. He had re-enlisted after his first term had ended, loving the secure life of the army. Many would wish to pay their respects. The regimental chaplain agreed to conduct the service.

On the day of the funeral, almost two hundred men, veterans all, were in attendance. Dudley found their numbers a moving demonstration of the quiet respect due a good steady man, a reliable man. Many others would also have come, but they were on duty. Lieutenant Arbuthnot was there, as well as Major Willis. Besides Dudley, no other officers attended.

Oakes was lowered into his grave, and the chaplain said his last comforting words. The guns of Sevastopol thundered in the distance, pounding the Quarries and the new trenches. Hester Oakes stood at the head of the grave, eyes wet and hands wrapped in a shawl. Dudley watched her. He knew she would do all right despite her loss. He had already decided he would keep her in his employ, and though she was middle-aged, she was still popular. The older men would soon come courting.

But not just yet, for she had lost a man she loved.

Although perhaps she had always expected to lose him one day.

When the service ended, the crowd dispersed. Hester Oakes remained alone, staring at the simple wooden cross at the head of the grave. As Dudley turned to go, Barker and Arbuthnot fell in to walk beside him.

Arbuthnot was still embarrassed about what Neville had revealed before the attack. He cleared his throat before saying, "It's a sad business, losing a loved one."

Dudley heard the sincerity in the portly lieutenant's voice and nodded. He had never lost a loved one, unless he counted his uncle's rejection as the hopeless loss it sometimes seemed. But he had lost friends in this war, and many comrades.

"Old Oakes was a good man," Barker said. "The most honest soldier I've ever known."

"I did not know him," Arbuthnot confessed, "beyond his duties as your servant, Mister Dudley. But he seemed like a good man."

"He was," Dudley said. A good man Dudley could have saved. He could have refused to allow him to fight, insisted he stay in the camp with Bill.

But Oakes had not wanted that. He had been a soldier. And he had died as a soldier. That would have to be enough.

They wandered back across the grassy turf toward the camp. They went in silence. At length Arbuthnot spoke again.

"I have heard that Miss Nightingale has recovered from her fever. She has already returned to Scutari on board Lord Ward's steam yacht."

"Well, that's good to hear," Dudley said. "Her nurses will soon have many new patients, from this attack and the one to come."

"Yes, that's true. I suppose the main assault will come any day now. Miss Nightingale will, indeed, have more patients."

Dudley grimaced. "And there will be more funerals."

A few days later, the bombardment again increased in magnitude. Everyone in the British Army was certain of its purpose, for the rumours had been flying ever since the capture of the Quarries and Mamelon. With those two obstacles at last in allied hands, Lord Raglan and General Pelissier agreed to a plan for an assault on the Redan and Malakov.

The plan called for the French to take the Malakov first. When the Tricolour flew from its walls, the British would take the Redan. If the French were unsuccessful, the British would not attack. If the Russians still held the Malakov, they could enfilade any attack directed against the neighboring fortifications, with deadly results.

The attack would begin the next morning at sunrise. The Light Division would take the far right of the British assault force while the Second Division would take the center. The Fourth Division would attack on the left, and the Third Division would make a diversionary attack even farther west.

With this knowledge, the army prepared for battle. In the afternoon, the Royal Hampshire Fusiliers paraded with the rest of their division. It was an inspection parade, a last chance for the generals to make certain their men were in the proper spirits. It lasted for more than an hour, and when it ended, the regiments broke off and went to supper.

For many, Dudley knew, it would be their last meal.

He tried to keep such morbid thoughts at bay, but they plagued him all evening. Almost all the officers in the regiment were present in the mess hut, and the mood was jovial; but Dudley's stomach rebelled. The death of Private Oakes had shaken him. Every cannon blast beyond the mess walls jarred his nerves, and he found eating difficult. For once, he decided to have wine instead of water. If he was killed in the coming assault, the expense would not matter anyway. When the assemblage toasted the queen and then drank again to "their success," he gulped down the contents of his glass and asked for more.

After dinner, he and Arbuthnot retired to their tent. The lieutenant busied himself cleaning and loading his revolver then sharpening and polishing his sword. Dudley cleaned his new rifle and checked its lock. With that accomplished, he lay on his makeshift straw mattress and tried to sleep. At some point, he must have managed to drop off, for the next thing he knew an orderly was at the tent flap. The battalion was forming and would soon go down to the trenches.

"What time is it?" Dudley asked Arbuthnot when the orderly had gone.

Arbuthnot lit the lantern and studied his watch.

"A quarter to two."

As Dudley dressed, he realized the guns had ceased firing.

"Why has the bombardment broken off?" he wondered aloud. "Is the assault cancelled?"

"If it were, why would we be forming now?" Arbuthnot asked. "And forming in such secrecy, with no bugles sounding reveille to alert the enemy?"

Dudley's concern mounted as he hurried to his position on the left rear of No. 3 Company. He saw that Lieutenant-Colonel Freemantle had called all of the captains together in conference. When the conference ended, Captain Neville approached and told Dudley and Arbuthnot, "There has been a change. General Pelissier decided that he did not like the plan. He wants to attack early, to surprise the Russians. Lord Raglan's agreed to the change, and that's why the guns have stopped."

He rubbed his hands and looked into the darkness in the west.

"I don't know what the delay is. As I see it, we ought to already be on our way across the ditch before the Redan."

Dudley had never known Captain Neville to display agitation—anger, but never nervousness—and the sight of it brought a furry knot to the pit of his stomach. He tried to shrug it off as a natural and meaningless reaction. Fear was the normal state before battle, something he had already accepted.

Yet if Neville was concerned, there must truly be something wrong. Maybe there was a rational justification for his unease.

He did not have time to brood. As soon as the battalion had formed in two ranks, Sergeant-Major Maclaren bellowed the command to march. They moved in file toward the trenches then down through the zigzags in the dark.

When they reached the Quarries, they found a gathering of other regiments from the Light Division. Green-coated skirmishers of the Rifle Brigade, who would cover the advance, rubbed shoulders with pairs of sailors carrying scaling ladders. Some soldiers carried ladders as well, while others held thick packs of tied wool that would serve as mobile cover for the riflemen. With all of these different units, the Quarries were so packed there was little room to move; the men jostled one another.

Dudley listened to the clamor of activity outside. The bang of Russian artillery and musketry rattling from the direction of the Malakov made him wonder what was happening. Most of the men with him watched the sky for the agreed-upon signal. Two rockets would tell them the French had succeeded and it was time for them to go.

Dudley glanced upwards, but what he saw was not a rocket, but a mortar shell, trailing fire and arcing down on the Quarries. It exploded somewhere to his left. In the light of its blast, he saw severed arms and legs thrown up into the air.

The sight made him close his eyes. He told himself that to die in battle or be wounded was an aspect of the glory he so much desired, the glory he knew was real. To die as Private Daniel Oakes had died...

"This is going to be a near-run thing," Sergeant Barker said.

Two bright stars appeared overhead, trailing luminous smoke. Two rockets. It was time to go.

The riflemen and wool carriers were the first out of the trench. The ladder-bearers followed at their heels. With room to move now, the men of the storming parties peered over the parapet to watch their progress.

The riflemen fanned out across the rocky ground, the ladder parties crowding behind. When they had advanced a half-dozen yards, the guns opened up, fire blasting from the Redan. Cannon also stabbed flame from the little redan and Malakov.

"The Malakov wasn't taken!" Barker cried in disbelief.

Waves of canister, grape, and musket bullets swept over the riflemen, flinging away bodies and splintered scaling ladders. Dudley saw a sailor fall, dropping his end of the ladder he carried. The man on the other end of the ladder dragged it alone, somehow managing to get through the storm of artillery fire to the abatis of stakes.

The abatis was intact, doubtless rebuilt in the lull following the end of the bombardment. The man dropped his ladder and started pulling the stakes out of the way. A red fountain shot up from his skull, and he jerked and fell. Behind him, some of the other ladder parties had crawled forward. Several of them managed to half-shove their burdens through the abatis, where they fell into the ditch.

Now aides were running to-and-fro in the trench, bringing orders to the battalion commanders. Dudley did not hear the orders over the din. The next thing he knew, Captain Norcott of the Grenadier company was leaping up onto the parapet. A second later Captain Neville was doing the same, shouting, "Number Three Company will advance!"

Here was the moment of action. A small voice in the back of Dudley's mind knew this was madness. The trench was not close enough, the Malakov had not fallen, and the Russians had once again repaired the Redan. But his tension had broken, and he dismissed his inner warnings. The sudden excitement carried him forward.

He clambered out of the trench after the company, Arbuthnot at his side, and surged ahead with the rest of the battalion. The other battalions were there with them, hundreds of men running. They ran in silence at first then began to scream. The waiting guns blasted smoke and flame, drowning the voices in their roar.

A group of men in front of Dudley disappeared in smoke, and now he was stumbling over bodies. The Redan was still more than a hundred yards away. Men screamed and were knocked down, and something heavy smashed into his right arm, making it go numb. He gripped his rifle with his left hand, knowing he was wounded but hoping at least some of the men had reached the ditch and were getting the ladders up.

Arbuthnot ran past him, spectacles gone, shrieking like a girl. As Dudley looked on, the lieutenant's stomach seemed to burst, torn open by a bullet or piece of grape. Arbuthnot stumbled and crashed to the dusty ground, still gripping his sword.

The feeling had come back into Dudley's right arm, and with it came pain, screaming pain and an intense burning. The pain was not enough to make him stop. He kept running, teeth gritted, until the smoke cleared and he saw he was almost alone. Sergeant Barker ran in front of him, but no one else.

Barker halted, shoulders slumping as if in disappointment. He turned around, a look of disgust on his face. Dudley stopped as well, for he knew there was nothing else to do. It was a total defeat. There was the abatis, still seventy-five yards away. Not one man had reached it, and the wounded were streaming back.

He wondered where the reserve infantry was but knew they would not be able to do much good. He could hear the Russian artillery officers shouting commands inside their fortress and imagined the gunners sponging and loading more grape and canister.

Sergeant Barker walked back, almost strolling, and said, "It's no good, sir!"

"I have to get Arbuthnot," Dudley said.

Together, they made their way back to where the lieutenant had fallen. They picked him up, Dudley using his left arm, and carried him back, out of the conflagration. Guns boomed behind them, but they reached the trench and dropped down into cover. Half-dragging their human burden, they kept going back through the zigzags, following the traffic of retreating men. Moving in no intended direction, they at last came out in the Woronzov ravine, the dividing line between the right and left-attack.

Arbuthnot still breathed, and they lowered him to the ground. Wounded men crowded the ravine, and the surgeons were there at work already, amputating limbs and binding wounds. Dudley saw a large pile of detached arms, a grisly mound of flesh and blood.

"We were not meant to attack the Redan," he said, "unless the Malakov had fallen. Why did we attack?"

"Don't know, sir," Barker replied, "but it was one hell of a disaster, if y'ask me. But you'd best have someone see to that arm, sir."

Dudley looked at his right arm and saw it was soaked with blood. There was a huge rip in his coat and, beneath it, a long gash in his forearm. He probed the wound with his left hand but found no sign the bone was broken.

"I'm all right, Sergeant," he said. "I'm all right."

CHAPTER 8

June 18, 1855

Sometime before dawn, Dudley fell asleep. He awakened to bright sunlight and the continued rumbling of the artillery. Above the sound of the guns came a plaintive chorus of moans, and cries for water and help. Wounded men filled the ravine from rim to rim, and the surgeons were still hard at work.

Barker was nowhere in sight. Someone had bandaged Dudley's arm and dressed Arbuthnot's horrible wound. A circle of red stained the linen wrapping on the lieutenant's torso, and his breathing was uneven. Dudley spoke to him, but his only reply was a feeble circling of his right hand. Then he closed his eyes and turned his face away.

Stomach wounds were usually mortal. Dudley had little hope for Arbuthnot's survival.

The position of the sun placed the time at close to noon. With its confined space, the ravine was like an oven. Whether from the heat or his loss of blood, Dudley felt too weak to move. He decided to stay there for now, on the rocky slope.

Time passed without his awareness. It was the middle of the afternoon before Sergeant Barker returned. The sergeant carried a sack containing tinned beef, dried peas, and some bread baked in camp. He had also brought two filled canteens.

"This doesn't seem to be over yet, sir," he said, dividing the rations for himself, Dudley and Arbuthnot. Dudley had assumed Arbuthnot was asleep, but the lieutenant's cracked lips opened and he said, "No food, please, Sergeant…I am in no condition…"

"There, now, sir," Barker said, voice raised as if Arbuthnot's ears were wounded rather than his belly. "Don't you worry about it. You just lie still, and we'll get you down to Balaclava as soon as we can. You, too, Mister Dudley. You stay put till the white flags go up, which I'm sure they will soon. You've gone and bled all over yourself."

Dudley ate slowly, using his left hand and trying not to vomit. His arm did not ache much, but his stomach rebelled. The glare of the sun was almost unbearable, and sweat trickled down his face and neck into his collar. It was strange how summer had come on so soon, so suddenly, after the rain and damp of spring.

"They're lying all over the ground up there," Barker said as he bit into a bit of bread crust, "up in front of the Redan." He shoved the crust into his cheek while he spoke. "The Russians must know the attack is finished. Looks like they had the upper hand this time."

He chewed for a while, then added, "I heard news o' the Third Division, under General Eyre. Seems the Royal Irish managed to push forward up to the cemetery and dislodge the Russians, all the while under fire from the barrack and Garden batteries. There's a gate or breach in the Russian wall there, just a section where it stops for a few yards around the gravestones then picks up farther on."

"I've seen it, Sergeant," said Dudley. "I know every inch of their earthworks now."

"At any rate, they then rushed from the cemetery into the town and got into some houses. Seems they held on there for over two hours, even though they were shelled and battered. The Russkies blew up some of the houses and set others on fire. But the fact is, sir, our boys held on waitin' for the reserves. They could've kept going, all the way into the town and taking the bloody Redan from the flank.

"But no reserves came, sir. No goddamned reserves were ordered forward, though we had 'em sir. We had 'em. And many a good lad slaughtered up there for nothing."

He spat, and Dudley shared his bitterness. Questions flooded his mind. Why had the bombardment cut off so soon, giving the Russians time to remount guns and repair the abatis? Why no support during the main assault or this successful diversion Barker had just described? Worst of all, why were they still lying here in the scorching sun?

But there was no use lamenting these blunders, he thought. He tilted his head back to rest it on the ground. It would be best if he just lay here for a while. Lay here and got his strength back...

He did not move for the rest of the day. When night fell, Barker covered him with a blanket. Still he shivered.

The artillery was still active the next morning, as if a further attack were still possible. Not until four in the afternoon did white flags appear on the allied batteries. Answering flags went up on the Redan and Malakov minutes later. By then, the wounded had been lying in the open for thirty-six hours. Many had died who could have been saved.

The burial parties went to work, carrying the bodies back to a new mass grave in the rear of the British trenches. Dead officers were taken to a cemetery on a low rise known as Cathcart's Hill. Other fatigue parties gathered almost two hundred mules to help transport the wounded. Sergeant Barker and two sailors hoisted Dudley and Arbuthnot onto the back of one of these sturdy animals. Barker and the sailors positioned the wounded officers back to back and roped them together for support.

"Thank you, jolly tars!" Arbuthnot said, head lolling. "What jolly tars."

Dudley was still weak from loss of blood, but he thought some of his strength had returned. His arm felt massive, and throbbed with a dull pain, while his nausea continued to wax and wane. On the loping ride to the end of the railway he kept telling himself he was better off than poor Arbuthnot. The lieutenant muttered to himself, at one point crying out, "I've lost my revolver! Sergeant Barker, you have to go back and find my revolver!"

"Never you worry, sir," Barker said patiently, walking alongside the mule to guide it. "I've got your Adams here in my haversack for safekeeping."

Dudley suspected this was not so.

It seemed like hours before they reached the railway depot, and then they had to wait as scores of other wounded struggled to board the flatcars. When they came to the head of the line, the train was full. They would have to wait some more.

At length, the train returned from its round trip. Barker lifted each of the officers onto a flatcar then climbed aboard after them. Again there was a delay as the train filled to capacity, but after that the journey to the sea seemed swift. The locomotive chugged along, spewing black smoke and carrying its human cargo past Kadikoi then down between the high bluffs to Balaclava where the gulls circled and cried.

When he saw the field hospital, Dudley almost wept with relief. There sat a collection of comfortable prefabricated huts, each with a little garden patch out front. The huts overlooked the sea from the eastern crags, below the ruins of the old Genoese castle. Dudley silently blessed the name of Miss Florence Nightingale, as he had blessed it before. Without her influence, the army would never have bothered to build a field hospital. The wounded would have had to endure the awful sea journey to Scutari, a journey that killed more men than Russian fire.

Dudley insisted he was strong enough to walk, although at a slow hobble. He followed as Barker and another man carried Arbuthnot into one of the huts on a stretcher.

The clean interior contained a double row of low canvas cots. Dudley sat on one while Barker placed Arbuthnot on another. All around them, the surgeons and nurses were at work, removing splinters from wounds, setting bones, administering bandages and splints. When they finished with each patient, they gave him a dose of brandy as a finishing touch.

"I'd best go, sir," Barker said, "lend a hand with some of the others."

Dudley nodded, and the sergeant moved off.

When Barker had left, Arbuthnot suddenly whispered, "Mister Dudley, Mister Dudley, I have something to say to you." His voice was faint but full of urgency.

Dudley tried to stand too quickly and fell to one knee. He winced as he jarred his arm but managed to move the few feet it took to kneel at the lieutenant's side. Arbuthnot's pinkish skin had faded to gray, and the blood on his bandage had dried a dark brown.

"Yes, sir?"

Arbuthnot stared at the ceiling, his eyes glazed and his breathing slow. One hand scrabbled for the hilt of his sheathed sword. Somehow, he found the strength to draw the blade and hold it against his chest.

"You have been a good friend to me, Mister Dudley," he murmured. "I know that I am not long for this world. I can feel myself slipping even now. I shall soon be with my Margaret, and have no more use for earthly possessions."

"You might still pull through," Dudley suggested.

The lieutenant shook his head.

"No, I am done for. But I want you to have my sword. Here, take it." He held the weapon up, his arm shaking.

Dudley reached for it, taking it by the guard. He placed it point-down against the sanded plank floor.

"I don't deserve this honour, sir. This sword has been in your family for many years."

"No one...for me to give it to, Dudley. I have no children. This sword...should belong to a soldier."

Dudley cradled the sabre in the crook of his left arm and took Arbuthnot's hand in his.

"Thank you, sir. Thank you."

"You may have...the scabbard...as well. It must be difficult...to be in your position. I would like to...make it easier...for you."

Arbuthnot's body relaxed as he spoke. His face had gone almost white, despite the tan he had acquired from the wind and sun. His hand grew limp and cold.

"Lieutenant Arbuthnot," Dudley said with force, "can you hear me?"

Arbuthnot blinked once, then said, "Do you think Miss Nightingale or one of her ladies will sit with me as I die?"

"Perhaps," Dudley replied.

But there was no chance of that. Arbuthnot had spoken his last words.

Dudley sighed and laid the lieutenant's hand on his chest then folded it together with the other.

"Is this one a goner?" said a deep and cultivated voice at his shoulder.

Dudley turned to see one of the surgeons, a man with gray hair that jutted out around his ears. He nodded.

"Yes."

"Ah, well." The surgeon shook his head. "Here, take this fellow out," he shouted at two privates then turned back to Dudley. "I'm Doctor Jeffries, and this is my hut. You'd best lie back on your cot, my good man. You're looking rather pale, and that arm does not suit me at all."

Dudley complied, first laying the sword on the floor. The doctor gave his bandage a brief examination then shook his head.

"No time to look at it properly, but I'll be back. You stay put. The nurse will be along at teatime, which is later than it ought to be, but that can't be helped."

The surgeon departed, and the two privates moved in to take care of Arbuthnot's body.

"Wait," Dudley said.

Again he rolled off his cot then struggled to detach the scabbard from the lieutenant's belt. When he had succeeded, he sheathed the sword and leaned it against his own cot. He had not just acquired a sword, he thought. He had fulfilled a dying man's wish.

As the privates carried Arbuthnot away, Dudley felt the beginnings of loss. He lay back on the cot and turned his head to stare down at the floor. A deep, slow, heavy sadness filled him.

A male orderly came in and served tea to every patient, but Dudley left his untouched. From the corner of his eye, he noticed that a female nurse had come, just as the doctor had said. She was moving from patient to patient, changing their bandages, giving kind words, and offering arrowroot and port wine. When she came across to where Dudley lay, he turned to look at her.

It was Elizabeth Montague.

"Miss Montague," he breathed, wondering if maybe he was dreaming.

But it was she after all, and for some reason, tears began to pool in his eyes and roll down his cheeks, and a few silent sobs welled up in his chest.

"There, there, Mister Dudley," Elizabeth said, leaning forward and whispering in his ear, "Fancy seeing you here. Let me just see to that dirty bandage."

The next day, Doctor Jeffries came to see Dudley after dinner. With him was another surgeon. Jeffries removed Dudley's bandage and examined the wound. It was livid and had begun to swell.

"I don't like the look of this," Jeffries said. "What do you think?"

His colleague puffed on a pipe and peered over the top of his spectacles.

"Looks like it's corrupted in this heat. I'd advise amputation."

"I agree." Jeffries looked at Dudley. "You understand that this is to prevent the spread of the blood poisoning, which will kill you if we don't act soon."

Dudley nodded. For a few seconds, the idea of losing his arm meant nothing to him. Then he wondered how he would write if he lost his right arm. It also would be difficult to use his new sword, although he supposed Lord Raglan got along all right with one arm. And Admiral Nelson had also been a one-armed man.

These calm considerations offered little comfort when his jaded mind at last grasped the reality of what Jeffries had said. With understanding came a deep sense of horror. No, he thought, this was no good. How could they take away a part of him? It made no sense. He could not bear the thought, nor the mental image of the surgeon's bone saw cutting into him.

The doctors continued to discuss his case, but he did not hear them, nor did he notice when they moved on. He stared at the ceiling and endured the throbbing pain in his ruined limb.

That evening, Elizabeth returned on her rounds. She brought a tray of arrowroot and wine to cheer the men. Setting this down at the head of the room, she began moving from patient to patient. When she came to Dudley, he turned and stared into her eyes.

"The doctors wish to take my arm off," he said.

Furrows appeared on her smooth brow.

"Oh no, no, no. The bone is not touched. I would not advise you to accept such a proposal."

She sat on a stool next to his cot and began to cut away the bandage.

"You would not advise it?" he repeated.

She removed the old bandage with gentle fingers.

"It is not swollen to a great degree, not at all, and merely needs proper cleansing. Here is what you will do. There is a spring of clear water that gushes from a rock at the bottom of the hill, towards the village. You are strong enough to walk about, so must go down to the spring every day and hold the wound in the water for as long as you can bear it. Do this at least once a day, beginning tomorrow."

He trusted her. She would save him again.

As she sponged the wound in clean water and applied a fresh bandage, he said, "Thank you, Miss Montague."

She smiled—her wonderful smile—and went to her next patient.

Later, Jeffries returned to announce, "Ensign Dudley, we shall operate tomorrow morning at nine o'clock."

"No, sir," Dudley replied, "I refuse to consent to the operation." He almost added that Nurse Montague had advised against it but held his tongue. At Scutari, he had seen the jealous rivalry many doctors harboured towards these young women.

The surgeon's next comment proved the wisdom of that caution.

"Who told you to refuse?"

Dudley met his eye.

"No one, sir. I have had ample time to consider it, and I still refuse."

"It is for your own good, Ensign. I realize the prospect of losing a limb is not a pleasant one, but you must understand you have already lost it. If we wait until the gangrene sets in, it shall be too late. You will die."

Dudley held fast.

"No, sir. I had a swollen bayonet wound after Inkerman, and though I did come down with a fever, the wound healed well and I am still alive."

Jeffries sighed in irritation.

"I don't have time for this, Ensign."

"With respect, sir, you'd needn't worry. This is my decision, and I have decided to take my chances."

Jeffries's jaw clenched, but he did not press the matter.

"Very well, Ensign. I will respect your objections. For now, at least."

Dudley followed Elizabeth's instructions the next day, and every day after. He spent as much time as he could at the bottom of the bluff, staring out to sea and letting the flow of the spring run over his arm. He kept the arm stretched out and resting on a slab of flat rock.

In the heat of the early summer, the cool water was refreshing, and he could bear it for hours. During those hours, he imagined the steady washing away of the corruption. He only removed his arm when someone else wanted to use the spring to fill a barrel, canteen, or wash some linen. As soon as the spring was free, in went his arm again.

Within a week, the swelling had decreased and the redness was fading. Doctor Jeffries confessed he was amazed, that he had not had any faith in Dudley's chances for recovery. Dudley did not tell him why he was recovering, and Jeffries did not ask. The doctor simply declared, "You must have an unusually strong constitution."

Since his wound was healing, Jeffries allowed Dudley to come and go almost as he pleased. Dudley continued to spend much of his time at the spring, but he also took walks through the hills above the village. Many of the wounded preferred to wander about between meals, and the hills and cliffs were favoured destinations.

Dudley strolled with his wounded arm in a sling, wearing the light linen shirt and trousers the army had issued for the summer campaign. He kept his head shaded with his straw hat. On several occasions, Sergeant Barker ventured down from the front, bringing news. Barker explained the war had stalled, that Hester Oakes was looking after Bill, and that the army had called for more reinforcements. There was as yet no talk or rumours of a second assault.

Dudley had already heard that Lord Raglan had taken ill, possibly due to the stress of the defeat. Of course, no major decision could be made until he had recovered.

"Just endless trench duty again, sir," Barker said on one of his visits, "and no apologies." He chuckled. "It's the army I've come to know and love."

"I thought you had recovered from your bitterness, Sergeant."

"No, sir, I'll never recover from that. I've just learned there's more than one way to fight the enemy, and more than one enemy to fight."

"A master of riddles, now?" Dudley grinned. "Am I meant to decipher what you mean?"

"Don't bother, Mister Dudley. I'm not entirely sure myself."

Captain Neville also paid Dudley a visit one evening, sitting on a stool next to Dudley's cot.

"A shame about Arbuthnot," Neville began, "but then, he was an odd sort of fellow. No one was ever entirely certain what to make of him." He lit a cigar and gave Dudley a sideways glance. "What did you make of him?"

"I thought he was a fine officer, sir," Dudley stated without hesitation. Then he tempered his tone, adding, "...though I admit he was somewhat strange. One had to get to know him, I suppose. He certainly did not lack for bravery, charged the Redan with the rest of us."

"Excuse me, sir," Elizabeth Montague broke in, glaring at Neville, "but there is no smoking of cigars allowed in here."

"Oh?" Neville said with astonishment. "Well, forgive me, my dear, I had no idea. I shall, as always, comply with the rules." He stamped out the cigar on the bottom of his shoe. As Elizabeth moved off, he watched her go. "I say, Dudley, having one of those creatures look after you must certainly make up for being wounded, eh?"

Dudley found this remark irritating. He did not like hearing anyone, including his captain, refer to Elizabeth in such terms. It demonstrated a lack of respect for her abilities.

"They certainly do a world of good," he managed, forcing a light tone. "The men fairly worship them, and bless the name of their superintendent, Miss Nightingale."

"Miss Nightingale, yes." Neville lowered his voice. "I have heard she is somewhat of a dish as well. Perhaps I should have contrived to have myself wounded. But alas, the Russians can't seem to shoot in a straight line."

A few minutes later, Neville announced he had to leave. Dudley had appreciated the visit but was not sorry to see him go.

———————

In addition to her medical duties, Elizabeth saw to any special need a man might have. One evening, she brought Dudley pen and ink, a parcel of notepaper, envelopes, and postage stamps. She placed these items down beside his cot then set about changing his bandage.

"The swelling is almost completely gone, Mister Dudley," she declared.

"I have you to thank for that."

She prepared a clean bandage.

"Cleanliness, Mister Dudley, is the key to survival for many men. Few soldiers need die if their wounds are not immediately mortal."

"I shall remember that, and spread the word if I can." He touched the notepaper. "Thank you for this. I am behind on my correspondence. They will be wondering what has happened to me, at home. Wondering and worrying."

"Your home in Hampshire, that is." It was the kind of statement a nurse made to a patient, a bit of trivial chatter to fill the silence.

"Yes. My aunt worries for my safety. And I think I will write to my uncle at last. I have not spoken to him for some time. We...have not been on speaking terms since I entered the army."

He paused, waiting. He had not told Elizabeth anything about his family troubles before. He hoped to pique her curiosity now. He wished for some indication he was of interest to her.

She glanced up from her work.

"I am saddened to hear that, Mister Dudley. Yet he did purchase your commission, did he not?"

He had not told her this before, either. He had just let her assume he had become an officer in the most common manner.

"No." He paused again, wondering how she would react to the truth. But it was the truth, and if she thought less of him for it then there was no hope. "I enlisted as a private soldier. I received my commission as a promotion, after Inkerman."

Elizabeth did not reply for a moment.

"You astonish me, Mister Dudley. You must be very brave."

"I believe I was lucky, actually. Lucky, a bit foolhardy, and educated, which made me more attractive to those who grant promotions."

"You are too modest. You have been wounded twice, and I think that is a sure sign of bravery."

She did not say this with her usual professional demeanor. Her voice had softened, and a hint of a smile appeared on her lips. Dudley realized he was staring at her so shifted his gaze to the row of cots across the room. Most were occupied, the men knitting, reading, or mending pieces of uniform. One man was making a quilt of colourful patches.

"My uncle does not think me brave," he said. "He had arranged for me to attend the university at Cambridge. He considers my actions a betrayal, that I have disgraced our family." He met her eyes again. "He is the Reverend Robert Mason. I don't know if you have heard of him, but he has written several pamphlets and a treatise on the education of children. He is a strong believer in the responsibility of the individual. I am afraid that I have proven to have forgotten my responsibilities to my family's expectations."

Elizabeth had completed her task, but she did not leave his side yet.

"You are full of surprises, Mister Dudley. I have read your uncle's treatise." She studied him for a moment then added, "Does he not say that we can all better ourselves through learning, whether we are peasant or king? That does not sound to me like the philosophy of a man who would not forgive a mistake. Or what he might view as a mistake, in your case."

"Yes, perhaps you are right. That is what I hope for, at any rate." He knew she had to move on to her next patient, but he did not want her to leave him yet. "He has always said that we are all equals in God's eyes; it is learning that sets us apart. Though, of course, he has many critics who believe the exact opposite."

"I daresay he would." She stooped to retrieve her tray of bandages and implements. "Perhaps we could discuss it sometime. Now, Mister Dudley, if you will excuse me?"

She moved to the next man in the row. Dudley took up his notepaper and tried not to pay attention to her. He could see the shape of her simple purplish-brown dress from the corner of his eye, and found himself glancing in her direction every few minutes. Other men watched her as well.

Other men, with serious wounds, had recovered under her care, and her mere presence was enough to soothe their anxieties. When she was not in the hut, their speech was that of rough soldiers, loud and filled with profanity. The moment she entered, they became instant gentlemen. They did not wish to offend her, nor make her think less of them. They all idolized her. Many had wondered out loud if she ever slept, for there did not seem to be a moment when she was not attending to someone.

Dudley had to remind himself he was not special. Yet she had offered to discuss his uncle's writings with him sometime. If she had meant it, that was the spark he had wished for.

When she had finished her rounds and left the hut, the corporal next to Dudley turned to him.

"Beggin' yer pardon, sir, but were ye acquainted with our angel from before your time here?"

Many officers would have taken offence at a personal question from an enlisted man, but not Dudley.

"Yes, Corporal, I knew her when I was in hospital in Scutari. I was assigned to her ward then, and I have been assigned to her hut now."

The corporal grinned. "Must be God's will, sir."

Dudley frowned at the man. "What do you mean?"

The corporal's grin vanished. "No offence meant, sir. Just that she seems to look at you a mite different from the rest of us. Not that she don't care for us, for she does. But there's a bit o' somethin' else when she stands over you, sir. I hope I haven't over stepped myself by sayin' so, sir."

Dudley shook his head. "No, Corporal, you have not."

He leaned back in his bed. The corporal returned to his knitting and said nothing more. Dudley wondered if the man could be right.

He returned to his letter, but instead of carrying on with the last line, his pen scrawled the name *Elizabeth*.

He stared at it for a moment. Then, suddenly ashamed, he crumpled the paper and stuffed it under his pillow.

While Dudley recovered, Lord Raglan at last succumbed to his illness. The Commander-in-Chief of the British Expeditionary Force died on June 28, at nine o'clock in the morning.

The day of his funeral, the walking wounded left the Balaclava hospital and made their way down the coast to the little inlet of Kazatch Bay. There, they gathered on the shore, some with hats in hands, ready for the arrival of the funeral procession. In the bay waited the transport ship *Caradoc*, which would take the body back to England.

Some said that Lord Raglan had died of a broken heart after having sent so many good men of Britain to the slaughter. The full weight of the failed assault on the Redan had crushed his will to live. Now that he was gone, his men expressed nothing but sadness at the loss. All talk of fault or blundering had ceased, although such talk had been common almost from the beginning of the campaign. The old general's good qualities now rose to the surface of many memories. The men spoke of how he had smoothed relations with the French to maintain the alliance, and how they had appreciated his frequent cheering visits into the camps. These last he had done out of a deep sense of duty, for he had been a shy man, uncomfortable making public appearances.

Dudley went to the bay, but once there, he decided to walk up from the water and meet the procession partway. He followed the route of march, a long avenue stretching from the shore to the French headquarters then to its starting point at British headquarters on the uplands. Lining the entire route was a guard of honour formed of fifty men from every British regiment. The guard stood in a single rank with arms reversed, the muzzles of their rifles to the ground. Behind them sat squadrons of cavalry and batteries of field artillery. The bands of each regiment stood between the detachments, playing the mournful strains of the "Dead March."

French troops also formed a section of the guard extending down from the French headquarters. Dudley stopped to examine the Zouaves for a moment, satisfied with their appearance. Their steadiness was every bit as good as the British. He was not so happy with the Imperial Guard and detachments from the regiments of the Line, who looked right and left in ranks, licking their lips and shifting their feet. Not one officer or NCO did a thing to stop this behavior. Dudley hoped this was not a deliberate insult to Lord Raglan from his one-time enemy. He knew the French army had never been as much for parade discipline as the British. Maybe this was their usual performance.

The French field artillery provided minute guns, firing as the procession crept along the avenue. When the flag-draped coffin came into view, Dudley doffed his straw hat, gripping it with his left hand.

The coffin lay on the soldier's traditional hearse, a gun carriage. At each side rode the commanders of the allied armies. Behind them followed all the generals who could be spared from trench duty. The horses took one deliberate step after another and seemed to hang their heads in sorrow.

Dudley accompanied the hearse back down to the water. The process took almost two hours, but he felt no inclination to return to the hospital. He had not expected to find this event so moving. He had never thought much of the general and had seen him only about a dozen times, from a distance. Yet none of that mattered.

Widespread opinion held that Lord Raglan had been a good man, good-intentioned, more of a diplomat than a soldier. For Dudley, his death stood for all who had died here in the Crimea. As the coffin ambled along, he imagined that every soldier in the guard of honour thought of friends and comrades who had gone before.

In Kazatch Bay, marines and sailors stood at attention on either side of the wharf. The seamen in the longboat had dressed in their best white frocks. They waited with their sennet hats in their hands as a party of soldiers lowered the coffin into their boat. With it in place, the boatmen took to their oars. The longboat set out toward the waiting ship, the national flags of Britain and France streaming from its bow.

Dudley watched the boat go for a few minutes. Then he put his hat on and returned to Balaclava.

Mid-July brought days of hot, still air and a plague of pestering flies. Every day, new patients arrived at the hospital, some the victims of disease, most the victims of gun and mortar fire. Dudley's arm was healing well, although it was stiff and the wound had begun to itch.

Sergeant Barker continued to visit. On one occasion, he complained that reinforcements had still not arrived, although the ongoing trench duty in the Quarries had further reduced the size of the company.

"Our artillery keeps up a pretty display, though," he said, "just to keep the Russkie gunners off the infantry and sappers. Soon as reinforcements come, we'll assault again, sir. The French sappers have done a fine job, better than we have. Their trenches will be on the Malakov's front doorstep before long."

"Good," said Dudley. "We should push ours farther, too. As I see it, that was one of the greatest reasons for our defeat."

"I don't know if our engineers agree with you, sir. Leastways, they haven't bothered to do any new work. Everyone's preoccupied with what the Russians are up to in the north, beyond the Tchernaya River. They've been pretty busy widening a road down from the hills almost to the right of our position. If they make some kind of push there, the French will have to deal with it. We haven't got enough men on active duty. Or maybe the Sardinians can finally make themselves useful."

"Perhaps you should tell them that yourself, Sergeant," Dudley suggested.

Barker chuckled. "Oh, sir, you may come it the sarcastic, but I know you'd be lost without my little visits."

Dudley kept a straight face.

"Indeed, Sergeant, I would be lost without you in general."

He meant this in jest, but he did appreciate Barker's visits. It was good to know someone in the regiment still cared that he was alive. The only other person to visit had been Captain Neville, who had only come the once, and had been rather annoying.

On another level, Dudley was thankful for his lack of contact with the regiment. He could hear the guns every day and preferred to keep them at a distance. He wished to make the most of this temporary detachment from the war. The danger of losing his arm was long past, so his time here had become more of a holiday than a necessary convalescence. This was a chance to rest his spirit.

He spent his hours walking along the headlands, exploring the ruins of the castle, or sitting in a quiet spot to read or stare out to sea. He relished the solitude. His only semblance of privacy before this had come on his rides with Bill on the uplands, but even then the war and duty had never been far away.

Often when he went walking, he would come upon Elizabeth sitting on the headland. He had discovered her favorite perch, a place where she sought refuge from her exhausting duties at the hospital. He would talk to her when he found her there. She seemed to welcome his company, and he was beginning to believe there was a real friendship growing between them. A friendship she did not share with the other patients.

Although she no longer needed to change his bandage, she still chatted with him when she made her rounds. Whenever he encountered her near the hospital, she would stop to exchange a few words whether she was busy or not.

One day late in the month, he came upon her at the spring. He had gone there to soak his arm, a practice he maintained to prevent the corruption from returning.

"Good afternoon, Mister Dudley," she said as he came along the path.

He raised his hat and said, "Good afternoon, Miss Montague." They greeted each other the same way every day. "What a delightful surprise to come upon you here."

She was carrying two large pails to fill with water.

"Oh, not so surprising, I should think, Mister Dudley. You know my habits by now."

He watched her fill the first pail.

"I wanted to thank you again for the loan of the novel *North and South*. It isn't the sort of thing I normally read, but I am quite enjoying it. I had forgotten how much I missed reading."

"I am glad that you like it, Ensign." She had remembered his shelf full of books in Scutari, and how he had read the same ones over and over to pass the time.

He sat on a rock as she filled the second bucket. It had seemed a contradiction to him, this practical young woman reading frivolous novels. Yet that apparent contradiction only confirmed his belief that she hid her true self, that there was a romanticism in her, powerful and passionate. It lurked beneath the surface, but he had seen it revealed many times.

For a few minutes, they spoke of books, a subject they had discussed on several previous occasions. She liked to tell him how much she had enjoyed stories as a child, especially stories of foreign lands. Often, she had curled up in a favorite window seat with a huge atlas. There She would stare at the maps while rain beat on the window. In later years, she had discovered more adult works, although by then her life of reading and leisure had begun to wear thin. She had never wanted for anything in life, but in time that life had come to seem quite senseless.

"You were surprised to discover that I read novels," she said. "But I ask you what else is there for a young lady of my class to do besides paint, sing, do fancy work, visit friends, and read? The answer is, not very much. I had become an ornament in my own home.

"My papa is a Radical, Mister Dudley, and he and I are alike, after a fashion. I was determined to go my own way, no matter what society said I should do, and in him I had some support. Mama wished for me to sit prim and pretty at home, waiting for the proper gentleman to come along. Then I could marry and sit and read at my husband's fireside.

"But there comes a time when a good story read in one's favorite window seat ceases to be a pleasure, and when the days lose their spark."

Dudley could hear the resentment hidden behind her words.

"It is very bold of you to tell me this."

"Is it? Well, I suppose I feel comfortable with you, Mister Dudley. It seems we share some of the same interests, and we are familiar with each other, after all."

He grinned. "Then you must call me William, rather than Mister Dudley all the time. That makes me feel like an old man."

She met his eye, and his breath stopped for a moment. He saw dimples, sun-bleached hair, curving lips forming a somewhat devious smile, pale-blue eyes.

"Very well, William. Then you may favour me by calling me Elizabeth."

She lifted her filled buckets, one in either hand. He shook his head.

"As long as I have one good arm, I can help a lady carry water."

Her smile wavered, and she replied, "Thank you for the offer, William. Nevertheless, I would not want it said that I was not capable of doing my own job, nor that I had a patient do it for me."

Her tone had been kind, but Dudley felt his face begin to burn.

"I'm sorry if I offended you."

"Of course you didn't," she said quickly. "I…I am the youngest of three sisters. I was always the baby, and everyone did everything for me. My sisters were always older, wiser, stronger, even prettier. That is why I…find satisfaction in doing things on my own, even difficult things."

Dudley considered these words before commenting.

"Your sisters are prettier than you? They must be pretty, indeed."

The corners of her mouth raised, then crinkled, then raised again.

"Was that a compliment, Mister Dudley? I mean, William?"

"Well, I think it might have been."

She bowed her head then looked back at him. Her cheeks were red, and for a moment, he thought she was about to laugh. Then she said, "I also find it easier to carry two buckets instead of one, for the balance, and you cannot carry two. But you may walk with me, if you like."

His embarrassment fading, he accompanied her back to the hospital. His plan to soak his wound was forgotten.

CHAPTER 9

July 1855

Near the end of the month, Captain Neville came to see Dudley a second time. Dudley appreciated the sentiment, although the captain's company was something he knew he would have to tolerate rather than enjoy. After the comment about Elizabeth, Dudley did not think he and Neville could ever become friends, despite their agreeable association as company officers. Their level of consideration for the feelings of others differed by too great a degree.

Dudley suggested they take a walk along the eastern headland, and Neville said he thought that a splendid idea. They climbed the path leading past the castle, and when they had gone beyond the last broken tower, the captain drew in a deep breath of sea air.

"Ah, it's good to get away from the stink of the camps," he said, "with the ever-present reek of gunpowder, rotting flesh, rats and death. You feel as if you are miles away from it here. Well, many more miles away than it actually is."

"Yes, sir," Dudley agreed, "it's a fine place for the men to recover."

"Yes, recover. Your arm is almost healed, is it not?"

Dudley flexed the wounded limb.

"Doctor Jeffries says another week or two of rest, sir."

"That's good. I doubt there shall be any movement before then. General Simpson is still getting the feel of things, I hear."

Simpson had served as Lord Raglan's chief-of-staff and was now his replacement. He was another ancient Peninsular War veteran, with a reputation for caution.

"Anyway, we don't have enough men to mount another assault. A few reinforcements have at last arrived, but nothing yet for the old Royal Hants."

"That's unfortunate, sir."

"Yes. Unfortunate." Neville turned and looked at him. "You know, Ensign, I have always had a difficult time imagining you as a sergeant. You are almost a gentleman in some ways."

This was typical of Neville, but Dudley tried to take it as a sincere compliment.

"Thank you, sir."

"Sergeants are usually recruited from an inferior class of men," the captain continued. "It must have been difficult for you, serving in the ranks with those fellows."

"Not really, sir. We had good men in my company of recruits. Mind you, many of them spent their evenings in rather base pursuits, but they had other qualities. I would read the newspaper to them every day. They were very keen on that. I am proud to have served alongside our fellows in Number Three Company."

Neville shook his head in amazement.

"You are altogether too diplomatic. I should have found it unbearable, myself. Perhaps you were not in the ranks long enough. After all, your rise was remarkably swift, perhaps even a new record. As for me, I have been in the army for many years. I have seen the kind of low characters we sometimes get. You may have served with good men, Dudley, and their valour here in the Crimea is proof of that, but I have encountered some truly rotten fellows marching in our ranks. Fellows who required harsh treatment, for the good of the regiment." Neville paused to light a cigar. When he had drawn on it once, he declared, "Fellows like that blasted Brian Barker."

He said nothing else, and Dudley realized he was meant to reply. Neville had never offered to discuss his hatred for Barker before.

"Why do you say that, sir?" he asked. "I realize Barker has exhibited some questionable behavior in the past, but his attitude has improved—"

"Questionable behavior!" Neville cried, laughing. "It was not questionable, Ensign. The man has no respect for authority, no respect for his betters, and no respect for the British Army."

Dudley did not know how to answer such a sweeping judgment.

"I see."

Neville narrowed his eyes and drew on the cigar. He blew out a gray jet of smoke, like a gun firing.

"I want you to understand what sort of man Sergeant Barker is. You haven't known him as long as I. His presence here is a danger to the company. Soon, we will be getting new men, a draft of recruits recently trained in Fairbridge. Uncorrupted men, who will go into battle the minute the generals are ready to try again. I don't want those men to come into contact with any bad influences. And to that end, I want you to watch Sergeant Barker very carefully."

To "watch" Sergeant Barker could mean many things. Barker was a subordinate whom Dudley "watched" in the normal course of his duty.

"I will, sir. I have watched him for two years now."

Neville shook his head.

"I don't think you understand me, Dudley. I want you to watch Barker in particular, as a special case."

Dudley sighed. Neville was at last trying to drag him into his campaign against Barker. He wondered whether he should disagree or hold his tongue and comply with the request. But to say nothing, he realized, would allow an old injustice to go unchecked. After all this time, Barker deserved the support of those who recognized his merits.

"May I voice an opinion on this subject, sir?" he asked, knowing this was dangerous ground. He could not simply refuse the instructions of a superior, no matter how irregular.

"By all means, Dudley," Neville said cheerfully. "I value your opinions, after all."

Dudley paused, choosing his words with care.

"Well, sir, when I knew Sergeant Barker as a private, he was, indeed, a bad character. Though, as I believe I have said before, the men respected him for various reasons.

"Since the beginning of this campaign, he has come to recognize how shameful his conduct was. He told me that he feels great remorse for not living up to the standards required by duty. In my observation, he has performed very well as a result of this change of heart. Many other officers have also seen the improvement, as evidenced by his return to the rank of sergeant.

"He is not a bad influence at all, sir, but a good one. I have observed this first-hand. He reinforced my authority when the men were hesitant in assaulting the enemy battery at Inkerman, and he helped the men through the recent disastrous winter."

Neville's eyes hardened, although he continued to smile.

"Are you telling me that you will not watch him, Ensign?"

Dudley blinked, taken aback by this question.

"No, sir. I watch all of my subordinates. I was just suggesting that making Barker a special case is not necessary."

"Oh, but it is necessary, Ensign. A man does not change overnight, even though he may appear to. I know Brian Barker better than you and understand his capacity to manipulate. Evidently, he has succeeded in pulling the wool over your eyes! You must trust my judgment on this matter. I want you to watch Barker closely and report any of his misdoings directly to me."

"Misdoings, sir? Do you mean mistakes?"

Neville sighed in sudden impatience.

"Yes, Ensign Dudley, mistakes as well as deliberate improper behavior on his part, such as excessive drinking of alcohol, insubordination, negligence—anything."

Dudley knew it would be unwise to debate the point further. Barker would continue to perform well, and he would make such a report to Neville. But Neville was playing the same underhanded game that had led to Barker's demotion, and he wanted no part in it. He searched his mind for a solution, a way out.

"What if I don't find anything?" he asked. Maybe Neville would accept that and leave it alone.

"That is a possibility," the captain agreed, "but I have already considered it. As I have said, Barker is an expert at avoiding punishment for his crimes. We must move fast if we are to deal with him before our reinforcements arrive. Why wait for him to oblige us when we know what sort of character he is? There are ways to ensure that you *do* find something, Ensign." He paused, a sly glint in his eyes, then added, "Or at least appear to find something."

Dudley stared at him for a moment, trying to understand this last statement. Neville had asked him to lie, to plant false evidence. It was the same thing Barker had refused to do for him.

Neville took his silence for partial acquiescence.

"Consider it for a while," he said. "See what you can come up with. I shall come again in a week's time to hear what you have to say."

A week would give Dudley a chance to form some kind of defence. He cleared his throat and managed to croak, "Yes, sir."

Neville had turned his attention back to the sea.

"What a fantastic view! I daresay you must find a more recreational use for your new telescope up here."

"Yes, sir," Dudley repeated, understanding the implication.

Neither man spoke again for several minutes. The sound of breaking surf rolled up from the foot of the cliffs, mingled with the cries of the seabirds. Then Neville said, "Well, Ensign, I must be off."

"Goodbye, sir," Dudley said.

Neville nodded and turned to stroll back down the path. When he had passed the castle, he stopped to call back, "I shall see you again in a week."

Dudley carried a parcel of letters to the Balaclava post office. The late summer morning was fine and warm, with a gentle breeze from the water. He wore his straw hat and a clean linen shirt, his sleeves rolled to the elbows. The sun shone on his bare right arm, the long red scar standing out against the white skin. The scar had begun to itch, although the wound had completely healed.

He reached the post office and presented the letters. Two were for his aunt and three for Jane. They told of his stay in Balaclava. He made no mention of his dilemma over Captain Neville's awful request. He did not want to worry them with his personal troubles.

The postal clerk took the letters, and Dudley asked if anything had arrived for him. As usual, there was nothing. He emerged from the post office disappointed and apprehensive.

He made his way along the waterfront, weaving between piled stores and lumbering bullock carts. He passed a pair of camels and their drivers, and from behind him came the shriek of the train whistle. The whistle made him start, and at that moment he saw Captain Neville coming toward him along the crowded street. He stopped, and Neville waved. A week had passed since their last meeting, but Dudley had not expected to see him until the afternoon.

"Ah, Ensign Dudley," Neville greeted, "they told me you had gone to the post office. I thought I would come meet you halfway. I see I have not missed you."

"No, sir."

Neville glanced at the camels in irritation.

"Perhaps we should get away from all this noise. What do you say to our heading back towards the castle? I found it very peaceful up there."

Dudley nodded, and they made for the eastern bluff, following the main street, passing the low plaster houses. As they found the path and began their ascent, Neville commented, "You are surprisingly silent, Ensign. Have you considered our plan?"

"Yes, sir, I have," Dudley said, a thickness growing in his throat.

Neville halted and turned to face him. He had taken a cigar from his pocket and was spinning it between his fingers.

"Well, what do you say?"

Dudley took a deep breath to steady himself. It had not taken him long to decide that he could not agree to Neville's plan. He could agree to watch Barker in the normal course of things but never to anything illegal. He risked making an enemy of his company commander, but he had to stay true to what he considered right and moral.

"Captain Neville," he began, "I'm afraid that you will not like what I have to say."

Neville stared at him.

"What do you mean?"

"What I mean, sir, is that I will certainly hold Sergeant Barker to a high standard of behaviour, but I cannot invent a crime where none exists. I can see no justification for such an act."

"No justification?" Neville repeated. "But I have given you the justification. It is a preventive measure, for the good of the company."

Dudley did not hesitate to make his case.

"It is an illegal measure, sir. It can only undermine the spirit of the company."

"Undermine the spirit of the company?" Neville wandered a few feet along the path then turned back. "No, no, Ensign. This is not what I want to hear. Why are you saying these things?"

Dudley sighed. "I don't think I can give you what you want to hear, sir."

Neville was shaking his head. His voice was hollow with disbelief as he muttered, "You are actually refusing me. I can't believe that I waited all this time, and you are refusing me."

"I'm sorry, sir," Dudley offered, although he knew that an apology was out of place.

"Sorry?" Neville. "How absurd. This is so completely absurd."

"But don't you see the danger, sir?" Dudley asked in an attempt at reason. "How can we combat the alleged bad behaviour of one man with bad behaviour on our part?"

"Damn you, Ensign!" Neville suddenly cried. He crumpled his cigar and flung its remains to the ground. "I won't listen to any more of this. How dare you question me? How dare you lecture me?" His face had turned a deep purple. "I am not asking you do these things, I am *ordering* you to! Do you understand? You are to watch Sergeant Barker and report his every infraction to me. And if you do not find any infractions, I will know that you are lying!"

Dudley's heart pounded in his chest. He had known Neville would be angry, but he had not counted on such a savage outburst. He knew the situation was precarious, but his own anger suddenly flared. Neville had no authority to issue such an order.

"I understand that you dislike Sergeant Barker, sir. The entire company knows it. This order is personal in nature. I have no choice but to obey at least in part, but I will not invent infractions nor produce false evidence. You cannot demand that of me."

Neville's fists clenched at his sides.

"You miserable, insolent ingrate. I gave you every opportunity. I gave you a gift. I made sure you were welcome, despite the fact you are nothing but a bumpkin, a tutor, raised by a schoolmaster. You are a nothing. How dare you betray my good will in this way?"

"The only part of your order I refuse to obey, sir, is the illegal portion, therefore—"

Neville waved his hand in dismissal.

"There's no sense in trying to escape from your corner now, Dudley. Perhaps you will watch Sergeant Barker. Perhaps you will find he is all that I say he is. But it is too late for you. I gave you a chance, and you threw it away."

Dudley did not care for the ominous nature of these words.

"I'm sorry if you believe I have betrayed you, sir. But I think things would not go well for either of us were we to follow your plan."

Neville had gained some control of his temper. He shook his head.

"This will not go well for you, Dudley. You must learn to trust your betters. This will not go well for you."

That was his final word. Shoving past Dudley, he stalked away down the path. Dudley watched him go, but Neville did not look back.

On August 16, a great battle raged along the high banks of the Tchernaya River. When the smoke and dust cleared, news of the outcome quickly spread through the camps and along the supply line to the hospital. The Russians had attacked the French and Sardinian positions on the far right of the allied lines. Fighting uphill, the Russians suffered heavy losses and were forced to withdraw.

For Dudley, this was a welcome turn of events. He would return to the trenches in the wake of a victory, and the mood of the men would be running high. That would offset the tension of his next encounter with Captain Neville.

Even more welcome was the letter he found waiting for him two days later. The letter was from his aunt, addressed in her flowing hand. He could not keep himself from tearing it open as he left the post office. Making his way towards the eastern bluff, he read as he walked.

The letter was months old, dating from the spring. It was a reply to one of his descriptions of life in Scutari. His aunt condemned the state of the Barracks Hospital, expressing relief that its deprivations had not affected her nephew. She had nothing but praise for Miss Nightingale's nurses.

"We are also shameless in our praise of you, William," she wrote, again telling him how proud she was of his success as a soldier. She never ceased in her efforts to force Uncle Robert to change his attitude. He was stubborn, she explained, although at one point he had said, "William will do all right, it seems. He does not need me." Those were his exact words, Aunt Bronwyn insisted.

Dudley read the last paragraph over again. His uncle's exact words had mentioned him by name. After a year of denying his existence then referring to him as "that boy," there was this.

His shoes crunched on the sand and debris of the seaside path. After Captain Neville's abrupt turn, this news was like a healing salve. Here was another sign that his uncle was softening his stance.

He stopped on the path and turned to look back the way he had come. Below lay the crowded harbour, the port with its brown houses, the rail and telegraph line. The train was moving up from the water, the engine blasting black coal smoke as it journeyed towards the front. He watched the smoke rise and dissipate into the high August sky. Something about that kind of sky, with its deep blue and bunches of cotton-bale clouds, had always filled him with hope, and a yearning for what the future might bring. Strange thoughts for a soldier in the middle of a bloody war.

He resumed his progress along the path, wandering without heed to where he went. He ached with a mixture of promise and rejection.

Without thinking, he headed towards Elizabeth's favourite perch on the bluff. He crested a low rise, and there he saw her. She sat alone, clad in a gray-green dress, staring out to sea. He was not surprised to find her here. Most of the wounded from the failed assault had improved and would soon return to duty. She had more time for herself now.

As he approached, she turned in his direction, shading her eyes with one hand. A few strands of her hair had come loose, and they danced in the breeze from the sea.

Dudley took off his hat and said, "Good afternoon." He was glad to see her, despite his inner turmoil. Perhaps because of it.

"Good afternoon, William." A smile flashed across her face then disappeared. Just as quickly it returned, as if she had realized it was all right to show pleasure in his company.

It warmed him to see that smile and to hear her use his first name. He stopped beside her and turned to gaze at the horizon, where sky met ocean.

"It certainly is a lovely day," he remarked.

"Why don't you sit?" she said gaily. "We can't have you standing there and me craning my neck."

"Are you certain? Please don't think you have to give up your privacy on my account. I can continue my walk happily."

"Nonsense." She patted the rock next to her. "Come and keep me company."

Dudley complied, and for a moment they sat in silence, watching the water and the swooping gulls. He wondered if he should ask her advice about how to deal with Captain Neville. He needed a sympathetic ear. But that, he decided, would be presuming too much. Elizabeth was a friend now, but she was still a recent friend. He had no right to burden her with his personal struggles.

He could, however, tell her about his successes. She already knew of his family troubles. She could well understand what his uncle's developing forgiveness meant to him. Her family also disapproved of her ideas and ambitions, of her coming here to serve in the dirt and blood and sorrow.

"That does sound like a promising sign," she said after he had read to her passages from his letter. "I think you should be happy."

He nodded, encouraged. He valued her opinions, her judgment. She had, after all, saved his arm from the butcher's saw. She had done much for him in a short time.

There was a rumbling in the distance, the sound of guns bombarding Sevastopol. They listened for a moment. Dudley would return to that struggle tomorrow. It would be his second return to battle, his second time leaving Elizabeth.

He suddenly realized that he did not want to go, that he wished the war would end. The defeat at the Redan had been a hard blow, while the unpleasantness with Neville had further eroded his enthusiasm.

But he needed to see the conflict resolved. All of the courage and endurance the men had displayed in the face of such horror, all of their triumphs, could not go down to defeat. They would prevail, he was certain, and he could not let his old comrades do it without him. He needed to be there at the end.

"It is a terrible war, isn't it?" Elizabeth said, her words echoing his thoughts. She studied the distance from where the sound of the guns seemed to emanate. "I wish there were more that I could do. I sometimes even wish I were a man."

"Why would you wish such a thing?" he asked, surprised.

"Then I could be a soldier, or a statesman. I could have more of an effect upon this world."

"You do affect it," he insisted. "By saving the men here. I would go as far as to contend that Miss Nightingale has turned the tide. We could not have taken much more of what we suffered last year. We would have had to withdraw, and lost the war for certain."

"Yes, perhaps." Her smile returned. "The soldiers have to bear so much. When I read the reports of the hardships, I thought that I could help. And you are right, we have helped. But the war itself—men living in holes and killing each other day after day." She looked at him. "Do you wonder sometimes what it's for? Is the outcome worth what you must do to achieve it?"

"I believe so, yes," Dudley said without hesitation. He had gone over these arguments so many times himself. "I admit this campaign does seem harder than anything I was ever told about war." He shook his head at the memory of his old folly. "I had always imagined crisp and shining-clean uniforms, infantry in tall hats taking a position with the bayonet, led by a gallant officer with his sword in the air. That sort of thing does exist, in some ways, but only if you look for it. I have had to adjust my notions of what gallantry and bravery are." He touched the lump under his shirt where his tin soldier rested. "This is a dirtier and far more brutal conflict than anyone had imagined. But I think war must always have been that way, only now more people are beginning to see that truth. Before, it had been the soldiers who knew what war was while the kings and politicians and citizens did not, unless they were directly involved."

"You have not answered my question, Mister Dudley," Elizabeth said. "I also think war is worse than most of us imagine. I have seen that with my own eyes. And that is my concern—Is it ever worth the outcome?"

"Let's hope something comes of it."

"Victory, you mean? We are told Britain has enemies, and I realize that is true. And as long as we have enemies we shall be forced to fight them, if they would fight us." She drew her legs up, hugging her knees. "But I wonder if there is not another way, and if I were a statesman, I could find it."

"Maybe one day there will be another way," Dudley said. "Maybe one day nations will become more reasonable institutions. Yet even then, all nations would have to agree on a solution when there is a dispute. If even one would have war, the others would be forced to follow."

Her mouth twisted in a sardonic grin.

"I suppose that sort of behaviour is all too common. Villains have a habit of spreading their discontent within the world."

Dudley was not enjoying this line of conversation. Lowering his voice, he said, "I am to be discharged tomorrow. I may never see you again, Elizabeth."

She did not reply for a moment.

"I have met many people here that I will never see again when the war is over."

He looked at her, stunned. This was not the sort of answer he had expected. He wondered if he had been wrong, that he was not more than just an acquaintance. Maybe he was just someone to pass the time with while she was here. Someone to forget when she returned to England.

He could not believe that. He scolded himself for being too sensitive, for imagining a dismissal that was not there. She could be waiting for him to say the appropriate words, to tell her what he wanted.

He wanted to see her again. He liked and admired her, and anticipated a reunion when the next chance presented itself. He did not want to lose contact with her.

"When the war is over," he said, "hopefully, the regiment will be returning to Hampshire, to Fairbridge or Portsmouth." He drew in a deep breath, mustering the courage to continue. "I must tell you how much I have enjoyed making your acquaintance, Elizabeth. I consider you a friend. I hope I am not being presumptuous, but I wonder if I could write to you? Or pay a call if I manage to obtain leave?"

For a second, he feared she would say *But I am just your nurse.* As before, she shaded her eyes with her hands, her brow furrowed.

"Mister Dudley, you certainly may. I would enjoy hearing from you."

The tension binding his chest relaxed, and his relief became a lightness, a threatening delirium. It was true.

"After the war, then."

She turned back to face the ocean.

"The sea makes one feel very free, don't you think? Such a wide-open space. Sea captains must be very happy people."

Dudley nodded. Yes, despite the war, he felt as free as the gulls. He would write to her. He could visit her. He could not yet afford a wife, but he could begin a courtship. When the war was over.

Tomorrow, he would have to face Captain Neville, but for now that did not matter.

Dudley arrived in the Light Division camp late in the afternoon. Hester Oakes greeted him outside his tent.

"It's good to have you back, Mister Dudley," she said, plump cheeks rising in her delight. She was bearing up well in spite of her loss. She had also kept Bill in good health, and Dudley thanked her as he stroked the pony's long nose.

"It's what my Daniel would have done," she said. "Prided himself on doing 'is best, he did. It's not for me to do any worse."

"You always do your best as well, Mrs. Oakes," Dudley told her.

He left her and Bill and entered the tent. The familiar quarters now seemed a sad and empty place. Arbuthnot's things were still there, lying on the floor and hanging from the center pole, just as they had so many weeks ago. No one had bothered to have them auctioned or shipped to the dead lieutenant's family. Dudley supposed he would have to see to that himself, although it was Neville's responsibility.

"The cold-hearted bastard," he muttered. He reached down to his left hip, feeling the hilt of Arbuthnot's sword where it hung at his waist. He gripped the new wire until his knuckles were white.

He would go to the mess hut, he thought, and have a decent supper. He would not have to associate with Neville there tonight, for the company was on picket in the trenches. They would not return until after dark.

The evening sun cast long shadows as Dudley approached the hut, still wearing Arbuthnot's sword. The door stood ajar to let in the summer air. He heard conversation and laughter. Several officers were already here. He stepped inside.

A few heads turned his direction. He took off his straw hat and smiled. The laughter and conversation stopped.

Dudley's smile faded. More than a dozen men occupied the hut, most of them subalterns from the other companies. Captain Rowntree was there, and he stared at Dudley with widened eyes, thin lips pressed together. The others seemed uncomfortable, and one young lieutenant stared at his feet. It was obvious something was wrong.

Rowntree cleared his throat.

"Ah, Mister Dudley. Back in one piece, I see."

"Yes, sir," Dudley replied, suddenly wary. "Completely healed."

"Yes." Rowntree's eyes strayed to the sword at Dudley's side then made their way back to his face. "You will be wanting to join us."

"Yes, sir," was all Dudley could say, frowning.

"I'm afraid that would not be prudent, Mister Dudley," Rowntree continued. "Captain Neville will be here soon. I think you had best leave before he arrives."

Dudley's ears began to burn, and his jaw clenched. He looked from man to man then fixed Rowntree with such a hard glare the other man blinked.

"I see," Dudley said. "Captain Neville."

There was another awkward silence. A few men shuffled and cleared their throats, while others glared at him with open disapproval. Then one young ensign, one of the children who carried the regiment's Colours, piped up from the back of the room.

"Captain Neville doesn't want you in here."

Dudley turned to the other ensign, his indignation flaring.

"What do you mean, he doesn't want me in here?"

"Just that, Dudley," Rowntree said. He shrugged. "Doesn't want you in here."

Dudley swallowed. He knew Neville could be vindictive, but he had not expected anything like this.

"Then I shall have to speak to Captain Neville about that, shan't I?" he declared.

There was no sense in standing there and debating with these fellows. He clapped his hat on his head and stormed from the hut, somehow managing to curb the urge to slam the door behind him.

He halted in the well-trodden camp street. The sun had set, and No. 3 Company would be coming off-duty. Then Neville would come here.

"What did he say to them?" Dudley wondered aloud. Had Neville accused him of a false crime, as he had done to Barker? Could the man really prevent him from entering the mess, from enjoying the company of his fellow officers?

It did not matter. Neville did not even have to invent a charge. All he had to do was voice his disapproval of this ensign who had been raised from sergeant, from the ranks. All he had to do was accuse Dudley of not behaving as a gentleman should. The other officers would side with his opinion because of whom and what he was, and whom and what Dudley was.

He refused to accept this outrageous insult. He would wait. When Neville arrived, he would demand an explanation.

He paced outside the hut. If anyone inside noticed him still there, they made no effort to get rid of him. He lost track of time. Perhaps an hour passed before he saw the familiar form approaching along the camp street. There was the upright bearing, the long sword dangling at his side. A cigar glowed in his hand. He gave no sign that Dudley's presence in the street surprised him.

Dudley raised his right hand in salute. Neville halted and returned the gesture, although he maintained a grip on his cigar with his left hand.

"Good evening, Ensign Dudley," the captain said, his tone congenial. "I see you are healed and ready to resume your duties."

"Yes, sir." Dudley found it difficult to keep an edge of contempt from his voice.

A slow glow of triumph spread across Neville's face.

"You look as if you have something you would like to say, Ensign." He took a long drag on his cigar, making its tip flare bright red.

"Sir." He searched for the appropriate words, "I am told that I am not welcome in the mess hut."

Neville said nothing for a moment, then: "No, you are not."

"May I ask why, sir?"

Neville chuckled.

"You know as well as I why you are not welcome. You failed to obey my instructions. You would not support me. We have already been through this."

Dudley cleared his throat.

"I am an officer of the Royal Hampshire Fusiliers, sir. I am a member of the mess. If I have been accused of some crime, I am entitled to defend myself at an appropriate hearing."

"You have not been accused of any crime, Mister Dudley. By your own behavior, you have demonstrated a lack of solidarity with the officers of this regiment. I have made this clear to the others. You still hold a commission—I cannot revoke that. You were promoted from the ranks, and so cannot turn in your papers for ten years. You still hold a position in my company. However…" He took the cigar from his mouth and stamped it out on the ground. "…you are no longer welcome in our society."

"The others agree to this, sir? What of Colonel Freemantle? Major Willis?"

"I am trusted by those men." Neville chuckled again. "Did you think you had some influence with them? You bloody fool! You are nothing! An upstart, a jumped-up sergeant. Now, get out of my way."

Dudley stood his ground for a moment, but there was nothing he could do. For a fleeting second, the urge to strike this man almost overwhelmed him—strike him and knock him flat. But that would mean the end of his career for certain.

He stood aside, and Neville carried on toward the hut.

At the door, the captain paused.

"You will, of course, carry out your duties as usual. When the war ends, we can arrange your transfer out of the regiment."

He turned and entered the hut. Exclamations of welcome greeted him.

Dudley stared at the half-open door. A few minutes passed before he spun away and wandered back through the camp, aimless. He did not know where to go or what to do now.

As he walked, he became aware of the men around him, the men of No. 3 Company, returned from the trenches. They shuffled among the tents, stacking arms and taking off their belts and pouches, preparing for their modest suppers at the campfires. One of them glanced in his direction and started in surprise.

"Welcome back, sir!"

It was Johnson. Dudley saw that he wore fresh corporal's chevrons on his right sleeve.

"Thank you, Corporal. Congratulations on your promotion."

"Thank *you*, sir."

Dudley nodded once and continued walking. He knew he should stop for a few minutes to chat, but he couldn't face a cheerful reunion with the men right now.

He made for the glow of one of the fires, needing its light. He didn't know whose fire it was, but when he drew nearer, he saw that Sergeant Barker sat there, alone.

Barker stood, a grin splitting his bewhiskered face.

"I didn't know you'd left the hospital, sir."

"Well, I have," Dudley said, trying to sound cheerful. Despite the mildness of the evening, he held his hands out to the flames. "Not messing with the other sergeants tonight, Sergeant Barker?"

"Don't know where the other lads are. Off doing this and that. Most are on duty anyhow, and I don't associate with that bloody Hoskins."

Dudley sat on an empty biscuit crate.

"Do you mind if I join you, then?"

"Not at all, sir. Bit stuffy in the mess hut tonight?"

Dudley stared into the twisting flames.

"I am no longer welcome there, it seems."

If anyone deserved to know what Neville had ordered him to do, it was Barker. It was Barker Neville really wanted to destroy, not Dudley. He told the sergeant everything that had happened, what Neville had said on the headland above Balaclava, and the consequences of Dudley's refusal to cooperate.

Neville had cut him off from what he considered best about the army, from what had kept him going since the beginning of this campaign. That was the sense of belonging, being part of a group bonded for a common purpose, to remain loyal to the Crown and to each other. Neville was trying to deny him that bond. Dudley now understood why Barker had considered military loyalty and honour a sham.

He could make an appeal to Lieutenant-Colonel Freemantle, he thought, defend himself. But to go running to the commanding officer seemed undignified. If Freemantle trusted and agreed with whatever Neville had said then there was no point. The fact remained that the other officers did not want his company.

Barker's face had clouded as he listened. When Dudley finished, the sergeant said nothing for a while. Then he declared, "He'll have you, too, sir."

Dudley's throat constricted, and he had to fight back a wash of despair.

"I never thought...I had worried about this sort of thing, but everything had been going so well for me."

"Neville's a bastard. He's got no honour, Mister Dudley. He ain't fit to call himself a British soldier, as far as I'm concerned. He's everything that's wrong with this army."

"But he can't be dismissed as just a bastard, Sergeant. He means to force me out of the regiment, first by poisoning the others against me. He has already taken a step in that direction. He has made this a personal battle, and there's little I can do to fight him."

The fears he had known in Scutari were coming true after all. The officers of his regiment would reject him for not being a gentleman. Meanwhile, O'Ryan had already rejected him for being an officer. Most of the other rank-and-file saw him as their superior, one of their commanders. They liked him, but he was no longer a member of their society.

Neville was right. What would be the point in remaining a member of the Royal Hampshire Fusiliers after the war? Maybe transfer *would* be the best solution, in the end.

But that, a part of him insisted, would be admitting defeat. He had gone through too much with the Royal Hants to give them up, let them go. It was his regiment. He would have to find some way back into the fold.

There must be a way to handle the situation. It was a problem, but problems could be solved. He wondered how another officer, one born to the class, would approach it.

Barker grunted and threw a twig on the fire.

"You've at least got your reputation on your side, sir. And then there's the lads in Number Three Company. There's plenty of us still left who followed you into that battery at Inkerman, and the others all know about it. It's a legend now. We won't let you go so easily."

Barker's words provided the tiny scrap of hope Dudley needed. He was no longer certain what Colonel Freemantle thought of him, but he still had the respect of the men. He was still the hero of Inkerman.

He faced Barker across the flames. The sergeant looked back, and in his eyes, Dudley saw nothing but support. It was then he realized for the first time that the sergeant, once his enemy, had become his friend. Perhaps the truest living friend he had.

"Thank you, Sergeant," he said.

CHAPTER 10

August 26, 1855

Dudley leveled his telescope and focused on the distant shapes of the Russian engineers. Waves of heat from the earth distorted the image, but it was still possible to see that the engineers were constructing a bridge of boats. When finished, the bridge would stretch from Sevastopol towards the north side of the harbour. It would give the Russians an escape route if they had to abandon the city. That meant they feared an allied victory.

It seemed the enemy was on the verge of giving in.

Dudley lowered the telescope. He turned it in his hands, letting the sun glint off its polished brass. The telescope had been Neville's gift. He had thought about giving it back, but he was reluctant to part with it. It was too useful.

"This instrument is the one bit of good to come from my knowing the man," he said to his companion. "That's something to console myself with, at least."

"What man is that, sir?" Barker asked.

Dudley had never told him the origin of the telescope.

"Our Captain Neville. He gave me this spyglass. I realize now he was trying to purchase my loyalty."

"Ah, yes." Barker nodded. "Well, it's always advisable to try to see the good side of things, Mister Dudley. I'm glad you've got your telescope."

Dudley gave him a curious glance. Sometimes he did not know whether Barker was having him on or not.

"I do try to see the positive side of things, Sergeant. It's good advice. Perhaps you should heed it."

"Oh, I do." Barker scratched his mess of beard. "But you must admit, sir, that it's hard to see much good in what's happening to our old company."

"Yes," Dudley agreed, feeling a wash of bitterness. "It is hard."

He had not spoken to Neville since the confrontation in front of the mess hut. The captain was a constant presence in camp, but he behaved as if Dudley did not exist. Dudley received his orders from an orderly every morning then carried out his duties alone. Other officers in the regiment spoke to him only as necessity demanded. He would come upon groups of subalterns muttering to each other, and the muttering would cease as soon as they noticed his presence.

That was why he had not gone back to the mess hut to fight for his right to attend. There was no point if most of the others would take Neville's side every time. Maybe they would even toss him out into the street.

In the gulf created by this rejection, he found himself thinking of Elizabeth more and more. She had occupied his thoughts ever since their farewell on the headland above Balaclava, and now her memory was his sole comfort. He missed her more desperately than he could have imagined.

Two days ago, he had tried to visit her in Balaclava. He had not expected to see her again until after the war, but there was nothing to prevent him from trying when he was off-duty. Trembling with hope and excitement, he had taken Bill across the plain and down to the sea to seek her company.

His hopes had been for nothing. She had not been there. She had gone back to Scutari three days after his discharge.

Now more than ever, he wished the dragging campaign would end. Everything seemed to be crumbling around him, and Elizabeth's departure had been a further blow. The triumph of Inkerman seemed long ago.

Somehow, he needed to repeat that triumph. He needed to gather his strength. He could not let Neville win, not without giving him a fight. The war presented one sure way to do that. He had already distinguished himself as a soldier, and now he could prove himself a worthy officer, in the trenches and in the next assault. In time, the others in the mess would recognize his ability and realize Neville was wrong. And if they did not, they were a stupid and shallow lot, not worth the effort of befriending. In that case, he would have to leave the Royal Hants and seek an assignment with another regiment.

For now, the Russians were the enemy not his fellow soldiers. He would strike at the enemy first.

With a new sense of direction, a renewed drive, he collapsed the telescope and thrust it into his coat pocket. Turning to Barker, he announced, "I'm going riding, Sergeant."

"Say hello to Bill for me, sir."

Twenty minutes later, Dudley was on the plain, the wind in his face and hair. Out here on his pony's back, he could still catch a glimpse of elusive freedom.

***

At long last, the reinforcements arrived, a draft of three hundred men from the training depot in Fairbridge. Twenty went to fill the thinned ranks of No. 3 Company.

Sergeant Barker took charge of the new men. He formed them in two ranks, stood them easy, and regarded them with mixed feelings. Their presence almost doubled the company's effective strength, but they were recruits who had received minimal training thanks to the army's desperate need. They had drilled together for half the usual time and were unfamiliar with their new unit. None of them had ever experienced enemy fire, and no one had ever asked them to charge a fortified enemy position. These were the men who would storm the Redan during the next assault, just weeks away.

Barker sighed and shook his head. The recruits darted him nervous glances, and some flinched at the distant banging of an artillery exchange. Unlike the veterans who had seen and heard so much, these men found the routine noises of war strange and terrifying.

"Ignore the guns," he said. "We all do. They pound away off and on all day and night. Just wait till you hear a real bombardment."

The men stared at him with increased horror. These words were no comfort, and he realized it at once.

"All right, lads," he began again, "it's a hard, slogging war, but there are ways to get through it, see? Before Corporal Johnson shows you to your tents, there are some things I'd like you to understand."

He looked from man to man. All wore new and immaculate uniforms, boots and buttons polished, belts pipeclayed a bright white. They made a gleaming contrast to the NCOs who faced them, Barker and Johnson in their patched and faded jackets, their non-regulation trousers and shade hats.

"You look like a bunch of bloody toy soldiers," Barker grunted, "and that's got to change. Believe it or not, lads, I want your battle gear to be comfortable. Your days of spit and polish are over. Never mind badges, buckles and buttons—keep the things that really matter clean. Your rifle must be spotless and in perfect order. Keep your mess tin scrubbed or you'll catch something. Try to keep your feet dry and your shirts clean. There's women who'll do laundry here for a small fee. When the lice start to crawl, run a candle along the seams of your coats. Never mind anything else."

The men exchanged dubious glances. Barker knew what he was telling them went against their training. He decided to surprise them even more, and shouted, "Take off your shakos!"

One man complied at once, removing his stiff leather headgear. The others had no reaction at all.

"Are y' hard of hearing?" Barker thundered. "I told you to take off your shakos, so take 'em off!"

There was no hesitation this time. One thing the recruits had learned was to obey an angry sergeant, and in a few seconds, they all stood bareheaded, caps in hand.

Barker grinned. "Now, throw 'em away! I know you hate 'em, so here's your chance to get your revenge. They're nothing but a bother in this climate. Chuck them over here."

The recruits hesitated again, disbelieving. Then one of them returned Barker's smile and tossed his shako to the ground. At that, the rest obeyed, casting their shakos in a pile to the right of the front rank.

"Wear your forage caps from now on," Barker said. "And get rid of these bloody things, too." He stepped up to a man in the front rank, reached into his collar and pulled out his stock. It was an inch-wide band of leather designed to keep a soldier's chin from drooping. "Anything that makes it harder to fight is worse than useless. Now get rid of your stocks!"

A second pile joined the little mountain of shakos. Sight of it gave Barker great satisfaction, and he was about to offer more advice when he heard someone shout his name. He turned to see the unsavoury form of Sergeant Hoskins approaching.

"What the hell does he want?" he muttered to Corporal Johnson.

Hoskins halted next to Barker. He looked at the piles of discarded kit, and a malicious sneer spread across his ravaged face.

"What the bloody hell do you think you're doing, Sergeant?"

Barker stiffened. It was incredible to think that even Hoskins would question another sergeant in front of the men.

"Don't you take that tone with me, Hoskins. If you have something to say, say it. If not, then bugger off."

Hoskins stuck a dirty finger into his nose and chuckled. He pointed the finger at the shakos and stocks.

"That's the queen's property. You ain't got the right to tell them to chuck it away. It ought to come out of your pay, it should."

The recruits shifted their feet, and one man coughed. Barker stared at Hoskins, his disgust increasing by the second. He had never liked the man. Not only was he Neville's lackey, but he was an abusive and ineffective sergeant. This confrontation was a typical example. It would hurt morale for the men to see conflict between their NCOs. It would destroy their trust. Hoskins either did not understand the danger, or he did not care.

"Hoskins," Barker said, keeping his voice low so the men could not hear him, "mind your own business and get out of my sight."

"I'll do that, Sergeant Barker," Hoskins replied, voice at a normal level, "but it's also my duty to report this here incident. The captain mightn't care for it. And you know what the captain might do if he hears, don't you?"

Barker narrowed his eyes.

"The captain, eh?"

"Aye. He's watchin' you, he is."

Barker took hold of the other sergeant's arm and started to propel him away from the squad. Hoskins tried to shake him off, but Barker was too strong.

"Get yer bloody hands off me!" Hoskins shouted.

Barker let him go and turned his back to the squad. Stabbing a finger toward Hoskins's face, he hissed, "Threaten me, will you? Damn you, you son of a whore! You lackey dog!"

Hoskins drew himself up.

"What're you goin' to do about it? Yer the one that's in the wrong here."

Barker took a deep breath. He wanted to smash this man's face, to knock him down and kick in his ribs. It would be so easy, for Hoskins was no match for him. But it would also mean an end to his efforts to redeem himself. Were he to assault Hoskins, Captain Neville would rejoice. Barker would lose his stripes again for sure.

"Hoskins," he said, "you're a sergeant, and so am I. The lads are supposed to obey us both, and here you are questioning me in front of them. What'll that do for 'em, seeing us at odds? In a few weeks or days, we'll be going after Sevastopol again. We need every experienced man we've got, even you. And the lads need to keep their spirits up."

Hoskins backed off a pace.

"You presume to lecture me? The captain's told me all about you, oh, he has! You don't fool me, Barker."

"God damn ye, then!" Barker's fury rose again. "Go and make your report! Run along, you infernal spy. Kiss your master's arse and hope he gives you the scraps from his table."

"We'll see who gets what in the end, Barker." Hoskins managed to find his crooked grin. "We'll see about that."

Barker prepared another retort but held his tongue when he saw Dudley advancing along the camp street. The young officer appeared displeased by the sight of two sergeants bickering in front of the squad. Barker snapped to attention and saluted. Hoskins also managed a salute, although he delivered it with a limp hand and an uncomfortable grimace.

"See about what?" Dudley said, halting and returning the salutes.

"Found Sergeant Barker destroying queen's property, sir," Hoskins said. "The man's a criminal."

Dudley glanced at the piles of kit.

"Oh? Well, that may be, Sergeant, that may be. I'll get to the bottom of the matter. Off you go, Sergeant Hoskins. I'll speak to you about this later. For now, I'd like Sergeant Barker's side of the story."

Hoskins hesitated. "But, sir..."

"Off you go, Sergeant," Dudley repeated.

Hoskins flashed Barker one last baleful glance then left, tramping down the street and muttering to himself.

Barker gave Corporal Johnson charge of the recruits. As the squad moved off to find their tents, Dudley said, "Now, Sergeant, I saw some of that little exchange from a distance, but not the details."

Barker told Dudley what had happened.

"He's the captain's spy, sir. No mistake."

"I'm certain you're right," Dudley murmured. He stared at the discarded kit. "It would be best if you gave the caps and stocks into the quartermaster's care. Though even he may complain that they will just take up space."

Barker spat onto the dry ground.

"Bloody Hoskins. He's been waiting for something like this, waiting to take any little infraction and give it to Neville. Whether it matters or not."

"You did well to show restraint. I know how difficult it must have been. But you had best be extra careful from now on. Both of us must be. We're in similar situations."

Barker felt his stomach clench. After all he had worked for, he had to put up with this. After enduring the winter, surviving when so many others had not, after all the battles he had fought, on the field and within the army, clawing his way

back to sergeant, it seemed he would have to keep fighting.
Although, this time, he would have Dudley fighting alongside
him.

"I'll be careful, sir," he said, "if you promise me you'll do
the same."

Captain David Neville crouched over his writing desk, scrib-
bling a new entry in his journal. He had begun the journal
five years ago and intended to publish parts of it when the
war was over. It would become a fitting tribute to his efforts
on the part of Her Majesty.

"The final assault will begin soon," he wrote, "and there
is no other subject of discussion in the mess hut. Now that we
are up to strength, I am certain that we shall take Sevastopol
in the next few days, at most in a week or two."

He raised his pen from the paper, wondering whether he
should say something about Ensign Dudley. It did not take
him long to decide not to. Thoughts of Dudley's defiant attitude could still make him angry, angry and disturbed that
someone would question his authority. He even had to admit
to himself that the incident had wounded him. He had
thought Dudley looked up to him, but that had not been so.
It still did not make much sense to him, and he did not need a
written reminder.

Someone ducked in through the tent flap, and he turned
to see Sergeant Hoskins. Hoskins removed his cap and stood
at attention.

"Sir, I have something to report."

"Oh?" Neville studied Hoskins, frowning at his appearance. The sergeant was flushed and trembling with apparent
indignation.

"It's about time you observed something. Who is it,
Barker or Dudley?"

"Both, sir. But mostly Barker."

Neville smiled. That was excellent. Hoskins had been watching Barker for months, waiting for him to slip up. It was surprising he had not, until now.

"Let's have it, then, Sergeant," he commanded.

Hoskins told him what had happened, how Barker had instructed the new men to discard their shakos and stocks, and about Dudley's intervention. Neville chuckled when the sergeant finished his story.

"What shall I do about it, sir?" Hoskins asked, taken aback by Neville's reaction.

Neville dismissed the news with a wave of his hand.

"Nothing, Sergeant. You have brought me nothing but a trifle. Everyone has been discarding kit since this campaign began. It has always been a common practice. I would seem absurd if I questioned it."

Hoskins sighed and stared at the tent wall, his shoulders slumping. He wondered if the man would burst into tears of frustration.

"But I can see that you are disappointed. We can't have that, Sergeant." Neville snatched a blank piece of paper and began to write. "I shall note down your observation and the date. At least it is a start. Keep up your vigil, and don't you worry. Barker will keep. I have a new toy to play with."

Hoskins swallowed.

"A new toy, sir?"

"Yes. Something more diverting." He glanced at his journal, at the blank page next to his last entry. Then he looked back at Hoskins. "Thank you, Sergeant Hoskins. That will be all."

Hoskins hesitated, his dissatisfaction obvious. Then he nodded once and ducked out through the tent flap.

Neville watched him go with a touch of disgust. Hoskins was not only a fool, he was a useless fool. He had been a useless corporal, brutal and unpopular, but Neville had recommended his promotion to sergeant on one condition. The condition had called for Hoskins to provide his benefactor with information. Hoskins had agreed, but he had since shown no talent for gathering useful intelligence.

It didn't matter. He didn't need Hoskins. His early success in the matter with Ensign Dudley was, he had to remind himself, a potent indication that his power had not waned.

Dudley was a popular young man and something of a celebrity in the regiment. Freemantle liked and respected him, as did the men of the company. Yet Dudley had been no match for him.

One evening in the mess hut, he had said to his companions, "When Dudley returns from hospital, the lad is no longer welcome. He is not a proper officer, and no proper officer would associate with him."

He did not elaborate, but he had no need to. The others had seen his anger was genuine, that for some reason he had come to despise Ensign Dudley. They did not need to ask any questions. They trusted his judgment and would respect his wishes. A small group of junior officers had been especially supportive.

The one obstacle to his plan was Major Willis. Neither he nor Lieutenant-Colonel Freemantle had been present when Neville had issued his decree. That was as he had wanted it. They were the only officers in the regiment that outranked him, and would have wanted details. They would have demanded he make a case, that he prove Dudley's conduct warranted such harsh condemnation.

He knew it was only a matter of time before Willis discovered something was amiss. The major had even touched on the subject last evening. He had wondered aloud why Dudley had not joined his fellow officers since his return from the hospital.

"That ensign of yours has been shunning us lately," he had told Neville.

Neville had found a ready response.

"I don't think he feels comfortable here, Giles."

"Whyever not?" Willis had exclaimed.

He had feigned concern.

"Well, he was raised from the ranks, as we all know. I think he still prefers to mess with the sergeants."

Willis had shaken his greying head.

"It's wrong, I say. You tell him to come. He's an officer, by God! The colonel's own choice!"

"I've tried, sir," Neville had lied, "but I shall keep trying, if you insist."

He was satisfied with how the conversation had developed. Dudley would not come to the mess, and Major Willis would wonder why. He would begin to think the ensign had turned his back on his messmates. He might still ask Dudley for an explanation, but Neville's word carried more weight. If the situation forced Willis to decide who was a liar, Neville would make certain he chose Dudley. If he played a skillful hand, Willis might come to believe Dudley had no place in the regiment. It was not a perfect plan, but there was plenty of time to iron out the wrinkles.

Neville adjusted the papers on his camp desk, squaring them to the side of the tabletop. This was a drastic measure he was taking with Dudley, one that called for a twisting of the truth. He wished it were not necessary, that the ensign's behaviour could have been different. Dudley had not seemed like such a bad fellow. This was all so unfortunate.

Even so, he could not let it go. He could not allow Dudley to get away with what he had done. He could not allow his sphere of control to erode, to crumble. He received his authority from society itself, and without it there was nothing but chaos.

Barker would have to wait. For the next while, Neville would concentrate on that damned upstart of an ensign. He would show Dudley what happened to anyone, be he officer or man, who crossed him. They were his to command, and his to discard, if he wished.

With a surge of confidence, he dipped his pen in ink and wrote, "Once again, we are to man a section of the most advanced sap at dawn. It is sure to be more dangerous than usual, now that we are so close to the enemy's walls. In addition to the shelling, there are raids almost every day now."

There was always a chance that either Barker or Dudley would be killed. That would be a satisfactory outcome, if a bit sad in Dudley's case.

As for Barker, Neville would much rather do the job himself.

No. 3 Company huddled in the converted Russian access trench to the Quarries. The trench had become the British fifth parallel, two hundred yards from the Redan. It made a tempting target for Russian raiding parties.

Sergeant Barker hoped for a raid. He leaned on the trench parapet, staring across the open ground towards the enemy walls. He could hear Russian voices shouting back and forth. He could not stop the Russian attacks, but he could make use of them as training exercises for the new men. The more trench skirmishes they experienced and survived, the more fit they would be for the main assault.

The assault would be a tricky one, and not just because half the men in the British force were recruits. In Barker's estimation, this fifth parallel was not close enough to the Russian wall. Two hundred yards was far too much space for unseasoned men to cross under massed artillery fire. The *veterans* would find it difficult. It made no military sense, but the Royal

Engineers had so far made no effort to press the British trenches closer.

In contrast, the French trenches were so close to the Malakov they had begun to undermine the Russian ditch.

"Light's fading fast," Colour-Sergeant O'Ryan commented. The Irishman stood on Barker's left, staring at the remains of the sunset.

"Ivan will be out soon, then," Barker said. "Then we'll see what these boys are made of."

He held no sway over the Royal Engineers and their plans. All he and O'Ryan could do was try to prepare their company for what lay ahead. Their greatest task was to mend the confused state of morale. The men could see the tension between their sergeants and officers and did not know what to make of it. Thanks to Captain Neville, the company was more unfit to fight as a unit than ever before. Barker silently cursed Neville's name, for he feared the captain would lead these boys to ruin with his damned petty power struggles.

Barker was glad to have Dudley back. Dudley had command of the company today, his first official duty since returning from hospital. It was a welcome relief from having Neville—and that slinking dog Hoskins—breathing down his neck hour after hour. Those two were forever watching and waiting for an opportunity to do some mischief. He had encountered fellows like them in the workhouse where he had spent his childhood, but beating Captain Neville senseless would not solve any of his problems here. The army was not a workhouse.

Neville was now out to ruin Dudley. At least Dudley had the support of the lads, Barker thought, if that meant anything. The men trusted him, even the recruits, who had not known him as a sergeant. Despite his modest appearance, the ensign had a reputation for action. The recruits believed he could see them through this war alive. In contrast, they would never warm to Neville. Neville had all the trappings of a proper officer, including unquestionable courage, but the recruits knew he was responsible for the company's awkward discontent. They could see it in the eyes of the veterans whenever the captain was present.

Tonight, those confused recruits would get their first taste of enemy fire. A parcel of green men, none knowing what to make of the conflict within their company, would have to stand together.

"What a way to fight a war," Barker muttered to himself.

"Don't look now," O'Ryan said, "but here comes our holy prince." The colour-sergeant jabbed a thumb towards the rear. "Couldn't leave things to someone else, I suppose."

Neville was advancing along one of the approach trenches. Barker could not see his face in the twilight, but he knew the officer from his walk, the way he wore his forage cap cocked neatly to the right. He had come to hate the look of that cap.

He turned back toward Sevastopol. He despised the sense of helplessness Neville gave him.

Something moved across the open ground to his left. He started, his mind clearing of all worries and personal concerns. The first raid would be early tonight.

"Stand to!" he cried.

At his command, the men readied themselves, some leaping to their feet, others cocking their rifles. Some fixed their bayonets. Barker and O'Ryan peered over the lip of the trench. The Russians were coming from their left, a mass of shadows slithering from hollow to hollow, moving closer and closer. He supposed they knew they were not invisible but didn't think it mattered. These raids were not attempts to capture the British positions. They were meant to harass, to wear the British down, to make rest impossible.

"Hold your fire, lads," O'Ryan whispered, grinning to reassure the recruits, who gripped their rifles with white knuckles.

Twenty yards from the lip of the trench, the leading Russians broke their silence, uttering wordless cries and coming on at the charge. O'Ryan barked the order to fire, and his section of trench erupted in flame. Gray shadows fell, and the enemy charge halted. Barker watched the Russians slither back the way they had come.

"They never meant to get in here," O'Ryan said.

"Wait," Barker said. The Russians had regrouped. They were going to come again.

The dark shapes advanced, screaming and charging as they had before. Barker had not fired his rifle during the first charge, but he raised it over the parapet now.

"Independent fire!" O'Ryan cried, and Barker squeezed his trigger. Rifles boomed and flashed around him. He thought he must have hit his target, for the Russian had halted and stood with his musket drooping in his hands. Most of his comrades milled around him in confusion. Three others continued their advance until they reached the lip of the trench.

The Russians did not jump into the trench but stood on the edge, stabbing down with their bayonets. One British recruit reached out and grabbed a bayonet with his left hand then jerked the musket away from its astonished owner. Another recruit fired his rifle, and one of the Russians groaned as the bullet punched into his side. Clutching the wound, the Russian spun about and limped into the darkness. The other two followed.

"Just trying to keep us on our toes," O'Ryan declared as the enemy withdrew. "No doubt they'll be back later. Might be a rough night."

Barker stepped toward the private who had taken the Russian musket. He was young, not much above eighteen. He had placed the captured weapon against the wall of the trench.

"Well, done," he said. "You've got yourself a souvenir there, my lad."

The soldier held up his left hand, the one that had grabbed the bayonet. There was a long scarlet gash across the palm. The Russian had sharpened the edges of his three-sided bayonet, which were usually left dull.

"I guess I paid a price for it, Sarge."

"Just a scratch," Barker reassured him. "A badge of honour. But you'd best get to the rear and have it seen to anyway."

The soldier grinned. "I'll be back soon enough, Sarge."

Barker watched him go, relief flooding into him. They had beaten off an attack without a serious casualty, and the one injured man was not in the least disillusioned.

As long as there were spirited fellows like that in the army, he thought, things would turn out all right.

———※———

At daybreak on the fifth of September, the sixth allied bombardment began.

As he had done before, Dudley rode out on Bill to watch. The crash of the guns was a welcome upheaval. He felt almost as if he were sending that powerful energy himself, striking out against those walls and guns that had distressed them for so long. This was action, movement! He relished it despite the jarring noise, despite the danger and fear that he would face in a day or two.

After three hours of continuous fire, the Royal Artillery rested for twenty minutes to cool their guns. Barker joined Dudley, and they took turns examining the enemy walls with Dudley's telescope. As the bombardment resumed, the earthworks surrounding Sevastopol appeared to sustain little damage. No breaches opened, and no guns came tumbling out of their embrasures.

"We can't see the damage for the smoke," Dudley suggested. "Nor can we see what's happening inside. Our thirteen-inch mortars are probably pounding them to bits."

"Maybe, sir," Barker replied. "Maybe. Let's just pray the pounding keeps up until the minute we leave the trenches."

The bombardment lasted all afternoon and continued into the night. After sunset, the light from the screaming rockets and bursting shells outlined the Malakov and Redan in silhouette. At one point, a British rocket struck one of the Russian warships trapped in the harbour, setting the vessel alight. The fire grew until the ship became a massive torch, illuminating the buildings in the town and the masonry forts on the north side of the harbour. The ship burned to the waterline before the flames guttered and went out.

After midnight, there was another brief cease-fire, lasting until half-past five in the morning. With the new day, the allied guns again boomed and cracked, the shells and rockets hissing and screaming. The men in each battery paused for a brief spell during the afternoon to let their guns cool, but then the loading and firing went on. The gunners removed their jackets then their shirts as they laboured, the powder smoke burning their eyes and clogging their throats and nostrils. Their hands and faces became blackened with residue as another day fell into evening, and the guns lit the darkening sky.

For the second night in a row, sleep was impossible. Dudley joined a large crowd at the Light Division lookout and extended his telescope. Exploding shells and fires produced enough light for him to see Russians scurrying about in the town. They were herding civilians out of harm's way and clearing the houses of valuables. Squads escorted wagons of furniture, paintings, boxes and crates out of town and across to the north side, trundling over the completed bridge of boats.

Dudley watched the evacuation of civilians and materiel from Sevastopol until dawn then returned to camp for breakfast. As the guns crashed on, the men around him grumbled about the delay. There was no point in the artillery blasting away like this, some said. It had done little good before and was doing little more now than providing entertainment. Houses burned in Sevastopol, ships caught fire, and during the night, there had been a great explosion as if a magazine had gone up. It was all very fine to look at, but the men wanted to attack now.

That afternoon, the news spread that General Simpson and Marshall Pelissier had held a council of war. They had sensed the growing impatience in their armies and had come to a decision. There would be an assault tomorrow, September 8th.

On the heels of these rumours came their confirmation. The Royal Hants received orders to parade on the outskirts of the Light Division camp. Soon, the companies were marching into position.

Lieutenant-Colonel Freemantle sat his horse before his formed battalion and read aloud the general orders. Tomorrow morning at nine o'clock, he cried, the Light Division would parade in light marching order. At noon, the French would storm the Malakov, and the British would assault the Redan. The generals expected success, he added, for the bombardment had most likely destroyed the enemy abatis and much of their artillery.

Tomorrow, he declared, Sevastopol would fall.

CHAPTER 11

September 8, 1855

Dawn brought a clear sky but a keen north wind. The Royal Hants paraded as ordered while the guns and mortars continued to hammer at Sevastopol. No one paid the artillery much attention now, not even the recruits. All thoughts focused on the coming action.

The wind raised dust clouds that billowed about the Royal Hants as Colonel Freemantle rode past, smiling and looking from man to man as he inspected his regiment. When he had finished this formal task, the companies marched off one-by-one towards the trenches. Other regiments in the Light Division had already gone ahead, moving down to the Woronzov Road and into the old first parallel. Behind the Light Division came the units of the Second Division, and behind them the Third Division. The Light and Second Divisions would lead the assault; the Third would make up the reserve.

The Royal Hants halted in a stony ravine just outside the first parallel.

"We'll wait here," Sergeant-Major Maclaren announced, "until further orders. Everyone should sit tight."

At this news, the men sat or lay on the ground, breaking into little groups for conversation. The bombardment was to continue until noon, and it was now ten o'clock. There was plenty of time. Time to wait, as usual.

Dudley sat with Sergeant Barker and Corporal Johnson. From here, they could see the hump of the Redan, brown and gray in the intense morning sunlight. Now and then a pillar of dust would burst up from the structure as a shell struck. At other times, a Russian gun would fire, making a horizontal jet of white smoke.

"So their guns were knocked out, were they?" Barker scoffed when he saw the enemy return fire. "I hope our gunners did a better job against the abatis and the ramparts."

As if to mock these hopes, a Russian shell struck the crest of the ravine. It exploded, showering the company with dirt and debris, eliciting curses but no cries of pain.

"This will be one busy day, sir," Barker said. He brushed bits of sandy soil from his arms and shoulders.

Dudley said nothing. He did not want to discuss the coming action, for Barker was right. Their trenches were simply not close enough. He wished the engineers had followed the French example and pushed the British trenches within a few yards of the Russian wall. It would take the French storming parties only minutes to leave their cover and climb the parapet of the Malakov. They had no open space to cover, no killing ground for the Russian artillery. The Russian gunners would have to be satisfied with mowing down the British assault parties.

"It will be a slaughter, sir, with all these green men," Barker whispered to Dudley. "They're good lads, sir, but they just ain't ready. And after all we've been through in this god-forsaken place, we deserve better."

"I suppose I agree, Sergeant."

It was certainly a great deal to ask of any army, to charge into such a storm. He wondered if those in command had learned nothing from the first assault.

He went over the attack plan in his head, trying to convince himself it was sound. It was virtually the same as the plan for the first assault. Everything would depend on the coordination of the artillery with the storming parties and the reserves. And the Malakov would have to fall first. That was an essential ingredient.

The attack would involve detachments from eight regiments, with three more regiments in reserve. The first units to leave the trenches would be a company of the Rifle Brigade and a detachment of the Royal Sappers and Miners. The Rifles would provide covering fire while the Sappers destroyed what was left of the abatis in front of the ditch. Next would come the ladder parties and the assaulting companies. There were twenty scaling ladders. These were larger than those made for the first assault, and each was carried by eight men. When the ladders were placed across the ditch, the assaulting companies would rush across them and up the face of the Redan.

The plan sounded simple, but Dudley knew he might die within the next few hours. The casualties were certain to be heavy.

He contemplated the possibility, examining his feelings. If he were killed, he would never see his family again, never confront his uncle. He would never have a chance to resolve the intolerable situation with Captain Neville. He would never be commissioned lieutenant. He would never see Elizabeth again. He would never hold her, nor kiss her as he had wanted to so many times. In the next few hours, all his hopes and dreams might end in one quick blast of grape shot, scattered by the heavy guns of Sevastopol.

Somehow, he did not care as much as he thought he should. He did not have to fight impatience and panic as he had before the first assault. He felt calm, almost relieved. If he were to die then so be it. He had no control over fate. All he could do was his duty. All he could do was what he had done all along, and that was be the best soldier he could. Whatever Neville had said about him, he knew he had no reason to feel shame about any of his actions. If his career were to end this day, he knew at least it had been a good and honourable one.

He saw Captain Neville approaching from within the first parallel. He felt no anger or panic. There was nothing more Neville could do to him. Not until the battle had ended.

"Well, Mister Dudley," the captain said, grinning like an old friend and not a new-found enemy, "it's time to move forward. I have just received our orders to advance to the fifth parallel."

"That's good news, sir."

Neville chuckled, a deep and sinister rattle.

"Yes, it is."

He carried on to speak to Colour-Sergeant O'Ryan. Dudley watched him and thought, He's hoping I will die.

He realized that Neville might also be killed. This brought a sudden flash of hope, but overwhelming shame quickly moved to crush it. Neville had never threatened Dudley's personal safety, and it was a cowardly thing to wish for his death. That was asking fate to solve his problem for him. It was beneath his dignity.

"All right, lads," O'Ryan cried in response to Neville's orders, "it's time to move. On your feet!"

The company began to file into the trench, turning into the approaches. Dudley followed Barker and adjusted the sword at his side, Arbuthnot's sword. He also carried a new Enfield rifle. He planned to fire the rifle once, stab with its bayonet then discard the weapon in favour of his sword. By then, the storming parties should have overrun the Redan.

It felt like a good plan. He hoped he would get a chance to put it to the test.

In the French right attack, three thousand men crammed the advanced parallel, packed under the very noses of the Russians in the Malakov. Behind them, five thousand Sardinians waited in reserve. At noon, the allied bombardment fell silent and the French swarmed from their trench. They carried wooden bridges instead of scaling ladders, and these they threw across the ditch before the Malakov. After filing across the bridges, they had no trouble climbing the shell-pocked earthen ramparts of the fort.

The Russians, still under cover from the shelling, were not prepared to meet an attack. When the French tide swept over the escarpment, they did their best to form into lines to meet the threat. They fought back with anything at hand— musket stocks, bayonets, swords, handspikes, rammers, even rocks and bits of shattered planking. Many in the first French wave fell, but there were more waves coming behind the first.

After a quarter of an hour, the French Tricolour floated above the Malakov. Bloodied, in disarray, but victorious, the French cheered and shook their rifles in the air.

The Russians, pushed out of one of their key forts, were not content to let the French keep it. Their first counterattack began a struggle as savage as the first. The French general sent in his first section of reserves, and they beat back the Russian attack; but the Russians would come again, and again.

As the fighting went on, the Malakov's guns remained in French hands. The Russians in the Redan had lost their support.

Dudley leaned his back against the wall of the fifth parallel. Behind him stood Sergeant Barker and, on either side of him, the close-packed ranks of No. 3 Company. There was little room to move, and this was having an affect on the new men.

They feared and disliked the trenches at the best of times, and this was not the best of times. They stared with panicked eyes, and sweat ran down their faces and into their collars. Dudley could see they simply wanted out of the trench. He doubted whether they would care if that meant retreating or charging into a storm of grapeshot and shells.

Above the crowded trench stood the Light Division commander, General Codrington. Next to him stood his aide, Major Clifford of the Rifles. Both men were exposed to enemy fire, but neither showed any sign of minding. Codrington was studying the face of his watch.

When the allied bombardment ceased at noon, General Codrington put his watch away. Dudley settled against the trench wall, expecting more of a wait. The French would make their assault now. If they were successful, the British would follow. An hour perhaps, if the French were lucky. He could smell the dry earth of the parapet, so close to his face. He was grateful it had not rained for weeks, and that they did not have to fight the mud as well as the enemy.

He was surprised when he heard the cheering from the Malakov, a thousand voices raised in triumph. About ten minutes had elapsed since the bombardment had ended.

"The flag's up," Major Clifford announced. The green-clad officer was looking through his field glasses. "The Tricolour is flying on the Kornilov bastion."

"They've taken the Malakov," Dudley whispered. It was incredible. Relief fell over him, relief that there would be no more waiting. There was success at the Malakov. Now they could take the Redan. They could do it, at last. It was possible.

Relief became joy. He saw it in the eyes of those around him as well, the panic gone. There was eagerness as, one-by-one, the waiting British took up the cheer the French had first raised.

"Wait for the signal!" Colonel Freemantle called from somewhere in the packed trench.

It was too late. On his left, Dudley saw the Rifles already leaping onto the parapet. Officers shouted for them to stop, to wait, but it was no good. The men wanted out of the trench, both the recruits and the veterans. The recruits wanted an end to their terror, any end. The veterans wanted an end to all the long months of standing in the snow, the rain, the mud, and the heat. They wanted an end to the months of huddling in the trenches on picket, waiting for a mortar shell to find them, or a stray bullet, or a bayonet during a night raid. They wanted a final chance to fight back.

The ladder parties were climbing out now, lugging their long and awkward burdens. The Sappers had gone ahead. Dudley watched the sky, and there they were—two rockets fired from Chapman's batteries. The signal to storm the Redan.

"Sergeant Barker," he said, "it's time to go."

He found a toehold in the trench wall then, with one heave of his left arm, pulled himself over the parapet. He stood on the first foot of ground he would have to cross. Two hundred yards to go.

"Right behind you, Mister Dudley," Barker said.

The entire company was clambering out of the trench and forming a line. Captain Neville raised his sword above his head. Dudley raised his rifle, remembering Inkerman, when he and this company had rushed the Russian battery. There were different men here, new men, but some of the old faces were still with them. They would not let him down.

"Number Three Company," Neville cried, "charge!"

The assault companies advanced in a ragged wave. Dudley ran in front of his men, Sergeant Barker at his side. O'Ryan and Hoskins were near on his left. On the far right of the company ran Captain Neville, sword still held aloft like a rallying point.

Behind them, companies of the 41st and 62nd filed down into the trench then clambered out to form a second line. In all, the assaulting force comprised about fifteen hundred men, a third of the strength the French had utilized in their initial attack. Another thousand waited in reserve.

Ahead loomed the Redan. Its dark walls rose above the heads of the skirmishers and ladder parties in the fore. Dudley could see the Russian defenders waiting along the parapet.

The right face of the Redan suddenly erupted in dense smoke. Three heavy guns had fired as one. The blast swept away sappers and Rifles, cutting three great swaths in their loose formations. Two more guns fired from the salient angle, and a hail of musket balls began to rain down from the ramparts.

Clouds of sulphurous smoke drifted past Dudley as he sprinted towards the ditch. The surviving ladder parties were already there, halted on the edge of the abatis. The sharpened stakes were still intact. Allied artillery had not touched them. The ladder parties were trying to pick their way through the obstacle, lugging their unwieldy burdens. They had taken heavy casualties, but they had not made it this far during the last assault. This time there was no crossfire from the Malakov.

"Bloody hell!" Barker cried when he had run as far as he could. They had advanced to the abatis and could go no farther until the ladder parties had completed their task. The sergeant turned to the men behind him and shouted, "Take cover! Lie down!"

The men dropped prone. Dudley followed their example just as the guns in the salient angle fired a second time. A blast of grape shot engulfed a ladder party in front of him. The ladder shattered in a rain of splinters, and a severed arm landed near his right hand as the grape tore five of the ladder bearers to pieces. Two of the others fell to impale themselves on the stakes, and the last man slid into the ditch.

Commands rang out as the Russians reloaded their cannon. British riflemen knelt to shoot into the gun embrasures while the surviving ladder parties crawled forward. Dudley rose to his feet, amazed that he was unmarked. He motioned for his men to get up and advance.

Grabbing a wooden stake with his free hand, he pulled it loose. He moved into the abatis, tearing down another stake, and another, knowing he had only seconds before the guns at the salient were ready to fire again. A blast from one of the side guns plucked away men to his left; he heard the grape striking their flesh with wet smacks. He was almost to the edge of the ditch.

"Tear it down!" Neville was crying on the right. The captain waded through the stakes, ripping them away. He led the company on a converging path with another ladder party. Behind them, the Rifles kept up a steady fire as the great guns boomed on either side. The guns in the salient angle had not reappeared in their embrasures.

On the edge of the ditch, the ladder party pushed its burden over the chasm toward the face of the Redan. The ladder did not reach. Its far end fell ten feet and buried itself near the bottom of the ditch.

A corporal turned to Barker, eyes wide with shock, and cried, "The ladders are too short!"

"Bugger 'em, then," Barker replied. The ditch was full of loose debris from the bombardment, clumps of earth, bits of rope and wood. It was still about fifteen feet deep, but its sides sloped away. Barker grabbed the corporal's collar and propelled him toward the edge. "In we go!"

They slid down the side to the bottom. Above them, the muzzles of the two guns appeared at last. Dudley leapt into the ditch just as the guns went off. The grape whistled over his head, and a piece tore off his hat. Men behind him in the abatis groaned or cried out. Gasping for breath and clutching his rifle, he followed Barker and the corporal up the uneven face of the Redan.

He came to one of the gun openings, a square gap like a window. Screening it were curtains of thick rope lashed together. He wondered if he could get inside before the gunners finished reloading, but the idea of becoming tangled in the ropes did not appeal to him. He glanced up to see how far he was from the top. There the Russian infantry waited to receive the attackers. One aimed his musket in Dudley's direction.

Dudley rolled to one side as the man fired, and the bullet plucked at his trouser leg. He fumbled for his rifle, but the Russian had fallen back to reload. Dudley screamed and scrambled up after him. On his left came Sergeant Barker. Hoskins was with him, an odd companion-in-arms. Behind them, the remains of No. 3 Company were crawling out of the ditch and up toward the parapet.

Dudley gained the parapet and found himself facing the man who had fired at him. The Russian gaped in surprise then thrust upward with his bayonet. Dudley leapt aside, and the bayonet went past him, stabbing at air. As the Russian struggled to keep his balance, Dudley struck him in the face with the butt of his rifle. The man fell backwards and rolled off the firing step into the depths of the fort.

Dudley leapt down onto the firing step. He was inside the Redan.

To his left stood a gun crew in the act of loading. The gunners froze in panic as the assaulting British swarmed over the walls, surrounding them on all sides. Dudley brought his rifle up and pulled the trigger, shooting the gunner who held the rammer. The man spun and fell under the gun carriage trucks, and Dudley charged forward with his bayonet. No. 3 Company was with him. Barker and Hoskins came at the gun from the other side.

Dudley's bayonet punctured a gunner's green tunic, sliding between the man's ribs. The Russian cried out and fell to the wooden platform. Dudley let his rifle fall with the body and drew Arbuthnot's sword. *His* sword. He raised the blade to strike, but the rest of the gun crew had fled.

Masses of Russian infantry milled about in the center of the Redan, having abandoned the firing step to the attackers. More spilled from a long, low building, perhaps a barracks, that lay in the rear of the fort. They were disordered and confused but not beaten, and not in retreat.

Only about a third of the British who had left the trenches had made it to the parapet. Most had halted to form lines, an instinctive reaction. Those who had not formed in line were running along the firing step in scattered groups, fighting small isolated skirmishes with the few Russians who remained on the ramparts. A group of Russians had taken cover behind one side of a traverse, a clump of British huddled on the opposite side. The two groups exchanged sporadic fire.

Dudley realized the attack had stalled. He heard officers shouting conflicting orders, some to advance and some to form line. No one seemed in overall command. The confusion was giving the enemy time to regroup. If enough British reserves arrived now, they might still carry the day, but they would have to arrive soon.

"We can't hold 'em if they counterattack, sir," Barker said from his side of the abandoned gun. "There's not enough of us left!"

"Then why don't you run, you bloody coward!" screamed Hoskins.

"Shut up, Hoskins," Barker returned. "I don't have time to kick your arse, too."

The Russians were getting themselves into a semblance of order. Officers pushed and prodded their men into rough columns, and those in the front ranks began to fire up at the firing step. Dudley crouched low to avoid making himself a tempting target.

"Keep firing into them," he shouted at the clumps of men around him. "We have to keep them off-balance. Sergeant Barker, Sergeant Hoskins! Rally as many men as you can find and have them prepare to resist a counterattack. We shall hold here until our reinforcements arrive. I trust that will be any minute."

As he spoke, he heard the characteristic whine of bullets in the air close to his head. One struck the gun carriage, spraying tiny splinters. Another entered Sergeant Hoskins's mouth and came out the back of his neck.

Barker caught the other sergeant in one arm as he fell. Hoskins was already dead. Barker stared at the corpse for a few seconds then dropped it with a dull thump. With a look of disgust, he grunted, "Bloody fool!"

"Here they come, sir!" a private shouted, pointing down into the fort.

Dudley tore his eyes from Hoskins in time to see two narrow Russian columns charging, bayonets lowered. The columns were making for the ramps that led to the firing steps. Two other columns stood back to provide covering fire.

The closest ramp was a few yards to his right; it was only wide enough to allow the Russians a frontage of four men.

Dudley turned to face them as they gained the wall. Rifles banged around him, felling the foremost men. The others stumbled over the bodies, and he leapt forward, swinging his unfamiliar sword in a downward arc. The blade bit into a man's neck then slid away with little resistance. The stricken man slipped on the ramp, clutching at his wound. Dudley cut another on the hand, severing the fingers, then thrust at a third man's right eye. The blade missed, but its intended victim jumped back, upsetting those behind him.

"We can't hold 'em, sir!" Barker shouted. The column had become a tangled mess on the narrow ramp, but the British were running. The survivors of No. 3 Company had begun to leap back onto the parapet and scramble out of the fort. All along the firing step, men from other companies were doing the same.

Dudley and Barker exchanged stunned glances, but there was nothing they could do. They could not stand here alone. They had to follow the retreat.

With a cry of frustration, Dudley scrambled after his men.

"Stand and fight!" he shouted. "Stand and fight!"

Other officers and sergeants screamed at the men to hold. Their urgings had some effect, for the withdrawal slowed and then stopped, the men reforming a few yards down the escarp. Dudley and Barker halted with them and dressed the ragged line. Above, the Russian columns flooded onto the firing step.

Dudley's right arm ached, and his hands were slick with sweat. He was afraid he might lose his grip on his sword. He looked up at the Russians then at the ragged survivors around him.

The British reserve companies were arriving at last, minutes too late. They came in small groups, sections that halted to fill gaps in the line. They were still not enough, but Dudley would not give up hope. The British were not advancing, but they were no longer retreating. They were standing their ground, and their rifles were finding more targets than the Russian muskets.

"Here come more of our boys, sir," Barker announced, pointing across the killing ground toward the trenches. Dudley saw three more companies racing across the field toward the ruined abatis. He flinched as Russian guns west of the Redan blasted fire, leaving a red stain of fallen men on the ground.

But most reached the ditch and leapt in. Dudley watched as they clawed their way up the face of the Redan. He felt a surge of confidence. This was enough; they could move forward now. The British line would soon be four and five men deep, and they had made it past the artillery.

He moved out in front of the line, waving his sword and crying, "Come on! One charge!" It was just like Inkerman. He knew the men would follow him. They would take the Redan.

He turned and scrambled back up the slope toward the waiting Russians. Bullets whipped past him. The Russians were running low on ammunition, and some threw rocks. Barker was on Dudley's left with other members of the Royal Hants. The Russians disappeared, ducking behind the wall. Dudley neared the top of the parapet, standing and looking back to urge the charge on.

But there was no charge. With him were just five men. The rest had stayed on the slope, continuing to fire but not moving. Dudley guessed their strength at close to six hundred, but they had clustered around the salient angle and would not budge.

"Bloody laggards," Barker shouted, running back and grabbing a man by the arm. He dragged the man forward. "Advance, damn you! We've got to advance."

The man he held jerked and sagged, a dark hole in his side spurting blood. More bullets made tiny fountains of earth around Barker's feet. With a curse, he let the dying man fall.

Dudley crawled the last few feet to the parapet. The few men in his pathetic charge fired their rifles in the direction of the enemy then turned to scurry back to the main line. Dudley struck at them with the flat of his sword, but they would not stop.

When the last of his companions had withdrawn, a single figure remained on the parapet with him. The figure had not been part of his attempted charge and stood about ten yards away. He looked at Dudley, seeming to notice him for the first time. It was Captain Neville.

Neville stared with cold eyes. Dudley straightened from his crouch and returned the stare. At that moment, they were alone. No other battle raged around them. Neville stood with his sword sloped on his shoulder. Dudley met his gaze and did not look away.

From the corner of his eye, Dudley glimpsed movement as the Russians again appeared at the parapet. A ragged musket volley blasted. Rocks and thrown bayonets sailed past. In the face of this onslaught, Neville tore his eyes from Dudley and began walking down the slope. Not running—walking. Dudley stayed frozen in position and watched him go. Around him raged a world of smoke and shouting, the firing of muskets, the whine of bullets that plucked at his clothes. Caught in a maelstrom of sight and noise, he felt Barker pull him back by the arm, back to the crowd of green recruits who would not go forward.

"You'll get yourself killed, sir!" Barker shouted.

"We have to advance," Dudley insisted.

The meeting with Neville had thrown him into a daze. The sight of a red-coated man emerging from one of the gun embrasures added to his confusion. Two others followed, men who had managed to hold on inside the fort. None of them carried rifles. Others came scrambling back over the parapet. He could not understand how they could have survived all this time. More than an hour must have passed since they had first come out of the trench.

It was then that a single private in the clustered line turned and ran the other way. Sergeants and officers shouted at him to stop, but he did not listen. Seeing him go, two other men followed.

That was the end. The British line began to edge back. More men left, turning and walking the other way. The entire formation was breaking up. Like a dam bursting, the British line broke. The men turned and began to run.

Dudley watched in horror. A sudden rage filled him, and he cried, "Come back, you damn cowards!"

He struck at another man with the flat of his sword. Barker took hold of two at once and threw them down, cursing at them to stay and fight. The men just glared at the sergeant, picked themselves up, and continued back toward the trenches.

The Russians did not cheer just continued to throw rocks. A few muskets banged, and the guns went on belching hot grape and canister. Men died with their backs to the enemy.

This could not be happening, Dudley thought. They could not be defeated.

But Barker was looking at him with resignation.

"We have to withdraw, sir."

"Withdraw, hell," Dudley retorted. "I'll make them come back. Cowards! Damn cowards!"

He stumbled down the face of the Redan, into the ditch and out again. He climbed over the twitching bodies of the wounded, the still forms of the dead. When he came across a fleeing man, he struck at him with his fist, shouting, "Go back! Go back, damn you!"

He did this twice more, and each time the man ducked and continued running. He trailed after them, shouting all the way back to the siege lines.

When he noticed where he was, he looked down into the fifth parallel. Powder-stained, wild-eyed men crowded the bottom. Defeated men.

He reached into the trench and tried to pull a man out, crying, "One push and we've got them! Get out, get back out! We're going back."

The soldier ignored him, recoiling as a mortar shell burst nearby. Dudley uttered a wordless cry of outrage.

"You, there, Lieutenant," someone said, and Dudley realized the voice addressed him. He turned to see General Codrington approaching along the rearward edge of the parallel. Major Clifford was with him. The major, brow creased with anger, had his sword drawn.

"Yes, sir?" Dudley said.

"Calm yourself," said the general. "You've done your best, and there's nothing more you can do. The attack has broken off, and I have decided there shall be no second assault. These fellows simply will not go at it."

Dudley's shoulders slumped. That was the final word.

"Yes, sir."

"What's your name, Lieutenant?" the General asked.

"Ensign Dudley, sir, Number Three Company, Royal Hampshire Fusiliers."

"Oh, I say. Ensign, is it? You're one of Freemantle's fellows. Well, I'll see that he hears of your conduct. You've done all you can."

"Thank you, sir."

The general nodded and carried on his way. The attack was finished. It was two o'clock in the afternoon.

Dudley sat in one of the approaches, his back against the dirt wall. His clothes were torn in several places, but he was not wounded. Somehow, he had come thro   haring type."

Yes, Dudley thought, he was. O'Ryan had always kept a full flask of brandy at hand. It was good to discover he maintained that habit.

As the night wore on, Dudley refused to sleep. Orders came for the Highland brigade to storm the Redan in the morning. The entire army was awake, gathered round campfires built in and close to the trenches. Somewhere, a lone piper played a slow air. Elsewhere in the trenches, the men sang, trying to keep their spirits up. They felt the sting of the defeat. Many members of No. 3 Company remembered that Ensign Dudley had called them coward and were ashamed.

Dudley and Barker shared a fire with O'Ryan. Dudley was glad of the Irishman's company, although O'Ryan remained distant, his conversation with the young officer formal. He continued to pass his flask around until they had drained it.

When the piper finished his third tune, a stillness followed.

"Listen, sir," Barker said, "do you hear that?"

"Hear what?"

The night was silent without the distant mournful music. The singing had also stopped.

"Exactly, Mister Dudley. There's no sound from Sevastopol. No shots fired, no sound of work, no commands. There's been no sorties for the first night in weeks."

Dudley stood and gazed toward the town. No lights burned. It was strange.

"We have to investigate," he said. "I'll find the colonel. Do I have any volunteers?"

He should have consulted Neville first, but he did not want to deal with him. He sought out Lieutenant-Colonel Freemantle instead. Freemantle agreed to his proposed reconnaissance. A few minutes later, Dudley, Barker and O'Ryan threaded their way through the trenches and back into the fifth parallel. Before them stretched the killing ground, the dead still lying on the churned and bloodied earth. Beyond squatted the dark hump of the enemy fort.

They crept out of the trench. Moving like crabs, they crept towards the ruined abatis. Dudley suggested they go even farther, but O'Ryan shook his head.

"I wouldn't, sir. It could be mined."

They lay in the darkness, listening. The wounded and dying, unattended, moaned and called out to them in two languages, a chorus of laments. The hairs on Dudley's neck stiffened at the sound. Here, in the darkness, it seemed like the voice of hell. There were no other sounds of living men.

They crept back, over and around the bodies. When they once again found Lieutenant-Colonel Freemantle, they reported their discovery.

"Have they abandoned the fort?" Freemantle mused.

There was no way to answer that question, but Dudley hoped it was so. It would turn their defeat into a victory.

Another hour passed, and his certainty grew. He returned to the fifth parallel and stayed there with the Highlanders, watching. After a while, he fell asleep, leaning against the trench wall.

At about four o'clock in the morning, something jarred him awake. He opened his eyes to an enormous explosion that lit both the enemy walls and the allied works. Flame and smoke rose behind the Redan, a lurid pillar carrying mortar shells that burned and exploded in the sky. Several other explosions went up along the wall, casting heaps of stones, earth, logs, and the bodies of the fallen—British and Russian—into the air.

Behind the Redan, Sevastopol began to burn.

As the sun rose, the flames began to die. Dudley focused his telescope to watch the enemy fleeing the town. They had destroyed their stores and now crossed the bridge of boats to the north shore. The British batteries took the opportunity to lob shells at them as they went.

The destruction was not finished yet. The forts opposite the French left-attack, never assaulted, erupted in columns of dirty flame. Two of the stone forts on the seaward side, Fort Quarantine and Fort Alexander, threw up clouds of bricks and mortar dust. More explosions tore through the city, and a pall of black smoke rose to cover the sun. The air stank of gunpowder and burning.

Before eight o'clock, the waiting British troops left their trenches and returned to camp for some much-needed rest.

CHAPTER 12

September 9, 1855

Dudley stood in the Redan amidst the wreckage and the uncollected dead. Stiffened corpses lay alongside bits of rope, splintered planking, shell fragments, pieces of kit, torn gabions. The interior of the fort was an unrecognizable ruin. Jumbled cannon sprawled near broken carriages, bronze barrels still draped in rope mantlets. The Russians had spiked and abandoned hundreds of pieces of artillery. With the port of Sevastopol, these guns made a substantial prize for the allies. He wondered what would become of them.

But the prizes were cold comfort for the British forces. The nature of the victory had produced a profound sense of dissatisfaction. They had not wrested Sevastopol from the enemy. Instead, the enemy had given up, soldiers and civilians alike abandoning the town. Much of the credit for the victory had to go to the French for holding the Malakov throughout the night.

Dudley shared in the general disappointment, agreeing this did not seem like much of a triumph for the British. At least he had tried to do his personal best, which was some consolation. The recruits had fought as well as their experience and training allowed. They had bloodied the enemy, and the enemy had conceded. The Russians still occupied the north side of the harbour, but they controlled nothing important, and the war could not last much longer. The siege was over.

He was one of the few who had not yet gone down into the town—he considered it indecent to leave the dead and many of the wounded untended in order to do some sightseeing. He also thought it wise to wait until the engineers had cleared away any traps or mines the Russians might have left behind. This danger seemed obvious, although it had not deterred many. Great numbers of French soldiers had rushed into the city at the first opportunity. Looting seemed their primary objective, for most had returned to the camps carrying plundered chairs, tables, framed mirrors, curtains, and clothing.

The British were not as interested in plunder, although there were a few exceptions. Sergeant Barker was one of the exceptions.

As the men flowed back from their initial explorations, Barker saw Dudley in the Redan and approached him with a mischievous glint in his eye. His haversack bulged at his side, and he gave it an affectionate pat.

"What have you got there, Sergeant Barker?" Dudley said, not hiding the edge of reproach in his voice.

Barker reached into the haversack and produced a wad of paper banknotes. From the sound of it, the haversack also contained a large number of jingling coins.

"I didn't find any of your mines or booby traps, sir," he said, "but I did find this in a bank."

"Imagine finding money in a bank," Dudley replied. He did not approve. He considered looting an act beneath the dignity of the present-day British soldier.

"Well, Mister Dudley, the Russians couldn't have valued it very highly," Barker contended. "The bankers must have had plenty of opportunity to take it with them when they left. Or maybe they expected to hold out forever and were in such a hurry they forgot it. Either way, it's fair game." Barker winked. "A soldier has to survive any way he can, sir."

Dudley wrinkled his nose and shook his head.

"Find another way to survive, Sergeant. Captain Neville would be delighted to catch you at this sort of thing."

Barker was unapologetic.

"No orders forbidding a little scavenging, are there, sir?"

"Not yet, but I suspect there soon will be."

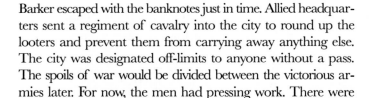

Barker escaped with the banknotes just in time. Allied headquarters sent a regiment of cavalry into the city to round up the looters and prevent them from carrying away anything else. The city was designated off-limits to anyone without a pass. The spoils of war would be divided between the victorious armies later. For now, the men had pressing work. There were graves that needed digging.

The grisly task took almost two days. Mule litters and ambulances ambled back and forth, transporting allied and Russian wounded into the temporary camp hospitals. Fatigue parties worked before the Malakov and Redan, digging mass graves for the rank-and-file. As before, smaller parties dug individual tombs for the officers in the cemetery on Cathcart's Hill.

Meanwhile, the engineers secured the city. They surveyed the remaining forts and the naval dockyard, discussing plans for their demolition. They cleared vast amounts of loose powder and discarded shells. As Dudley had suspected, they also discovered numerous Russian traps, which they dismantled.

One problem that defied the engineers was how to extinguish the many fires that still raged out of control. At last, nature intervened and solved the problem for them. Four days after the assault, a violent storm swept in, bringing wind, thunder, lightning, rain and hail. The storm lasted for more than six hours and completely doused the troublesome flames.

A week after the assault, Dudley and Barker went to headquarters to see if they could obtain passes to enter Sevastopol. French infantry was posted on the town perimeter with orders to shoot anyone without such authorization. When the secretary asked his reasons for going in, Dudley told the truth.

"I have not yet seen the city, and it's high time that I did."

The secretary thought this reason enough and issued the passes.

A rough road now cut across the trenches and into the Redan. Sappers had filled in part of the ditch and removed the gabions of one gun embrasure to make a huge breach. The Redan was now an open gate. Dudley showed his pass to the sentry then walked inside.

Not much had changed since the day after the assault, save that the bodies were gone. The abandoned guns still reclined in their sagging positions. In the rear, where the great explosions had taken place, the path down to the town was strewn with spent round shot, broken shells, and fragments of iron. The long barracks building was now a pile of rubble and great stones.

Dudley and Barker strolled down into the streets. They saw more marks of the allied bombardment, evidence that much of it had overshot the target. Great craters pitted the streets, the flagstones and cobbles shattered. Gaping shot holes made jagged windows in the walls of the houses. Many buildings stood roofless, their chimneys broken or leaning, while others remained standing despite having their lower stories burned or pounded away. Iron railings were twisted in fantastic shapes. Everywhere lay heaps of crumbled masonry, scorched timbers, broken muskets, artillery carriages, abandoned carts and ruined wagons.

Except for these signs of recent conflict, the city resembled some ancient ruin from a lost civilization. It was a city of ghosts.

Dudley and Barker stopped at a barricade the Russians had made across one street. Two abandoned field guns sat behind a few tables, a cabinet, and some timbers. There were more such barricades blocking other streets, each guarded by silent guns. It looked as if the Russians had planned to defend Sevastopol street-by-street.

"It's amazing they held out as long as they did, I suppose," Dudley remarked.

The ruined city and the absence of people fascinated him. It did not seem real. He felt as if he and Barker were witnessing the greatest work of some mad sculptor. On the edge of a small square, they found a large church with its steeple blown away. They stepped inside, moving with care across the broken window glass. They saw the pews in fragments, the chancel and alter half-burned, filled with broken plaster and masonry. Farther on in another square, they found a public building with the clock in its tower pierced clean through by a round shot. The shot had knocked out the back of the tower. Nowhere was there a structure not scarred somehow. Even the stones in the public cemetery were chipped and broken, the iron railings twisted.

"I remember reading about Quebec after Wolfe's conquest," Dudley said as they made their way to the harbour front. "Wolfe, of course, died on the field, but when our troops entered the town, they found it almost completely destroyed. Very much like this, I imagine. Though I'm sure that this must be worse, and far more quiet."

"It's damn impressive, that's for sure," Barker commented.

They came to the water. There lay the remains of the Russian naval ships, trapped, burned and sunk. Two thousand yards away lay the north side of the harbour and its coastal forts, still in enemy hands. On the shore, the Russians had built another battery, the gunners visible on its low parapet.

"Fat lot they can do to us from over there," Barker said. "They ought to know they're beaten."

There was a puff of smoke from one of the far embrasures, and a bang a few seconds later. An iron ball skipped across the water and thumped into a pile of brick five yards away.

"I think we'd best retire," Dudley suggested.

A moment later, the entire Russian battery erupted. Dudley and Barker ran, laughing at the poor fellows who would fire at two men strolling on the beach. Another ball struck a house, showering them with wood, splinters, and mortar. More balls landed behind them, but they made it back into the cover of the city. There they halted, their laughter verging on hysteria.

"Beaten, are they?" Dudley said; then the convulsions took him again.

Beaten, but still defiant.

With the siege ended, the need to man the trenches and batteries round the clock disappeared. Guards were still necessary in the camps and in Sevastopol, but so many regiments were available that a particular unit might draw the assignment less than once a week. Drunkenness and neglect of duty grew rampant as the men began to relax. The proliferation of commissaries in the camps and Balaclava was too tempting for those with not enough to do. Morning after morning, many a regiment paraded to witness punishment.

Often that punishment consisted of fifty lashes, sometimes even for minor crimes. It was still, after all, a time of war.

To solve the problem of too little work, the army turned inward in an effort to improve its own conditions. General Simpson ordered the construction of a proper supply road from Balaclava. The infantry divisions would take turns at the work. Meanwhile, every regiment set about improving its camp. The men dug drainage ditches around the tents, strengthened the tent poles with scrap wood from Sevastopol, and fitted storm ropes in anticipation of autumn gales. In the Light Division, fatigue parties brought up more prefab huts from Balaclava. There was no desire to repeat the mistakes of the previous winter.

Dress parades and reviews were another diversion to keep the army busy. The largest of these came on September 20, the first anniversary of the bloody battle at the Alma River. The entire British Expeditionary Force paraded together for the first time. The event celebrated the victory of a year ago and the ultimate victory that was certain to come. The general staff made speeches and gave congratulations then distributed service medals for the Crimea to every regiment. The medals came with clasps for the battles of Alma, Balaclava, and Inkerman. The men of the Royal Hants received clasps for both Alma and Inkerman.

The clasps reminded Dudley of the labels he had seen on pill bottles at the village chemist's. Still, he wore them with pride, as did everyone.

When the parade ended late in the afternoon, an air of festivity lingered. Informal entertainments sprang up—songs, sketches, and concerts by the regimental bands. Other groups of men organized shooting contests and other games.

Dudley wandered through the Light Division camp. He paused at some of these minor spectacles, watching for a few minutes then carrying on. He walked alone, aimless, until he saw Neville chatting and laughing with some of the officers. They were smoking cigars and passing round copies of the *Times* that announced the fall of Sevastopol. Rowntree was there, a few lieutenants, and the young ensigns. These fellows had become the core of Neville's followers.

He overheard one lieutenant declare he would have a closer look at the newspaper later in the mess hut.

The gathering was a physical reminder of Dudley's growing isolation. He was not part of what he witnessed. He would not get a chance to read the newspaper. All at once, the day was ruined for him. Although he had served the queen as well as he could and wore her medal on his chest, he was not considered worthy.

He turned and walked on, face set like stone.

When he saw Major Willis coming toward him, he touched the brim of his new straw hat, a replacement for the one lost at the Redan.

"Good afternoon, Ensign," the major hailed, returning the salute with a wide smile.

Dudley halted and returned the greeting, doing his best to hide his ill mood.

"Will you be taking part in the steeplechase tomorrow, Mister Dudley?" Willis asked.

"Steeplechase, sir?" Dudley repeated. "I hadn't heard."

The major's smile faded.

"Oh? You weren't in our little hut again last evening? I was unable to attend myself, but…still avoiding us, are you?"

Nonplussed, Dudley said, "Yes, sir. I mean, no, I was not in the mess hut."

Willis's cheerfulness changed to irritation.

"Now, really, Ensign, you must get over this. You are no longer a sergeant but an officer. I realize our hut is not much, but you must begin somewhere. It represents the center of our fellowship. You will never fit in if you don't make an effort."

It took Dudley a few minutes to understand the major's meaning. Then he said carefully, "I thought I was not welcome in the mess hut, sir. Captain Neville does not want me to go there."

"What? Captain Neville?" Now it was the major's turn for bewilderment. "No, no. You must have misunderstood. He was supposed to tell you that you must come, not that you must not." Willis shook his head. "Here, then. Tomorrow's steeplechase is just the thing to get over whatever it is that ails you. There shall be an inter-regimental tournament tomorrow. Not everyone can enter an event, of course, but the old Royal Hants needs more representation. You seem just the type, always off on that little pony of yours. What's his name?"

"Er, my pony's name is Bill, sir."

"Ah, yes. Well, I hope to see you and Bill there." He started to move away then stopped with a look of surprise. "Blue blazes, I nearly forgot. Allow me to shake your hand, sir."

Dudley took the major's hand, his confusion deepening.

"May I ask what I've done to deserve this, sir?"

"You may, and I will answer you. The general had kind words about you, young fellow. Our General Codrington, that is. Told Freemantle you did everything you could to move the men during the assault. Spoke highly of you. And of course, anything the general says about one of our officers makes the entire regiment look good, you understand."

Dudley remembered Codrington's words to him after the assault. It was incredible that anything had come of it. Every other officer had been doing the same thing, trying to urge the men on.

"Thank you, sir," he said.

"No need to thank me, Ensign. At any rate, perhaps we shall see you in the mess hut tonight. If not, at the races tomorrow."

"You certainly shall, sir."

The major nodded and strode off. Dudley stared at his receding back, trying to decide what had just happened. It seemed that the major had no inkling of Neville's actions. His concern over Dudley's absence in the mess hut had been genuine.

Neville must have said something to him, Dudley assumed, but what? Perhaps he had told the major Dudley refused to attend, that he was nervous or felt out of place. That would make sense.

Here at last was an unexpected ray of hope. He had to determine its best possible use. He could go to the mess hut tonight, challenging Neville to eject him in Willis's presence, but he did not want to face that sort of confrontation now. He did not want to sit at dinner, ignored, the others hostile to his presence. He could not force himself into their company.

The only course was the one he followed now. He would have to sway the others with deeds. Being in Major Willis's good books made that all the more possible. The younger officers, although they liked Neville better, could not ignore the opinions of the second-in-command.

He would go to the steeplechase tomorrow. He had become a competent enough horseman, and here was a chance to behave like a proper officer. He would race for the Royal Hampshire Fusiliers.

It was a fine day for a steeplechase. High clouds drifted overhead like massive balloons as Dudley rode to the course. He wanted to arrive early so he would not miss the chance to enter at least one event. Last night he had sought out the farrier Oakes had befriended, and Bill was freshly shod and in high spirits. Both pony and master were eager to perform.

Barker accompanied them, walking alongside Bill. The sergeant displayed almost as much enthusiasm as Dudley.

"Maybe bloody Neville will enter the same race you do, sir," he suggested, "and you and Bill here can whip his arse."

"You may be right," Dudley said. He had not considered that possibility. "It would be satisfying to race him, but I doubt he would wish to race me."

Neville's game was to deny Dudley the life of an officer. To race him would be to admit he had a right to be there. Neville would never do that.

The new racecourse lay on the plain between the British and French camps. It ran a quarter-mile in length, designed for both flat races and hurdles. The hurdles were fashioned from old canvas bagging stretched on wooden frames. A group of officers from several British regiments had organized the event. Their headquarters tent sat at one end of the course. Dudley made his way there.

He was a last-minute entry; most of the contestants had entered a week ago and had trained since then. Dudley insisted he had trained as well, for months, ever since the last steeplechase in the spring. The organizers told him not to worry, that in the spirit of good fun they had no authority to deny him. They entered his name in the first event of the day, one of the hurdles.

The sidelines were beginning to fill with spectators, some on horseback but most on foot. In the crowd were civilians, sailors, marines, and soldiers from every allied army, both officers and men. Many of the officers had come to watch rather than compete, and some had brought their wives.

Dudley lingered near the headquarters tent, whispering encouragement to Bill and waiting for word to take up his position. Barker spent his time sizing up the other contestants as they arrived.

"Don't look now, sir," the sergeant said, "but here he comes."

Neville had ridden onto the field, trailed by his usual entourage. The captain wore a fantastic costume of tight tan riding breeches and a multi-coloured checkered shirt. Strips of bright cloth fluttered from his forage cap, and he carried a leather riding crop.

"Fancies himself quite the pony jockey, don't he?" Barker commented. "I knew he'd not be content to sit this one out, Mister Dudley."

Neville took up a position near the head of the course. He appeared to be getting ready to compete in the first event. He could have no way of knowing Dudley was a last-minute entry.

Dudley swallowed, excitement giving way to trepidation. He was suddenly unsure whether he wanted to race Neville. It would take all the sport out of the activity. He would want to win too much, or at least beat the captain, and he was not sure that he could.

The other contestants were gathering near the starting line. Besides Neville, there were four other infantry officers, one a Highlander in trews. All wore flashy outfits that provoked smiles and cheers from their watching subordinates. Dudley decided it was too late to bow out now. He mounted Bill easily, feet settling into his stirrups, and moved towards his position.

Neville glared at him as he approached the course.

"What in blazes are *you* doing here, Dudley?" he snapped. "We're about to race."

Dudley ears began to burn, but he forced the anger down and said, "I'm racing, too, sir. Bill and I have entered this event."

Neville's eyes widened in astonishment.

"The hell, you say! No, you're not. Get out of here."

Dudley stared at him, sensing the beginnings of helplessness. Could Neville really bar him from this, too?

"Why should I leave, sir?" he demanded.

"Because I order you to, that's why," Neville stated. "I'm your company commander."

The Highlander, who had watched the exchange with curiosity, suddenly laughed and said, "What are you on about, Neville? Let the man race, for heaven's sake! He's off-duty, ain't he?" He leaned toward Neville and asked with a leer, "Afraid your junior will beat you, eh?"

At that, Neville turned purple. He chewed his lip and looked from the Scotsman back to Dudley. Then he slapped his riding crop into his left hand.

"Damn you, then, Dudley. Do your bloody worst!"

Turning his horse, he took up his place at the starting line. The Highlander laughed and winked at Dudley then followed. The race was about to begin. Dudley breathed a sigh of relief.

A grinning referee stood beside the starting line with a pistol in his hand. Bill seemed to sense something was up and pawed the turf in eagerness. Dudley could feel Neville next to him, on his immediate right, a hostile mass of man and horse.

The pistol cracked, and he dug in his heels. Bill shot forward.

Dudley concentrated on the upcoming hurdle. From the corner of his eye, he saw the man on his left topple from his saddle. Furious laughter burst from the crowd. The other horsemen fell behind, all save one, and that was Neville. He and Dudley rode neck-and-neck.

Bill sailed over the first hurdle and landed smoothly. Dudley stood in the stirrups, bending low over the horse's neck. The second obstacle hurtled towards him. He chanced a glance to his right.

Neville returned the glance. He rode closer to Dudley than was safe. His eyes smoldered. With a flick of his left wrist, he dealt Bill a stinging blow across the neck with his riding crop.

Bill screamed and turned hard. Dudley struggled to keep hold of the reins, and pain lanced through his arms and shoulders. Bill missed crashing into Neville's horse by inches then bolted from the course.

Spectators dashed out of their way. Dudley shouted at Bill to stop, but the horse insisted on running circles on the flat ground behind the crowd.

After a few minutes, Bill slowed to a trot then a walk. Dudley stroked his neck and made soothing comments, and the pony came to a halt. Dudley turned back to the course, but the race was over. Neville was already gloating and holding aloft his little improvised trophy, a thing made from a pewter cup and a block of wood.

Dudley did not bother to watch or even pause. He would be damned if Neville could force him out of this race! He turned back to the empty course and made Bill jump the missed hurdle then the next. Watchers in the crowd shouted at him in good humour, one man crying, "Go on, sir, you'll win yet!"

When Dudley had completed the course, he reined in at the finish line. A mass of grinning, laughing men surrounded him, all slapping Bill's flanks and shouting further encouragement. Dudley could not help laughing in return.

When the little crowd had dispersed, only Barker remained.

"Good show, sir," he said. "You would have had 'im if old Bill hadn't gone off like that. Guess he doesn't like Captain Neville any more than we do."

Dudley's laughter died, his face hardening.

"You didn't see what he did?"

Barker shook his head, and Dudley was about to tell him what had happened when he spied Major Willis approaching on horseback. Willis reined in. Unlike the others, he was not laughing.

"Deuced strange, your horse bolting like that," he stated. "Do you know what set him off?"

Dudley opened his mouth to tell the truth, but then he changed his mind. If no one had seen, it would be his word against Neville's. It seemed a petty thing to complain about, anyway. A practical joke. Not at all sporting and probably dangerous, but a joke, nonetheless, and in typical Neville character.

"I suspect it was an accident, sir," he said, "with Captain Neville's riding crop. We were too close together. I'm not much good with horses."

"Nonsense! Captain Neville's riding crop, you say? I thought I saw him give your pony a good whack. Damn strange, I thought, though just like the sort of damn-fool stunt he would pull. Not at all fair. It must have been an accident."

"I trust it was an accident, sir."

The major suddenly grinned.

"At least you have a chance at the Consolation Prize, eh?"

"Yes, sir," said Dudley, "there is that."

CHAPTER 13

October, 1855

As the weather grew colder, scores of men decided to build their own shelters instead of waiting to receive prefab huts. Scavenging parties ranged Sevastopol, tearing out planking, doors, windows, hinges, nails and screws. Trains of mules and pony carts carried the material down to the camps. Occasionally, the Russians fired on these processions from the north side of the harbour. No one paid much attention to the danger, but the firing was a reminder the war was not yet over.

A more serious reminder came with the beginning of a new campaign. Dudley was hard at work transforming his tent into a comfortable winter hut when an orderly brought him the news. At next reveille, the regiment was to parade in full marching order. They would march to Kamiesch, the French supply base, where they would join other regiments for a detached expedition.

The next morning, October 4, the Royal Hants trudged to Kamiesch and boarded the line-of-battle ship *Hannibal*. Lieutenant-Colonel Freemantle had not yet revealed the objective of the expedition. Thanks to the presence of thousands of sutlers and camp followers, the general staff were worried about spies. The regiments would learn their destination only after disembarkation, although everyone agreed on the obvious purpose of the campaign. They would attack some vulnerable point in order to force the Russians to terms.

It took several days to assemble the entire expeditionary force. The operation was a joint British-French affair, although command fell to the British Brigadier-General Spencer. The French contribution consisted of a sizable naval squadron, with four line-of-battle ships, several steam frigates, gun and mortar boats, and three floating iron-clad batteries.

The iron-clad batteries made an intriguing sight, unlike anything Dudley had ever seen. Each carried twenty-two French 50-pounders mounted in twelve gun ports a side. Four-and-a-half inch iron plating protected the sloping hulls of the batteries. The Allied navies hoped that Russian artillery would prove useless against that armour.

The British fleet contained five line-of-battle ships, each carrying a regiment of infantry and a company of marines. Accompanying the battleships was a collection of steam frigates and sloops, ten gunboats, six mortar boats, three steam tenders, and ten supply transports. The transports carried a detachment of the Royal Artillery, freight, a floating hospital with staff, stores, Commissariat Staff, Land Transport Corps and stores, shot and shell, and fuel. To Dudley, it seemed a far better prepared force than the original expedition to the Crimea more than a year ago.

The British fleet left the Crimea on a fine cool autumn day, the 7th of October. The fleet moved only as fast as its slowest vessels and met the French squadron the next afternoon. The rendezvous point was near the Russian port of Odessa. About three miles from shore, the allied vessels dropped anchor.

Dudley stood near the starboard rail waiting for Colonel Freemantle's address. The Royal Hampshire Fusiliers had formed on deck and now stood easy. He could hear Neville talking and laughing with Captain Rowntree nearby. He tried to ignore them.

Since the steeplechase, Neville had become even more wearisome and abusive. He had changed tactics, making humiliation and practical joking the order of the day. Several times, Dudley had returned to his modified tent to find his work ruined in some "witty" manner. Once, he found the floorboards taken up and stacked in tripods like rifles. Another time, the stakes had been pulled then the ropes wrapped around the slack canvas and secured in large bows.

Dudley knew Neville himself was not one of the culprits—Hester Oakes had seen Rowntree and the young ensigns lurking about several times. Neville had probably just offered encouragement, or an idea or two.

He tried to forget his frustrations and turned to watch the distant shore. This could be the expedition's objective—the capture of Odessa. The city spread up the slope of a gentle hill, covering more ground than Sevastopol. Dusk was coming on, bathing the wide, tree-lined avenues in its golden light. From out of the autumn foliage rose the spires of several great churches and cathedrals.

On one side of the city lay an extensive wood or park. Near it was an esplanade filled with citizens, all watching the invading fleet. More civilians crammed the rocks and outcroppings along the shore. Maybe they hoped to see the enemy repulsed, or perhaps they worried that the few gun batteries along the waterfront would not be enough to protect them.

Dudley took out his spyglass for a better look at the coast. Telegraph and semaphore stations transmitted messages to and fro in a panic; regiments of Cossacks galloped about in apparent disorder. A brigade of infantry had also appeared, their bayonets gleaming as they marched along a seaside road toward the town.

He hoped the fleet would not have to destroy this attractive place the way they had destroyed Sevastopol.

Lieutenant-Colonel Freemantle at last came on deck, and Dudley collapsed the telescope to listen to the address. Freemantle smiled then told his men why they had come here.

Odessa was not the objective, he explained. Anchoring here was a diversion to draw enemy troops from their true destination. That was the fort of Kinburn, which lay below the confluence of the Bug and Ingul rivers near the mouth of the Dnieper. This brick-and-mortar fort sat at the end of a long spit of sand that jutted into the Black Sea. The allies meant to take it.

In Odessa, church bells began to ring, pealing across the calm water. The Royal Hants gave three cheers in anticipation of success. More cheers sounded in the other vessels anchored nearby. It was to be war again, and a chance to do better this time.

That night, a heavy fog descended, and the next morning it still shrouded the shore. The Russian troops appeared as dim shapes gathered on the high ground, ghostly infantry and artillery waiting to oppose a landing. Above the mist, the semaphore stations continued to react, and Cossacks raced from place to place. The diversion had been a success.

By evening, fog and calm had given way to gale-force winds and an ugly swell. The weather delayed the departure of the allied fleet for several days. The combined squadrons did not get underway until Saturday, October 14.

That same afternoon, the fleet anchored again in full view of the star-shaped stronghold that was Kinburn fort.

The Russians had no reaction, and the allies waited for night. Under the cover of darkness, a detachment of French and British vessels moved through the narrow channel into Dnieper Bay to anchor above the fort. The rest of the fleet moved in closer the next morning. Despite the high surf, boats pushed off from the transports, the troops making for the shore. The Russians did not waste any powder, perhaps realizing the boats were beyond the range of their guns.

Each regiment tried to be the first in, racing for the root of the long finger of land. The 17th won the contest, their boats pushing up on the beach. The next regiment to land was the 63rd, and one of its ensigns leapt from his boat to plant a Queen's Colour in the sand.

The third regiment in was the Royal Hants. The first man ashore was Captain Neville.

The infantry had landed four miles from the fort. The finger of land was about a mile across here, and the men set to digging two trenches. One trench faced the fort, the other faced inland. The French were to man the former, the British the latter.

The soil was mostly sand, and the digging was easy going. When darkness fell, the work halted, and the infantry bivouacked under the stars. There was plenty of available wood for campfires, and no enemy activity save for the shouts from the walls of the fort as the Russians changed their sentries.

The next morning, stores and field guns came off the transports without mishap. The infantry completed the trenches and turned to constructing batteries for the field guns. By nightfall, all preparations were complete.

"What shall we see in the morning?" Barker wondered that night beside his bivouac fire. "Are we in for a weeklong siege, or something worse?"

"Something better," Dudley predicted. "Unless the Russian army appears to give them relief, the fort will fall within a day."

With dawn on the 17th, the sea calmed, and the sky cleared. The allied fleet closed in, paddle wheels churning and funnels belching black coal smoke. The ships made a half-circle around the fort as steam tugs towed the two ironclad batteries into range. The bombardment began at half-past nine.

Dust and smoke rose from the walls as the first shot struck home. Mortar shells burst inside the fort. When the Russian gunners replied, they concentrated their fire on the closest target, the iron-clad batteries. Their solid shot struck the armour plating, each ringing like a hammer against an anvil. The shot did no damage, bouncing harmlessly into the sea. The guns of the batteries tore huge gaps in the fort's stone walls.

Within three hours, the fort was a wreck, its walls several feet shorter and its guns dismounted. Thick black smoke poured from its interior. In the early afternoon, the fort surrendered.

The French infantry came out of their trench and formed in column to meet the defeated garrison. The Russian district military governor, who had taken shelter in the fort, threw his sword at the feet of the French general who advanced to meet him. Then the twelve-thousand man garrison, sullen and mortified, marched out of the fort to pile arms. The transports would take them to Constantinople that evening as prisoners of war.

It had been a quick and decisive little victory. Although of no great strategic importance except to hurry peace talks, it was still significant to the British troops. The efficient way in which the British command had planned and executed the mission went a ways in making up for the failure at the Redan. This was a miniature version of how the Sevastopol campaign should have gone, and proved that the British army and navy were still capable of running a good show. The infantry felt they had defeated a much larger body without having to fire a shot.

Dudley and Barker visited the fort the next morning after the fires had died. They found the stone walls reduced to tiny fragments and piles of dust. Several guns lay broken in the rubble, the cast bronze splintered, and almost every gun carriage was damaged in some way.

"A French officer told me a rumour," Dudley said. "Apparently, the garrison had wanted to surrender earlier than they did, but the incoming fire had been too thick. The flag was shot away, staff and all, so they could not haul it down. No one wanted to risk climbing the walls to show a flag of truce, either."

"Well, they got over that fear, didn't they?" Barker remarked.

Later that day, tents and baggage came off the transports. The allies made their camp near a small village a few miles from the fort. The people had fled at the first sign of the invaders, and the village stood empty. The French looted every house, but the British had orders not to touch anything.

In the evening, Dudley built a fire near his tent and enjoyed his first decent cup of coffee since the war began. A half-eaten plate of tinned meat, gravy, dumplings, peas and carrots sat on a crate next to him. The meal was hearty and fresh, free of taint or mold. He aimed to savour the rest of his excellent meal. He did not want anything to spoil it.

He had already drunk several cups of coffee and felt the need to relieve his bladder. Setting down his tin cup, he made his way to the latrine at the edge of the camp. When he returned, he sat on the crate and picked up his plate and fork.

He heard laughter and glanced towards Neville's tent. It was pitched about six yards away on the No. 3 Company plot.

The usual cronies were there—Rowntree, the lieutenants and young ensigns, messing with the captain. Dudley sipped his coffee. Now that the war was ending, he would have time to try to straighten out his affairs in the regiment. He would think of something. Then maybe he could go home for a time.

Home, to Hampshire, with its green meadows, hedges, fir forests and streams. He sighed and wiped a sudden and unexpected tear from his right eye. He tried to suppress how much he missed his fair England. He missed a life without constant danger, without rats and filth and dreary discomfort. He missed his aunt, and cousin Jane, and looked forward to confronting his uncle. And Elizabeth would be going home as well. He would find time to visit her.

He took a bite of beef and gravy. It had lost some of its heat. As he chewed, something ground against his teeth.

He stopped chewing and stared at his plate. With his fork, he searched through the remains of his dinner. Gray sand was mixed in with the peas and gravy, sand that had not been there before.

"I say, Mister Dudley," a voice called from Neville's tent, "is there something wrong with your supper? Our rations are excellent, I must say."

The voice was Captain Rowntree's. The other subalterns surrounded him, grinning like fools. They had been watching, waiting for him to take another bite, since his return from the latrine. Neville sat beside them in a folding camp chair, fondling his mustache and chuckling.

Standing, Dudley took the plate and walked toward Rowntree.

"Is something the matter, Ensign?" Rowntree asked, showing his teeth.

Dudley threw the plate at the man's feet. Rowntree danced out of the way in astonishment. Gravy splattered the bottom of his trousers.

"Of all the juvenile tricks!" Dudley cried. "You think this is funny? Do you think it takes wit to spoil someone's supper?"

Rowntree's face had gone red, but the others laughed all the harder. Neville pulled himself from his chair.

"Oh, don't be too upset, old boy. It may have been a juvenile trick, but you can at least take it like a man, after all."

"With all due respect, sir," Dudley replied, "condoning and encouraging such behavior is not becoming to a man of your position and rank."

Neville's expression clouded.

"Don't lecture me on such things, you damned upstart! This has nothing to do with rank." He managed to salvage his grin. "This is not an officer-to-officer affair, it is man-to-man."

"Man-to-man," Dudley repeated. "Man-to-man. I shall remember that, Captain Neville. Thank you, sir. Now, if you will excuse me."

There was nothing else he could do. Picking up his now-empty plate, he gave the assembly a last baleful glance then returned to his campfire. Laughter followed him.

Dudley stared at the fire and tossed the plate to the ground. He regretted letting his temper boil over. Confronting Neville's gang had just made him feel more helpless. He did not know what effective action he could take, but he could not endure much more of this.

He picked up his coffee tin and sipped. He would be hungry tonight.

Rumours spread that a large enemy force had been moving inland. An army of twenty thousand under the command of General Liprandi, the same commander who had struck at Balaclava, was preparing to attack the new invasion force. It was an odd rumour, for such an attack would be foolish. The allied fleet flanked the camp, and their combined guns could destroy any enemy force, no matter how large.

Foolish or not, General Spencer thought it prudent to find out for certain. He ordered a reconnaissance party of close to five thousand troops, including the Royal Hants, to move inland toward Kherson.

The column set out on the 20th, the cavalry fanning out ahead of the infantry. It was a difficult march, the soil and sand shifting under the feet of the marching men. They passed through several villages, all deserted, the hearths still warm and the doors hanging open. A few men broke ranks to raid the gardens for cabbages and the yards for poultry.

The column managed a mere ten miles before they had to bivouac for the night. The next day, the infantry stayed in the bivouac site while the cavalry ranged far ahead. When the cavalry had not returned by the third day, the infantry resumed their march as far as a village named Petrouski. Again abandoned vegetables, pigs, geese, and ducks became the property of the British Army.

That afternoon, the cavalry rejoined the column. They reported that a force of a few hundred Cossacks was retreating before the British advance and watching every movement. Allied gunboats on the river had sent a few shots after the enemy horseman, but the Cossacks had withdrawn out of range and halted.

That night, No. 3 Company drew picket duty, with orders to double the sentries in case of a surprise attack. Neville delegated the command of the picket to Dudley and wandered off, seeking a card game. Dudley considered the captain's behaviour irresponsible but was relieved to have a few hours away from him.

At midnight, Dudley made the rounds of the sentries with Sergeant Barker. The sentries had little to report. There was no sign of the enemy, nor even a sign this land was inhabited at all. Satisfied, He and Barker returned to the tent that served as their guardhouse.

Halfway there, they spied a dark figure approaching—a man holding a cigar with a bright orange tip.

"Look at you two, thick as thieves," Neville said, his words slurred. He must have been having a grand time with his messmates.

"Good evening, sir," Dudley tried, managing to keep the mockery in his voice to a subtle level.

"No, no, Dudley," Neville replied, shaking a finger. "That won't do." He spread his arms. "There's no one else here. There's no need for you to carry on a charade of normal relations in my presence. For it is you, you know, who carries on the charade, not I. Everyone knows I despise you, and you care little for me. You only make yourself look a fool."

Dudley stopped and gripped the hilt of his sword. Neville was right. There was no one else close enough to hear, save perhaps one of the sentries. It did not matter what anyone said.

"We'll see who's the fool, Captain," he snapped.

Neville seemed delighted.

"Ah, ha-ha! The imp finds he has some teeth, does he? Well, it's too late for that. You have shown you have no respect for your betters, and I mean to have your resignation from this regiment soon, my boy."

"On what grounds?" Dudley took a step forward. "On what grounds do you intend to force me to resign? As one raised from the ranks, I can't resign. I must serve a minimum term."

"Not with the Royal Hants, you don't. Just with the army. You shall quit the regiment on the grounds that it will be better for all of us. You may think you have a shot, what with racing that old nag of yours and getting chummy with Major

Willis, but it won't be enough. Neither will throwing your dinner at Captain Rowntree.

"As for you, Barker." Neville's eyes narrowed, and he blew a jet of cigar smoke. "I shall think of something special for you."

"Will you, sir?" Barker replied, sounding pleased.

Neville was already walking away, but he turned back to add, "Oh, yes, I shall use my imagination."

"Bloody madman," Barker muttered when the captain had disappeared.

He and Dudley returned to the guard tent in silence. Dudley sat on the single camp stool while Barker stood. Dudley rested his hands on the folding desk in front of him.

"Something special, sir," Barker said. "Makes me sound privileged, don't it?"

Dudley shook his head. He was trying to make a decision.

"We're both privileged, Sergeant. The privileged butt of a madman's whim."

Barker stroked his beard.

"Forgive me for saying this, sir, but it doesn't have to be that way. I'm a ranker, and there's not a lot I can do against him. I'm ashamed to admit it, sir, but the army has me at a disadvantage. But you, sir, don't have that disadvantage. And I think you keep forgettin' that."

Dudley looked at him and nodded.

"You're right. This persecution has gone too far. I've *allowed* it to go too far."

Barker was not done.

"What I mean to say is that you may not be as powerless as you think. If the captain's into making your life miserable, man-to-man, as he says, then you can strike back. Man-to-man." He gave Dudley a level stare. "If I'd had a decent chance to tell my side of the story all those years ago when that bastard had me demoted, I'd have taken that chance, sir. You've got that chance, Mister Dudley, and you haven't used it."

There was a tense silence. Dudley knew exactly what Barker meant. He had never spoken up for himself. Not once. He did not trust anyone to believe him.

"But," he began, offering another excuse, "what can I do when Neville has poisoned all of the others against me? What can I do against men who don't want me in the regiment?"

"Well, now, sir, I've been watching." Barker continued to stroke his beard. "As far as I can tell, it's not all the officers who are against you, it's under half. Besides Neville, there's only about five others, the same lapdogs that follow him around everywhere he goes. Rowntree and the like. All the others probably have no opinion of you at all, sir, if you'll pardon me for saying so."

Dudley ran his fingers through his hair. Maybe Barker was right. After all, he did have the support of Major Willis. And Willis had more influence than Neville, surely.

"You know what Neville expects?" he asked. "He expects me to allow him to continue until he has had his way. Well, I have played into his hands too long. Maybe I am afraid. Not afraid of Neville, but of what he stands for. Afraid of being an outsider, and not understanding the rules of a class that considers me beneath it.

"Maybe I've been afraid of speaking my mind amongst men of that class, and so had convinced myself it wouldn't do any good anyway. If that is so, it's time I stopped being afraid."

Barker nodded. "It may not do you any good, sir, but you've got to try."

Dudley stared at the single candle on the desk.

"Do you know the ironic twist to this? I remember having conversations like this about you, back when you gave me such trouble."

Barker grinned. "But I turned out all right, didn't I, sir?"

In the morning, the enemy finally showed themselves, but not in the manner expected. A single man, a Russian deserter, approached the column with his hands in the air. General Spencer took him in and pumped him for information. The man reported that large quantities of stores and fodder were stored up-country. There was also plenty of cavalry and infantry about, but he was unsure what they meant to do.

The column marched on and, later that day, saw thick columns of smoke in the distance, as if the Cossacks were burning the reported stores. The men speculated on whether the enemy intended to draw the column farther on, leaving behind an expanse of "scorched earth."

The countryside was deserted for miles, one poor peasant village after another standing empty. There were no goods of value in any of these places, save for the livestock, and these grew fewer and of poorer quality.

In one village, the column found an ancient peasant couple too feeble to run. They fell on their knees before the British officers, begging for mercy. They seemed surprised when they were left alone, their persons and meagre belongings untouched.

After this episode, General Spencer decided a further advance would gain them nothing. Liprandi was obviously not coming. He ordered the column to about-face and return to Kinburn.

The men were tired and dusty when they reached the vicinity of the captured fort. Although the sea was cold, they could not resist stripping off and frolicking in the waves. Their comrades who had stayed behind gave them news.

While they had been away, the naval squadron had patrolled the river and discovered several more forts the Russians had destroyed or abandoned. There would be no further fighting here. Even the native inhabitants realized this.

Many had returned to the village before the reconnaissance party.

On October 29th, the expeditionary force sailed back to Kamiesch, its goal achieved. General Spencer left a small garrison of French and British troops to hold the shattered fort for the winter. The Royal Hants were not part of this garrison. They would return to Sevastopol, and there, Dudley hoped, he would oppose Captain Neville as he should have done long ago.

His decision to prove himself by deeds alone was not working, at least not as well as it should. He would return to the mess hut, something he knew now he had simply been afraid to do. If Neville tried to have him evicted, so be it. He would come again, and again.

In the end, he hoped, it would be Neville who looked the fool.

CHAPTER 14

It took the squadron from Kinburn a day to reach Kamiesch. There, the troops remained on board the transports for nine more days. During that time, the allied commanders deliberated on the merits of a second expedition to Kaffa. At last, the new expedition was cancelled. The shipbound troops disembarked and returned to camp, where the preparations for winter continued.

Things in the Crimea had progressed while the Royal Hants had been at Kinburn. The new supply road was now hard-packed, well-drained, and wide enough for two-way traffic. A second steam locomotive was at work on the railway. The two engines brought stores as far as Kadikoi, and the recently formed Land Transport Corps employed its fleet of wagons to complete the journey to the camps. It had taken until the near end of the war to achieve this efficiency.

Every man in the Light Division was now to have the use of a prefabricated hut. Dudley found this welcome news, but he was content to remain in his tent. Each officers' hut held four men, and he did not wish to room with men who might not want him there. Not yet. At any rate, four men in a hut made for close company. Since Arbuthnot's death, he had come to appreciate having a dwelling to himself.

His tent still needed extensive modifications. Before going to Kinburn, he had dug a foundation four feet deep and set down a floor of planks salvaged from Sevastopol. He had then stretched a second tent over the first, fastening this double canvas wall down with four stout storm ropes attached to heavy wooden stakes. Now he completed the structure by adding a drainage ditch and a fireplace in one earthen wall. For a chimney, he cut an eight-foot smoke trench leading from the fireplace outside. At the end of the trench, he built a smoke stack of mud-plastered stones with an empty nail keg on top.

The work took him a day and a half. When he finished, it was evening. Supper would soon begin in the mess hut. The others would be gathering there.

For a few minutes, Dudley considered not going, putting it off as he had the previous night. It had been so long since he had been to the mess that the place had become unfamiliar territory. Hostile territory.

He felt a stab of self-disgust at his weakness. It seemed absurd that he could face a storm of Russian shot and shell, but not the society of his own regiment, however awkward the situation. What, he asked himself, would he have done if his uncle had bought him a commission, and the same thing had happened? Or if he had gone to Cambridge as his uncle had wished? There as here, he would have rubbed shoulders with the sons of privilege. If they had refused to accept his company, what would he have done?

There would never have been a way to avoid tonight's confrontation. There would never have been any other option than to fight. He had vowed to fight Neville but had shied away from a frontal assault. It was time to make that assault. His flank attack had failed.

There was no room for further argument. He would go tonight.

David Neville was enjoying the army's present situation. The regiment had been back from Kinburn for eleven days, and now there was little left for an infantry officer to do. The Land Transport Corps took care of supplies while the Royal Engineers were busy deciding how to destroy Sevastopol's docks and remaining fortifications. The Russians had even stopped firing from the north side of the harbour. The infantry's main responsibility was to see to its own needs.

For Neville this meant more riding on the plain, more time enjoying the company of his comrades, and more time to consider how best to finish off Dudley and Barker.

He stood near one wall of the mess hut, watching the door as the others arrived. It seemed odd, but thanks again to the light duties, this would be the first time every one of the regiment's officers would be together. Every one, that is, except William Dudley. Dudley, as far as Neville was concerned, was no longer an officer of the Royal Hants.

He had Dudley in his pocket, just as he had known he would. The wretch was helpless, completely unable to strike back. He seemed to hold out hopes that he could find acceptance if he just did his duty without complaint. Neville knew it was too late for that.

Dudley's one decent move had been his participation in the steeplechase. It had caught Neville by surprise, leaving him shaken for days. He had been left feeling powerless and foolish. Many had seen him whip Dudley's horse and thought it a damned unfair move.

The event could have been a major setback, but Neville had not seen any evidence it had changed anything. Certain facts remained. Dudley had been raised from the ranks and that was all there was to it. Whatever his true background or qualities, if old Neville said chuck him out then chuck him out they would. And they would soon enough.

He chuckled to himself then drained the contents of his glass. Victory was sweet when it was certain. Nothing could ruin this for him.

The door creaked open, and he waited to see who would come in. Everyone was here, so he wondered if perhaps this was a guest.

Dudley stepped through the doorway, letting the door bang shut behind him. He wiped his feet on the doormat. He had taken off his cap and held it in his hand.

Neville stared at him. For a moment, he refused to believe what he was seeing. Dudley did not come in here. He had just affirmed that fact. His shock gave way to rage. What the devil was he up to, barging in here like this—and now, of all times?

With three quick strides, he was at Dudley's side and leaning over him.

"What the bloody hell are you doing here?" he whispered.

"Good evening, Captain Neville," Dudley said, loud enough for everyone to hear.

Neville heard a faint quaver in the ensign's voice. At least he still knew enough to feel fear.

"I trust you are here on business, Ensign, and don't intend to stay long?"

"Why, sir, I am here for supper." Dudley smiled. "I hope I am not too late. I was busy putting the finishing touches on my tent."

Neville stared at him, his heart beginning to pound. Panic flooded him. This made no sense. This was not supposed to happen.

"Get out!" he cried.

"I say, Neville, what's this all about?" Major Willis asked as he approached. He glanced from Dudley to Neville then back again. "Ah, Dudley, good to see you finally. Did you tell him to get out, Neville? Why would you say that?"

Neville swallowed and faced the major. He had no ready response. He noticed that the chatter had died and glanced around at the faces in the small room. Some appeared as perplexed and indignant as he knew he must look while others retained an air of indifference.

He turned back to Major Willis, who still seemed to expect a response. He cursed himself for not keeping his voice down. Months ago he could have dealt with this, but now he was in a corner. How could he explain that he wanted Dudley to leave when he had given Willis a different story? His credibility was at stake. At the same time, if he let Dudley stay, as Willis desired, his authority would come under question from the junior officers. They might see him as all bombast and no substance.

In an instant, he realized, unexpected events had shattered his careful plans. *Damn* Dudley! Why didn't he stay away? That was what Neville had counted on; now things had taken a different turn.

"He did tell me to get out, sir," Dudley said. "He has been saying so for some time."

Neville felt himself stiffen. How dare he!

"Do not put words in my mouth, Ensign," he snapped. "I never said such a thing."

"What is all this commotion?" Lieutenant-Colonel Freemantle cried from the other side of the hut. "Supper will be ready soon. Let's have no more formality, gentlemen, and take our seats. It is too cramped in here to stand about the table for too long."

Neville stayed rooted in place, paralyzed by his uncertainty. In horror, he watched as Dudley followed Willis to the table.

It was too late. He took three long, controlled breaths then moved towards his chair.

Dudley sipped his water, marveling at how removed from the mood of the regiment both Major Willis and Lieutenant-Colonel Freemantle had become. To be unaware of the specifics of Captain Neville's antics was understandable—Neville would have told some lie that they could believe. Yet it was strange neither had sensed that something was not right amongst the regiment's officers.

The colonel looked tired and old where he sat at the head of the table. He had taken a wound at Inkerman, and Dudley wondered if his recovery had ever been complete. As for Major Willis, Dudley thought him brave and honourable but not the most astute fellow he had met. Both officers suffered from a lack of perception that was epidemic in the army.

Many of the senior officers had lost their sharp edge, perhaps because of the decades of peace in the wake of Bonaparte's fall. They were like old swords left to rust in their scabbards.

He wondered how he could think such thoughts. He would never have passed judgement on his superiors even a year ago. Neville had taught him something, at least.

He drank the last of his glass of water. His nerves were beginning to settle. It was a triumph to sit in this chair, to have joined some of the small talk, to have eaten the meal just finished. He had gambled well. Neville was unable to show his hostility before the watchful gaze of the major and colonel. Most of the captain's supporters had ignored Dudley during the meal, which was not unusual, though Captain Rowntree had smirked at him and raised his glass in mock salute at one point.

So, he was victorious in the first battle, but the tension in the air was palpable. He expected a renewed attack. He would have to prepare himself to meet it.

The orderlies were clearing the last bit of plate and cutlery. Dudley pushed back his chair. He wondered if he should post a sentry on his tent tonight, or one to watch over Bill. He would not want anything to happen to Bill.

As the servants dismantled the table and carried the pieces from the hut, the officers sat or stood, chatting, drinking, smoking or reading the latest editions of the *Times*. Freemantle and Willis arranged themselves on either side of the stove, the warmest spot in the hut. Dudley decided he would stay a little longer. He chose a newspaper from the pile and began to sift through it.

Someone pulled a chair up to his left side, and he lowered the paper to see Rowntree staring at him. Rowntree leaned in close, still wearing his smirk, and murmured, "What have we here, David?"

Neville positioned himself on Dudley's right, peering down and stroking his neat mustache.

"I think we have an uninvited sergeant in the officer's mess," Neville said, voice as low as Rowntree's. "I think it's time he was on his way."

Dudley glared into Neville's smoldering eyes, then turned to Rowntree.

"You're sitting rather close to me, sir."

"I was remembering that gravy stain on my best trousers," Rowntree replied. "I need someone to wash it out for me. Can you think of anyone?"

"Enough of this," Neville hissed. "Get out of here, Dudley. I've tolerated this long enough."

Dudley's ears began to burn, the paper crumpling in his hands. The counter-attack was coming sooner than he had expected.

"You shall have to tolerate it longer, sir. I have a right to be here."

Neville barked a laugh.

"You have a decent sense of humour, Dudley. Leave now, and things will be easier for you. Stay, or come back again tomorrow, and things may get very, very hard."

"They can't be much harder, can they, sir? Do your worst." Dudley rattled his paper to smooth the pages.

"You don't want that, Dudley. I assure you. Now get out."

"No." Dudley raised the paper so he could not see their faces. "If you want me out, you shall have to throw me out."

There was a pause; then, rough hands gripped him under either arm, lifting him straight out of the chair. At first, he was too surprised to react; then he struggled to throw off their grip. His newspaper made a furious rattling, and Neville and Rowntree released him.

"Here, what is going on?" Major Willis cried from his side of the stove. "Neville, what is the meaning of this commotion?"

Neville said nothing. Dudley trembled, dropping the newspaper and straightening his coat. He fought to hold his temper in check.

"Good heavens, Neville," Willis said, rising from his chair, "will you explain yourself? Is this another one of your jokes?"

"It's all right, sir," Dudley said. The evening had lost its charm. "I was just about to leave." He would come back tomorrow. Neville would have to learn to live with his presence. "Goodnight," he said to Freemantle; then he crossed to the door. Footsteps followed him as he stepped outside.

He turned to see Neville and Rowntree coming after him. Behind them, Neville's entourage had clustered, the

ensigns grinning and snickering, drawn by this latest bit of
fun. They pushed and prodded each other as they fought to
get through the door.

"Don't come back," Neville said.

Dudley did not want Neville to think he had won.

"I *will* be back."

"Then this scene will be repeated."

He shook his head.

"Then so be it. You will make yourself look a fool in time."

Neville took a step forward, eyes blazing.

"That's a fine little pony you have, Ensign. Quite the gal-
loper. It would be a pity if anything were to happen to him,
wouldn't it?"

Dudley felt the blood drain from his face. The anxiety
churning his stomach took a step closer to fear.

"I will have Sergeant Barker post a guard on Bill's stable."

"I will not authorize such a guard. Sergeant Barker will
have duties elsewhere."

"How dare you, sir!" Dudley suddenly cried. His anger,
contained until now, exploded at last.

Neville snickered.

"That's it, my good fellow. Lose your temper. It won't do
you any good."

Dudley was not finished. Without lowering his voice, he
said, "It's easy to hide behind rank and influence, isn't it, Captain? If not for the privilege that rank affords you, I would
deal with you on the spot. You know I'm helpless against you,
and that makes you nothing but a coward and a bully, and a
disgrace to this army that I hold dear to my heart."

Neville stiffened, his jaw clamped shut. Dudley turned to
the others gathered round the mess hut door.

"You're all very eager to follow Captain Neville," he said,
"and doubtless think him a fine officer. Well, he does, indeed,
possess courage in battle but little honour. Imagine the sort of

man who would threaten the life of a helpless animal—my pony Bill—in order to get his way!

"He has made it his business to ruin me in this fashion, and his reason for this cowardly behavior is the worst part of all. He does this because I would not help him destroy another man. I would not spy for him nor plant false evidence. Now he proposes to punish me. He has said it to my face—he would force my resignation from the regiment. He has denied me the privileges of this mess, and he has poisoned you all towards me with lies."

Neville was unable to speak. His mouth snapped open and shut, and a gurgling sound came from his throat. At his side, Captain Rowntree looked as if someone had slapped him in the face.

"This is slander," Neville finally managed to croak. "Slander! How dare you call me a coward! How dare you tell such lies!"

"You deny it?" Dudley said, facing him. He was no longer afraid, the churning in his stomach gone. The same wild energy that took him in battle took him now. "You deny that you asked me to gather information about Sergeant Barker and plant false evidence that you could use against him? You deny that, when I refused on moral grounds, you warned me never to come to the mess? You deny that you have promised to have me ejected from the regiment?"

"Enough! I deny it all." Neville raised his right fist. "By God, I'll teach you to say such things about your betters, and in front of my peers. You—nothing but a jumped-up sergeant!"

Dudley's shoulders relaxed.

"I have said my piece. You can deny it all you wish, sir. At least those gathered here know my side of it." He looked at Rowntree then at every other man who had followed Neville. The two young ensigns bowed their heads when his gaze fell on them.

"You have slandered me," Neville repeated, voice now level. "You profess to being a gentleman. Will you fight like one?"

Dudley hesitated, not understanding for a moment. Then a voice from the doorway cried, "Here! This has gone too far!"

It was Major Willis.

Dudley's face coloured in sudden mortification. It was fine for this pack of brats to see him ranting like a madman, but not for anyone whose respect he wanted. That Major Willis might have heard his angry tirade took some of the liberating joy out it. It had felt good to strike back in so bold a manner, but still it was unseemly for a soldier to lose such complete control of himself.

The major pushed his way through the others.

"What is this, Neville? What are you saying?"

Neville faced his superior with a cool lack of emotion.

"I am saying, sir, that I will not tolerate this." He turned back to Dudley. "Retract what you have said, or I will have my satisfaction from you, Ensign Dudley."

"Satisfaction?" Dudley repeated. "You mean that you're challenging me to a duel?"

The sudden change in Neville's outward attitude was uncanny. Now he was calm, collected, and even smiled. He was a man who had made a decision.

"You understand what I mean. Retract what you have said or meet me on the field of honour. With the permission of Colonel Freemantle, of course, sir," he added to Major Willis.

"Neville, this is your career you are endangering!" Willis warned.

"It is my reputation that I am upholding, sir," Neville insisted. "I will not have this upstart make a mockery of me. It is my right as a gentleman."

Willis looked pained.

"But you're an acting captain—a major, for the love of God! Dudley's a junior officer. It's damned irresponsible for you to put him in such a position."

"Ah, but he pretends to be a gentleman, sir," Neville stated. "Therefore, he must act like one. He thinks his company commander has wronged him, but I say that he has wronged me. There is no worse insult for a soldier than to be called coward, and to have one's honour questioned. I will have satisfaction for your lies, Dudley! Will you apologize, or will you accept my challenge?"

Dudley's mind raced. To fight Neville in a duel seemed ridiculous. By challenging him, Neville had endangered his career as an officer. By accepting, Dudley could be doing the same thing. A court of inquiry would decide when the battle was over. Neville could be cashiered, and Dudley could be reduced to the ranks. Worse, he realized, he could lose his life. He had no doubt that a duel with Neville would be to the death.

But to apologize was unthinkable. He might just as well admit his accusations were false. In that case, his career in the Royal Hants would be finished for sure. He had no choice but to back up his statements with action.

And a duel seemed almost...natural. It was one way to vindicate himself.

"I cannot apologize for the truth," he said.

"Then you accept my challenge, I take it?"

His anger boiled over again.

"Yes, I accept! If you will have it no other way, I accept." He jabbed a finger at Neville's chest. "But you are the one who forces this on me. I would not fight you if you would make amends for what you have done, but I will not apologize for the truth."

"Major Neville," Willis interjected, "you are taking a grave risk. Things are not the way they were in my day. Will you not consider some other option to this dispute? Much is at stake here."

"The credit of the regiment is at stake here," Neville insisted. "What do you say to pistols, Dudley?"

Dudley nodded. He had practiced with Arbuthnot's pistol only about a half-dozen times, but he could not back down now.

"Pistols, aye."

"Good. Who will stand for you?"

Dudley again glanced at the gathering of officers.

"I have no friends here, thanks to you. Therefore, Sergeant Brian Barker will have to do me the honour."

Neville sneered.

"Normally, I would object to such a choice, but for you it is fitting. Captain Rowntree?"

Rowntree clicked his heels. "Yes, Major?"

"Will you stand for me?"

"I will, sir," Rowntree declared with pride.

Neville nodded.

"Good. Captain Norcott, would you be so good as to make whatever other arrangements are necessary?"

Norcott, captain of the Grenadier Company, was not one of Neville's cronies. Curiosity must have drawn him out of the mess hut. He hesitated to answer Neville's request but then stepped forward and bowed his head in an affirmative reply.

With that, the gathering burst into an uproar of support for Neville. Some threw disgusted looks at Dudley, although not Captain Norcott. For a second, Dudley imagined he saw admiration in the grenadier's eyes, but he could not be certain.

Major Willis pushed back through the gathering to the door.

"I have to inform Colonel Freemantle," he said. "He may still put a stop to this."

Neville took Norcott aside to discuss the details. Dudley sat on the low step beneath the door. His head was pounding.

A few minutes passed; then Neville approached with Rowntree and Norcott close at his heels.

"It is settled," he stated. "At dawn tomorrow. In the MacKenzie Ravine near the river. That should keep it away from prying eyes."

Dudley nodded.

"Agreed."

"I will supply the weapons. You may have first choice, if you wish." He turned to Rowntree. "Come along, lads."

They marched past Dudley and back toward Neville's hut. He would not see them again until the morning.

———❦———

Sergeant Barker woke well before reveille. Under the cold autumn stars, he donned his dress coat and forage cap then made himself a quick breakfast of tea and biscuits. When he had finished eating, he went to see if Dudley was ready.

Dudley stood outside his modified tent with a steaming tin mug in his hand.

"Good morning, Sergeant."

"Morning, sir," Barker returned. He studied the younger man for any sign of agitation, but saw none. That was good. He knew Dudley was afraid, but he was keeping it under control. That was true courage, in his opinion. Only a fool would not fear a duel with a crack shot like Neville.

There was a good chance Dudley would be killed today. Barker did not care for that prospect, but he approved of the fight. Dudley had to face this madman. If he lost, so be it. He would at least go down like a good soldier, fighting.

If that happened, Barker knew he would have to watch his back. Neville would come for him next. He had not yet decided how to defend himself.

Dudley set his mug down on the ground. It was half-full of tea, still hot, but he said, "Let's get this over with." He had already saddled Bill and brought him around.

Barker noted Hester Oakes was nowhere in sight. He wondered how she had reacted to this turn of events. Not well, he imagined.

He walked alongside Bill as Dudley rode. They made their way across the plain of brown grass and shrubs toward the MacKenzie Ravine. The ravine was a dry streambed, a funnel that drained rainwater into the Tchernaya River. It had not rained since the storm. It was a sheltered and secluded place, a good location for an illegal duel.

Bugles were sounding in the camps when they arrived in the ravine. The air was still. Neville, Rowntree and Norcott were already there, along with the regimental surgeon. They made dark shadows under the high, sloping western bank. Near the north end stood another knot of officers. Major Willis was there, and Lieutenant-Colonel Freemantle in his cocked hat, looking damned uncomfortable.

Barker was the only sergeant present, as he had suspected. This was not a business for enlisted men. The junior officers cast many a distasteful look in his direction. His presence here was wrong, but no one else would dare stand for Dudley. It was an odd situation. A sergeant would have to do.

Dudley dismounted, and Barker stepped forward to take Bill's bridle. Dudley whispered something to the horse then advanced to meet Neville, his back straight and his shoulders squared. Barker swelled with pride for the lad. To think of how much trouble he had given Dudley before the war.

Captain Norcott positioned himself between the combatants. Neville exuded arrogant confidence, while Dudley's mouth was a cruel line slashed across his boyish face. Norcott looked as if he had not slept.

"Will you not resolve your quarrel?" he asked, a question required of the referee.

"If Mister Neville thinks there is another way," Dudley said, "I would prefer not to fight."

"There is no other way," Neville stated, as cool as ever. It was obvious he was enjoying this. He ran his eyes over Dudley's grubby uniform and said, "I see you still wear Arbuthnot's sword. Well, that is fitting. He was a fool. A man lost in a world of his own imaginings, as you are."

"Lieutenant Arbuthnot was an honourable man," Dudley retorted.

Norcott cleared his throat. He seems a decent fellow, Barker thought. Most of these officers could be decent enough fellows if they were not so easily swayed by a bastard like Neville. None of them had any backbone.

"I'll take that as a no," Norcott said. "Then it is time to choose your weapons."

Barker stroked Bill's nose and muttered, "Well, here we go." He looked into the pony's right eye. "Wish your master luck."

Dudley followed Norcott and Neville to a camp table set up on the other side of the ravine. The surgeon stood next to the table with his bag tucked under his arm. On the table rested a handsome mahogany box.

Norcott lifted the box and opened it. Inside was a pair of brass-framed .36-calibre Colt Navy revolvers. Neville's revolvers. The box also contained a small powder flask, a bullet mold, wadding, and twelve bullets.

"I shall load each," said Norcott, "then you may choose your weapons."

Dudley swallowed. Now that several hours had passed, he wished that events had not taken this course. He regretted his outburst, regretted calling Neville a coward. He wished he could have kept his head, but the captain's despicable threat against Bill had been too much for him.

He had to steady himself. It was too late to brood on what he might have done different. He reminded himself that here was a chance to fight in the most direct fashion. This was no different from marching into battle.

He had sworn to fight the queen's enemies and had joined the army with the fanciful notion that a soldier fought for justice whenever possible. Neville had broken the code of British justice and British values of conduct and dignity. Today, Dudley thought, he would strike a blow for those values, and for the regiment. Neville was a disgrace to the profession of arms. He was not just Dudley's enemy, but an enemy to all soldiers.

As Norcott prepared to load the pistols, Neville put a hand on his arm.

"Wait," he said. He looked at Dudley. "Two rounds, Mister Dudley? It is the classical form, after all."

Dudley took a deep breath. Things were going from bad to worse. Neville was confident he would win this contest. Asking for two rounds proved he meant this to end in his opponent's death.

He decided his first shot would have to count.

"Why not?" he replied, nodding. "Two rounds."

"That's rather extravagant, gentlemen," Norcott protested, but he carried on with his loading all the same. When he was done, he spun each cylinder to place the loaded chambers in the proper position.

Turning from the table, Norcott held out the revolvers butt first. Dudley chose one and held it in his right hand. Neville took the other.

"Take your positions," Norcott commanded.

Neville flashed Dudley one last baleful glare, then took ten paces towards the north end of the ravine. Dudley marched ten paces in the other direction, halting close to where Barker stood with Bill.

"You'd best get out of the field of fire, Sergeant," he said.

Barker took Bill's lead, but before he moved he murmured, "You can beat him, can't you, sir?"

"Afraid I'll lose, sergeant?"

"No, sir. Just concerned."

"Well, I'm a good shot with a rifle, aren't I?"

Barker nodded. "The best. But these things are different."

Dudley hefted the revolver, measuring its weight.

"Not very. And I have a plan, Sergeant."

Barker gave him a sad smile.

"Just shoot fast and straight, sir."

Norcott took a position next to the surgeon. Rowntree stood with them.

"If you are ready, gentlemen?" Norcott called.

Dudley turned to face his enemy as Barker led Bill towards where Norcott stood. He reached into his jacket with his free hand, gripping Wellington, trying to pull some strength from the cool metal. Strength and luck.

"Will you not resolve your quarrel?" Norcott asked a final time.

Neville said nothing from his end, and Dudley had no intention of backing down. He released Wellington and adjusted his feet, thinking back to his practice sessions with Arbuthnot's heavy Adams revolver. He wished he could take a few preliminary shots to see how this weapon fired. For all he knew, it might have a pull to the left or right. It was a good thing he had agreed to two rounds.

Norcott reached into his jacket pocket and took out a handkerchief. The white handkerchief looked like a tiny flag of surrender. Norcott held it high.

"You may fire," he cried, "after I have dropped my handkerchief."

Dudley heard Neville cock his pistol. It sounded like a bone cracking. Reaching with his thumb, he also pulled back the hammer of his revolver. He chanced a glance down to watch the cylinder revolve, the first loaded chamber coming into line.

Norcott still held the handkerchief aloft.

The handkerchief fell.

Dudley watched Neville's arm shoot up, the gaping black muzzle of his revolver coming into stark view. He began to count then raised his arm.

He remembered the shooting contest so long ago now. Neville always aimed with care, counting about a dozen seconds before he fired. That was all the time Dudley needed. He tracked his target, moving the revolver from left to right, and all the while counting six...seven...eight...

He drew in even breaths. Neville still had not fired. Dudley squeezed his trigger, and his pistol barked.

The bullet struck Neville in the right shoulder. The force of the blow knocked him backwards, and he stumbled. A gasp went up from the assembled officers. The sound filled Dudley with sudden electrifying energy. With his thumb, he pulled the hammer back a second time.

Neville maintained his balance for a few seconds then dropped to his knees with a crash.

"Damn you!" he cried. His right arm sagged, but he forced it back up and continued to aim.

Dudley saw Neville's pistol spit smoke. The crack came later, and the bullet whipped past his ear. The wad struck him a stinging blow in the neck. Neville fumbled to cock his revolver again.

Dudley kept his pistol at his side. He thought the weapon had pulled to the left a bit. He knew he could kill his adversary with his second shot, destroy this man who had tormented him for months. He could destroy this man who had tried to recruit him for a dishonourable purpose then had punished him for refusing. He could destroy this man who had tried to rob him of his rightful place in the regiment.

His arm wavering, Neville fired his second shot. The bullet whined away somewhere to Dudley's left.

Neville's head sank to his chest, and he pulled in a long sobbing breath. It sounded less like a sob of fear or despair than an expression of frustration and disbelief over his impending defeat. When he raised his head again, his look of arrogant defiance was back.

Dudley raised his revolver and aimed at Neville's skull.

"I could have killed you," he whispered, "but I chose not to."

He shifted his aim and fired toward the eastern crest of the ravine. The bullet stabbed out toward the empty uplands.

At first, there was no reaction. Then a shout went up from Rowntree and the others. They dashed forward to crowd round their fallen comrade. The surgeon damned them to let him through, and they made room for him.

Dudley slowly walked toward the little group. He halted a pace away. Rowntree turned to look at him then stood from his crouch. Neville lay on his back. The captain's eyes stared and his lips were moving, but Dudley could not hear what he said. The surgeon was trying to stop the blood flowing from the shoulder wound. He threw Neville's revolver to the stony ground.

When in the midst of battle at the Alma, a feeling of immense power, almost of invincibility, had coursed through him. That feeling had been even greater when he had taken the guns at Inkerman, and had returned to him again at the Quarries and on the Redan, thrusting aside his fear.

But he had never felt as strong as he did now, standing over Neville's prone form. He had bested his enemy.

He addressed those assembled.

"I regret having had to do this, but I had no choice. I shall see you gentlemen in the mess hut tonight."

He turned and strode back to where Barker waited with Bill.

"Looks like Number Three Company is yours again for a while, sir," Barker said.

Dudley did not return to camp. Instead, he took Bill across the uplands. After riding a short way, he decided too many other officers were out riding and walking this morning. He did not want their company just now.

To be free of them, he headed north, toward Russian-held territory. If the Russians spotted him and tried to take him prisoner, he would welcome the chase.

He rode through the old Inkerman battlefield then down towards the Tchernaya. He crossed the river by the hump-backed Tractir Bridge then continued on for miles, making for the scene of his first action. He wanted to visit the heights of the Alma.

When he reached the old battlefield, he stopped on the ridge above the river and stared at the brown autumn land-scape. He could make out the outlines of the Russian redoubts, and the place where the victorious British had camped. Out to sea rose the smoke trail of a steamer, perhaps an allied transport. The ship threaded past a squadron of smaller ves-sels. The low morning sun reflected from their sails, which shone a blinding white.

It seemed a peaceful country now. A peaceful country of fading colours.

On his way back, he startled three fat quail as he passed. They made him think of hunting, and the food in the mess hut. He would return there for the second time in a row to-night. He wondered how everyone would receive him. Nev-ille would not be there to egg on his fellows, having gone to hospital.

But he would be back. Their quarrel would not end here. Neville might even insist on resuming the duel when he recovered, the next time carrying it through to the end. If he did so, Dudley would refuse. No one could question his courage and conviction now.

He wondered what the outcome of the duel would do to Neville's followers. Would they remember Dudley's accusations and see the truth in them? He might have taken a step toward earning their respect, if not their friendship. Or he might have earned their undying contempt. They might testify against him in the inquiry that was certain to come. They might try to lay all the blame on his shoulders. He had solved nothing today.

He leapt Bill over a small gully. He needed friends now more than ever.

CHAPTER 15

December 1855

Three days after the duel, a court of inquiry convened in the parlour of a small villa near British headquarters. The court included a major in the Rifle Brigade as president, two captains, and an orderly-sergeant as clerk. The officers sat at the head of the room behind a rough table, and the clerk occupied a chair to one side. A second chair opposite the clerk's served as a witness stand, while a third, alone in the middle of the room, gave the subject of the inquiry a place to sit. Those scheduled to take the stand waited in an anteroom.

Ultimate responsibility for the duel lay with the commanding officer of the Royal Hampshire Fusiliers, but the focus of the inquiry was Ensign William Dudley. Dudley was certain Lieutenant-Colonel Freemantle would never know the embarrassment of an investigation. It was common knowledge that General Simpson was eager to avoid providing more fuel for the fires of Reform, and there had been too much bungling already. Freemantle would never face a court martial nor the judgement of his peers. It was bad enough that the ad-

ministration of the British Army had come under close public scrutiny for the first time in history. The court martial of a
battalion commander who had allowed two of his officers to
fight a duel would have made scandalous news in Britain.

That left Neville and Dudley. Each would face a separate
inquiry, and Dudley feared the outcome of both was forgone.
With a certain amount of bitterness, he knew the army would
seek to keep things quiet. The condemnation of William
Dudley, an obscure subaltern with no connections, would make
the least noise of all those involved. The blame would fall on
him.

With resignation, he listened as the president opened the
proceedings by stating their purpose.

"We are here to determine whether there has been a
breach of Article Ninety-eight of the Articles of War. Article
Ninety-eight states, 'Every person who shall fight or promote
a duel, or take any steps thereto, or who shall not do his best
to prevent a duel, shall, if an officer, be cashiered, or suffer
such penalty as a general court martial may award.'"

Dudley was the first witness. He had done his best to improve his appearance, mending the nicks in his coat, brushing
the worn cloth, and polishing his brass buttons and belt buckle.
He was determined to answer the questions with as much
truth and dignity as he could muster. He would not disgrace
himself during his final act as an officer.

The members of the court wanted to know everything
about him. They asked his name and rank, how he had obtained his commission, why he had enlisted in the army and
when. They demanded to know how he had met Captain
Neville, and Dudley related every event from Neville's gift of
the telescope to the incident at Kinburn.

Finally, he described the recent affair in the mess hut and
the actual duel itself. He told the truth as he saw it. This was

his vindication. Here was his chance to tell his side of the affair in an official capacity.

"Did you refuse to fight the duel?" the president at last demanded.

"In the end, obviously, I did not," he replied.

This was what his case would hinge on, but he did not know how to make it look good for him. His heart sank as he watched the clerk jotting shorthand notes on a sheet of foolscap. Everything said here would go on a permanent record.

"According to your testimony today," the president said, "you suggested to Major Neville at least twice that you could find some other way to resolve your dispute. But the fact is, Ensign, that you fought the duel." He nodded with apparent satisfaction. "Perhaps you did not do enough to prevent it."

When he left the witness chair, Dudley struggled to keep his legs from wobbling. He did not feel his testimony had gone well.

Lieutenant-Colonel Freemantle was the next witness. Dudley feared he would have nothing good to say about his young ensign.

It turned out otherwise.

"Ensign Dudley did not wish to fight," his commanding officer insisted. "He is a fine young officer. Twice wounded in action. He did all he could to avoid a confrontation with Major Neville. I do not know if honour would have allowed him to do any more."

When Major Willis testified, it was the same.

"Ensign Dudley did all in his power to avoid confrontation. Major Neville had subjected him to a campaign of vilification. Ensign Dudley did nothing to defend himself for months, hoping Neville would back off or see reason. I believe Ensign Dudley acted for the benefit of the regiment, so as not to cause a rift among the officers. In the end, Major

Neville persisted in his efforts. He pushed the ensign into a corner."

Dudley listened with increasing wonder. He had convinced himself he was the scapegoat, but the words of his superiors did not fit that theory.

When Captain Rowntree took the stand, Dudley's hopes mounted.

"The ensign eagerly agreed to the fight," Rowntree said. "I observed no reluctance on his part."

"Your statements do not match those of your commanding officers," the president interjected.

Rowntree looked puzzled.

"Oh. I, er...would not presume to question their judgement, sir. But that is how I remember it."

The Artillery captain eyed Rowntree with evident distaste.

"You were Neville's second, were you not?"

Rowntree hesitated.

"Yes, I was."

When he stood from the witness chair and crossed the floor, he refused to meet Dudley's eye.

Neville was never called as a witness. The members of the inquiry deliberated for fifteen minutes. Dudley could not sit still in his chair as he waited. When they were ready, he stood to hear their decision.

"We have listened to the evidence as provided by the eye witnesses," the president stated. "We can come to only one conclusion. It is clear that Ensign William Dudley was the man challenged. He did not initiate the combat. According to the testimony of his commanding officers, he did his best to avoid the duel. To his immense credit, he refused to deal a killing blow when given the opportunity. According to a strict interpretation of Article Ninety-eight, we find that Ensign William Dudley is not responsible for the occurrence of the duel in which he took part.

"Based upon the evidence heard, it is the recommendation of this court that the charges against Ensign William Dudley, Royal Hampshire Fusiliers, be dismissed."

The proceedings concluded, he wandered outside into the yard. A groom brought Bill around from the stable, and Dudley led the horse toward the gate. Halfway there, he stopped. A slender oak tree grew beside a water trough, and he leaned on it for support, resting his forehead against the bark.

He had fought, and he had survived. This was a victory, yet somehow it seemed unclean, like the victory at the Redan. The irony of the situation did not escape him. Lieutenant-Colonel Freemantle and Major Willis had done all they could to promote his innocence. Maybe they had exaggerated. Maybe he could have done more to avoid the duel. He could no longer say for certain.

After a few minutes, he took a few shuddering breaths and turned away from the tree. Bill nudged his shoulder. The horse knew his moods. Dudley stroked the animal's neck and whispered in his ear, "It's all right, old fellow. I've just been through hell and back, that's all."

Before he could mount, Major Willis emerged from the house. Dudley waited for him. The major extended his hand. Dudley shook it.

"Well done," Willis said.

"Thank you, sir." He appreciated the support the major had given him, but the show-like quality of the inquiry still made him uncomfortable. "What of Captain Neville, sir?"

Willis's face hardened.

"What of him?" He turned and walked back toward the house.

At that moment, Dudley knew Neville was finished. He would take full responsibility for the duel. Dudley's victory was complete. He had met his adversary, and with the help of that adversary's own actions, he had destroyed him. After all that had happened, this seemed incredible.

He felt an unexpected touch of guilt, of remorse. Neville never stood a chance. He, not Dudley, had become the scapegoat.

But he deserved it, Dudley thought, for he had disgraced the ideals of the army. That the army itself would find him out was just, after all. It was just.

———◆———

Neville could not face a court of inquiry until he had recovered from his wound. Days passed, and as he waited, Dudley built a snug stable for Bill. Over a wooden frame, he stretched a layer of discarded bagging, a layer of canvas, then a coating of tar against the rain. A parlour door and hinges from Sevastopol made a fine barn door, and there were now enough blankets available to allow Bill to have one.

While he worked, the weather worsened, bringing rain and sleet, a high wind, and more mud. Another harsh winter threatened, although no one would starve this year, and no one would freeze. The camps were bursting with supplies, and day after day the Land Transport Corps brought up more.

By the middle of the second week in December, Neville's condition had improved. The second inquiry was held in the same villa as the first. Dudley testified again, relating the same stories he had told before. He tried not to look at Neville as he spoke. The captain sat before the officers at the table, right arm in a sling, face pallid and expressionless. He never blinked.

Having already testified, Dudley was permitted to watch when Neville took the stand.

The president asked, "Did you challenge Ensign William Dudley to a duel?"

Neville's reply held the force of conviction.

"He insulted me. He called me a coward in front of my friends. He pretends to be a gentleman, so I demanded to know if he would defend his accusations as a gentleman would."

The president shifted with impatience.

"I didn't ask *why* you challenged him, Captain. I simply wanted to know *if* you challenged him to a duel, yes or no."

Sweat appeared in beads on Neville's forehead.

"I had no choice. He told such lies. Him, a jumped-up sergeant. I demanded my satisfaction."

The president glanced at Neville's sling.

"Too bad you didn't get it."

The members of the court did not take long to make their recommendation. They decided there was no need to proceed further. Neville, a long-serving officer, deserved the honour of a court martial.

The court convened the following morning in the same room. General Codrington sat at the head of the tribunal. Dudley, marvelling that the wheels of military justice were spinning so fast, told his story for the third time. When his examination and cross-examination were finished, he left the court and waited on a bench in the yard.

It would be a few hours yet, but no more. He knew the verdict already and was glad for it. A fine drizzle fell, soaking his straw hat and seeping into the collar of his greatcoat. The door to the villa opened, and Captain Rowntree emerged. Rowntree returned the door sentry's salute then crossed the yard to settle on a tree stump. Dudley nodded in acknowledgment. The other man glared at him, saying nothing, then turned his face away and did not look back again.

It was mid-afternoon when Neville came out of the house. He stood on the step for a moment, but when he spied Dudley he came towards him. Rowntree leapt up from his perch and rushed to his side.

"What has happened?"

With his left hand, Neville grabbed Rowntree's collar and pushed him away. Rowntree stood in the drizzle, speechless. Neville halted before Dudley, who rose from his bench.

"Yes, sir?" He half-expected Neville to strike him. The captain's face was as cruel and impassive as a statue's.

Despite the pain it must have caused him, Neville let his sling fall and drew his sword with his right hand. Dudley took an instinctive step back, hand flying to the hilt of his own weapon. But Neville did not strike. He jammed the point of the sword into the mud at Dudley's feet. When he let go of the hilt, the sword stayed upright, swaying slightly.

"You have made a grave error, William Dudley," Neville said.

"No, sir," Dudley replied, "you have."

Neville turned and strode back toward the stables. Rowntree chased after him.

Dudley did not touch the sword.

The following morning, Neville boarded a steamer and left the Crimea for Scutari. From there, he would transfer to a mail packet that would take him to England.

On Christmas Day 1855, Dudley joined the other officers in making the rounds of the camp. The men had decorated their huts amid a flurry of competition, tying spruce and fir boughs over their doors and on their ceilings. In amongst the boughs hung ribbons, paper streamers, bunches of calico, and flowers made from folded tissue paper. Paper flowers also sprouted from "vases" made from covered meat tins.

The denizens of each hut expected their officers to toast the day with them. They passed round tumblers of mulled wine and mugs of warm cider, and when Dudley had gone through the entire regiment, he was warm inside and unsteady on his feet. It was his finest Christmas since joining the army.

That night, he ate Christmas dinner in the mess hut. He was still not an integral part of the company, and most treated him with the usual polite indifference. Captain Rowntree and Neville's other close friends did their best to pretend he did not exist. He knew some harbored a lingering resentment that he, a man promoted from the ranks, had destroyed a fellow gentleman. That Neville had deserved destruction was inconsequential.

For all this, no one treated him with open hostility, and no one would try to force him out. Perhaps some even feared him. They would not cross him, for they knew he would fight. In time, they would come to accept him. They would have to. He would not fear them anymore.

He retained the support of Major Willis, a man who held honesty and fair play in high regard. In Willis's view, Neville had almost disgraced the regiment, not Dudley. The major would not tolerate any more discord amongst his junior officers.

But this was Christmas, and the stain of near-scandal was fading. It was a cheerful occasion, and Dudley could allow himself to enjoy it. For this night, at least, he drank wine instead of water. When dinner and the toasts were over, he sang and laughed with the rest.

"I say, Ensign Dudley," Captain Norcott began after the last raucous notes of a carol had ended, "I hear several perverted versions of your story are making their rounds of the camps."

"My story, sir?" Dudley repeated in the silence that followed. The entire room was listening. They might not care for him, but they could not help finding him an intriguing character.

"Yes, the tale of Ensign William Dudley's having beaten a superior officer in a duel then having beaten an official inquiry. You're becoming notorious, my dear fellow!"

"I'm not certain I care for that!" Dudley cried. Such a reputation would go against everything he had worked for.

Norcott clapped him on the shoulder. With Willis, he was a man whose respect Dudley seemed to have earned. Norcott was a tough soldier who did not care what others thought.

"Oh, don't worry. So many outrageous things have happened since this campaign started, it will blow over soon enough. At any rate, Happy Christmas!"

He raised his glass. Feeling a wash of unexpected gratitude, Dudley returned the gesture, and they drank together.

"I wonder what old Neville is up to now?" Norcott suddenly added to the room at large. "I suppose he is snug at home in Kent, a log on his fire and his best hounds at his feet."

This proved a conversation stopper. There were a few grumbles of agreement, but most just stared at their glasses. Then Major Willis changed the subject.

"Oh, how I wish to return to my own fine hounds! It has seemed so long."

There was an eager murmur of agreement, and the talk moved on to the pleasure of the chase. Then another song began.

Halfway through the second verse, Captain Rowntree, who had not joined in, cried, "How can you all stand here as if nothing has happened?"

At once, there was another silence. All heads turned to look at him, many in displeasure.

"This regiment has been dealt a terrible blow!" Rowntree insisted. "How can you all forget him so easily?"

"Sit down, Mister Rowntree!" Freemantle commanded. "Have you forgotten that David Neville brought his fate upon himself? Have you no shame?"

283

"No shame, sir?" One long finger shot out and wagged in Dudley's direction. "You give up on one of our finest and bravest officers for *this*? Well, I want no part of it!"

He shoved his chair back so that it toppled over with a bang. Then he stormed from the hut, slamming the door behind him.

"Insolent dog!" Major Willis shouted. "Behaving like a spoilt child!"

Many voices joined him in condemnation. That sort of outburst was unseemly, they said. A few eyes flickered in Dudley's direction, but no one spoke to him.

Neville's name was not mentioned again.

Soon enough, the revelry continued, but Dudley felt sick. This would take time. For now, his very presence was enough to cause a disturbance. He downed the contents of his glass and asked for more.

The mess hut never again saw use. In January, a group of senior officers hired a large warehouse from one of the sutlers. The group invited every officer in the British army to pay a subscription to help furnish the building with tables and benches as a common mess, or "Symposium." All officers from brigadiers on down could attend.

The Symposium was an instant hit. Like the mess hut, it was a dry, comfortable place where one could have a decent dinner and smoke a pipe or cigar. Unlike the mess hut, the warehouse was large enough to house a small stage for evening entertainment. Anyone could sing a popular song if no one booed them off the stage.

The Symposium organizers formed a Dramatic Club, and in his determination to embrace this officer's life, Dudley volunteered. He had some dramatic experience from his school days. Because of his youth and smooth features, he was often asked to play the women's parts, as were the other subalterns involved. The plays they attempted were popular farces such as *The Mustache Movement, Going to the Derby,* and *To Paris and Back for Five Pounds.* The performances began after supper at seven o'clock and were over by ten. This frivolous activity helped to fill the weeks as the winter dragged on.

In February, allied engineers blew up the naval docks in Sevastopol. The harbour front strongholds of Fort Nicholas and Fort Alexander soon followed. The allies had met their objective at last.

On the last day of the month, word came that the war had ended.

The news was only a rumour, but the truth was every bit as good. The allied and Russian generals in the Crimea had arranged an armistice pending the outcome of peace discussions in Paris. The opposing generals would meet the next day at ten o'clock in the morning. On the Traktir Bridge crossing the Tchernaya, they would discuss the terms of the ceasefire.

Dudley rode out on Bill to witness the event. He was one of thousands of spectators from the allied side. From the Russian side, there were no spectators at all.

A large tent sat on the Russian bank of the river, and next to it flew a white flag on a pole. On the allied bank waited the allied staff—General Windham, Chief of Staff for the British forces, General Martimprey of the French, and Colonel Count Petitti of the Sardinian Army. A flock of aides and other officers hovered around each man.

At exactly ten o'clock, the Russians emerged from their tent and mounted their horses. In the fore rode General Timoieff, Chief of Staff of 4th Corps. A body of cossacks formed his escort, and with him rode a large group of staff officers.

They made their way to the bridge, and the allies rode to meet them.

With much doffing of cocked hats, the allies gave the proposed terms of the armistice to the Russian general. The River Tchernaya would form a boundary, and all offensive military operations would cease. Both armies would post sentries along the river to prevent anyone from either side crossing.

General Timoieff was to take these terms to his commander, General Luders, whom the allies had fought for so many months. Timoieff politely agreed, and with more doffing of hats, the conclave broke up, each side riding their separate ways.

An official peace did not arrive for almost a month. When it did, on Wednesday April 2, 1856, midday salutes rang out from all of the allied batteries while the ships in the harbours celebrated with colourful flags and decorative bunting. In contrast, not one gun fired from the Russian side and no extra flags flew. They had suffered a humiliating defeat.

Now that the treaty was reality, it was time for the British to go home. Preparations began, but they were slow. No one expected to board a ship for at least another month. In the meantime, armies that had once been enemies began to mix as friends. The Tchernaya ceased to function as a border.

In mid-April, the allies held a grand review for General Luders. The lines of infantry, squadrons of cavalry, and batteries of field artillery stretched for eight or nine miles. When the parade was over, Luders announced that it had been magnificent, that his former adversaries looked quite splendid.

Dudley discovered he had no animosity towards the Russians now the shooting had stopped. He had not forgotten that they had killed British wounded as they lay on the Alma and Inkerman battlefields, but that no longer seemed to matter. His sense of outrage had dimmed while his understanding of war had brightened. War was not a polite business. He could not blame the enemy for the loss of so many friends and comrades. The Russians had been defending their homeland. The British and French were the invaders.

He could even admire the Russians as soldiers. Last year, he had not considered them very effective, but they had been fighting superior weaponry in the form of the Minié and Enfield rifles. They had fought well enough from behind their walls and had given up only after months of siege and deprivation. They had suffered as much as the British from disease, cold and starvation. Perhaps more so. Perhaps this was why he now felt nothing but sympathy for his former enemy.

One spring afternoon, he rode to the north side of the harbour to visit the forts there. He came across a large body of Russian soldiers living in crude huts, and holes dug in a hillside. They would once have been big, fine-looking fellows, but now they seemed unhealthy, sallow, underfed, their once-smart green uniforms soiled and worn. Most watched with downcast and sullen expressions as he rode past. A few others offered relics for sale—Russian caps and bayonets—or begged tobacco.

On another occasion, Dudley met a Russian officer who was a guest at the Symposium. The officer explained that the past winter had not been a comfortable one for them. After the final British attack on September 8, they had expected an assault on the north side of the harbour the next day. The officer admitted they had been on their last legs and had feared such an assault. When it never came, it was too late for them to evacuate to the interior for the winter.

Then, hunger became their enemy. Their food and supplies had to come from distant St. Petersburg, and they had been unable to provide their men even with common black bread. Thousands had died while the allies sat snug in their huts, the British officers enjoying their comic plays in the Symposium.

But that was over. Now, a large Russian band of more than one hundred-and-fifty performers played each spring afternoon across from the Inkerman battlefield. Russian officers made frequent visits to the British camps. They admitted to being upset over the loss and destruction of Sevastopol but were pleased with the road and railway to Balaclava.

Those who had built the road were pleased as well, and had erected a monument in Kadikoi to their endeavor. The monument was a smooth-faced stone engraved with a message. The message read, "This road was made by the British Army assisted by the Army Work Corps under the direction of Mr. Doyne, C.E., 1855."

<hr>

In late May, Lieutenant-Colonel Freemantle announced that the regiment would leave for England within days. Dudley received this news with a mixture of joy and heartbreak. The heartbreak was for Bill. He would have to sell him. Infantry officers were not permitted to transport horses purchased in the Crimea.

On May 29, he took a final ride—his last ride with Bill and his last look at this land he had known for a year and a half, this harsh land that had been his home. He made a tour of the Alma battlefield, the Tchernaya valley, and the uplands. He felt a need to pay his respects to the thousands who had fallen here, to visit the places where they had given their lives. In particular, he wanted one last look at the graves of the men he had known.

On the heights of the Alma, he tried to locate the grave of his friend Reginald Harris. There were so many grass-covered mounds above that river he could not tell one from the other. He comforted himself by saying a short prayer to the entire hillside.

Nearer to Sevastopol, he rode among the many cemeteries of British dead, scattered over the hills and plain. He followed no systematic route, zigzagging here and there. Some of the graves he encountered were unmarked, but most had a white stone or rude cross. In front of the Malakov, he discovered a huge mound covering the ditch. This was a mass grave where many French were buried. Above it stood a tall black wooden cross on which was painted in white letters:

Unis pour le victoire
Reunis par la mort
Dud soldat c'est la gloire
Du brave c'est le sort

[Coming together for victory,
United by the grave.
In this, the soldier's glory,
And the fate of the brave.]

A more permanent monument had been erected before the Redan, near the ditch at the salient angle. It was a white obelisk of stone bearing the names of every man who had fallen in the two assaults.

Back on the plain, Dudley came upon a number of enclosed plots, one for the Naval Brigade, one for the Army Work Corps, and a recent one for the Land Transport Corps. The largest and most elaborate cemetery was that for the Guards. It held more than two hundred graves, most marked with small white stones, others with headstones or wooden boards. A stone wall encircled it with a gate of wood and iron swinging between two stone pillars. A round shot crowned each pillar.

At this entrance stood a high stone cross bearing the inscription: *Grenadier, Coldstreams, Fusilier Guards, A.D. 1856.* On the other side, the words read: *To the non-commissioned officers and men of the Brigade of Guards who fell in the Crimea, this cross was erected by their surviving comrades, A.D. 1856.*

Dudley visited the Light Division officers' cemetery last. After dismounting, he walked among the stones and wooden markers. When he found Arbuthnot's marker board, he lingered for a moment, thanking the lieutenant again for the gift of the sword. Then he continued through the cemetery to a single plot detached from the rest.

The isolated gravesite already had a visitor. Hester Oakes stood with her back to him, her head bowed. She had not yet remarried, although he knew she had received several offers. She was not able to forget Daniel Oakes yet.

Letting Bill graze nearby, Dudley stood next to her and looked down at the weathered wooden board. Small spring flowers grew on the mound.

He mouthed the words, *Goodbye, old fellow.*

"I can't bear to leave him here," Hester said, voice broken. Tears smeared her lined face, and she wiped them with her wrist. "I can't bear to leave him alone in this barren place."

"But he's not here, Mrs. Oakes," Dudley said. He placed his hand on her arm. "That is just his body. Wherever you go, he will follow."

She said nothing for a moment then nodded.

"Yes, Mister Dudley, I know that. The old mugger will be with me always."

Although he longed for home, Dudley knew he would miss this place. Overhead a hawk cried, and a mild wind ruffled the wildflowers.

END of Empire and Honor Book 2

ABOUT THE AUTHOR

HAROLD R. THOMPSON works for Parks Canada, but in his spare time he writes. He also draws (cartoons, really) and dabbles in filmmaking. History, in particular military history, is his favorite subject. Though he has written non-fiction for periodicals such as *Military Illustrated* and *Canada's History*, he is also the author of the Empire and Honor series of novels, which star fictional Victorian hero William Dudley, an officer in the British Army. The first book in the series, *Dudley's Fusiliers*, was released in 2010.

ABOUT THE ARTIST

SHAUN LINDOW loves that he actually gets paid to draw pretty pictures. It's only his compelling need to eat on a regular basis and occasionally sleep indoors that causes him to charge his beloved clients money. He has been illustrating and 3D modeling professionally for the past ten years, and plans to stop when they pry the pencil from his cold, dead fingers.

TAMIAN WOOD is currently based out of sunny South Florida. Using art, photography, typography and digital collage techniques, she creates book covers that appeal to the eye and the mind, to entice the book browser to become a book reader. She holds degrees in computer science and graphic design and is a proud member of Phi Theta Kappa National Honour Society.

Lightning Source UK Ltd.
Milton Keynes UK
UKOW051417240412

191377UK00001B/10/P